THE WHISPER OF THE SEA

My Life of Sex, Crime, Loss and Love

LAINIE JANE GRAY

Publisher:
Australian Self Publishing Group, Pty. Ltd. / Inspiring Publishers
PO Box 159, Calwell, ACT 2905, Australia.
Phone: 61-(0) 2 6291-2904
http://australianselfpublishinggroup.com

A catalogue record for this book is available from the National Library of Australia

National Library of Australia Prepublication Data Service

Author: Lainie Jane Gray

Title: **THE WHISPER OF THE SEA:**
   My Life of Sex, Crime, Loss and Love

ISBN: 978-1-923250-98-7

Contents

Prologue 1995

I stand here on a beach in a quiet and beautiful corner of the world, where a soft sheltered sea laps gently on the clean white sand.

Only a short distance out to sea, dolphins swim along the shoreline, gently splashing as they break the water, travelling up or down the coast, oblivious to the complexity of the life that exists only twenty metres away from them on the shore. Sometimes there are whales, larger and further from the beach, but still with their own way of life, their own paths to follow, from when they are first born in the cold southern waters to when they die and are absorbed once more into the sea.

I live in a neat house with a neat garden that ends in a reserve with a jungle of seaside sedge and peppermint trees, and beyond that there is only a footpath and a few metres of dune before you reach the sand on the beach. I sleep each night alone with just my thoughts and my memories and the soft whisper of the sea.

This is the south west of Australia, thousands of miles from the place where I was born. I have lived here in exile, a fugitive from my past, using someone else's name, for more than five years. Yet I have come to love it here. I love the soft warm climate, slightly too hot in summer and slightly too cold in winter but perfect for most of the year. I grow vegetables and flowers in my garden, wave to my neighbours but rarely speak with them, and I belong to a birdwatching group, a native-flower society and an investors' club. I am twenty-nine years old, wealthy enough to work only three days a week, clever enough that I could have done much more with my life, yet in spite of the heartache that never leaves me, I am content just to be alive and here in this beautiful place.

But my life was not always this good, although I have never lacked money. Every day I check the newspapers from England at our local library, searching for news from the area on the south coast of England where I once owned a house, waiting for a headline to say a body has been found buried in a garden. The body of a young woman who met an untimely end. The newspapers are a couple of days late, but that does not matter.

If the body is found, I know that it will be only a few days before the police catch up with me, and I will be sent back to England to be questioned. My alias could never stand up to scrutiny; they would need only to follow the money trail from the sale of my house. Paul, who arranged the sale, would have no choice but to help them.

I did not kill the girl—I do not even know her full name— but I know where her body lies, buried in an icehouse in the wooded grounds of a beautiful house that borders the English Channel.

Then she was just a meaningless girl to me, one of the many au pairs and escorts that my uncle brought to the house for his own pleasure and that of his wealthy friends. Now I wonder why she was never missed. Did she have a mother somewhere in a northern European country? A mother who waited and waited for a letter from her daughter, for the small but regular payments of money sent home. A mother who has spent more than six years wondering what happened to her child, knowing in her heart that she is no longer alive.

My own mother is long dead, as is my father, my brother and my uncle. There is no one left but me to remember the house with the walled garden where we all once lived, or the long-ago days when we were still all together.

Simon still lives his separate life, far away from me in space and time. He was the only man I ever loved as a woman should love a man, with my whole soul as well as my body, yet he is as lost to me as they are, with thousands of miles and five long years separating us from the brief time we shared.

He is still a science teacher at Harton School, expensive and exclusive. The years have slipped away, but every year I send him a Christmas card, with no return address, to let him know I am still alive and I still think of him. I have newsletters from his school with photographs of him with some of the boys he teaches, privileged young men who will one day be leaders in the world, or business men, or simply good men who love their wives and raise their children to be good and useful and happy.

Every day I think about that magical summer when we were lovers, lying together in velvet darkness upstairs in a cottage, lost in a love that joined our souls, listening, as I still do now, to the whisper of the sea. But our love and any future we could have shared was already doomed from the very first day we met.

Last Christmas when I sent his card, I told him I sometimes spend hours looking at the photographs of him in the newsletters, I sometimes wonder if he still owns the cottage by the sea, and I hope he sometimes still thinks of me as I always think of him, every day of my life.

I will never send him a card again. I will let him slip out of my life, and I will slip out of his. I long ago realised that regret only eats into your soul and makes you discontented with the life you still have remaining.

He may have married someone else, have children of his own, a wife to cook his meals and sleep beside him at night. I have no way of knowing.

Tonight, I will write the story of my life—the story of how and why I came to this place—and I will leave it in my safe with a note for it to be sent to Simon one day when I am dead. And he will know then what really happened all those years ago, and why I had no choice but to leave him.

Perhaps the police here will one day read it and send it to the police in Britain, and my uncle's name will be cleared of the murder of one girl but linked with the manslaughter of another.

Our lives are not just how the world remembers us when we are gone—even that is fleeting—but everything we were and did and felt and thought, the choices we made that shaped our lives and those of the people we loved, our joys, loves, hopes and fears, our aspirations. And our dreams of things that might have been.

Sometimes I wish I could just walk out into the sea, keep walking until I am out of my depth and the soft salt water closes over my head, then swim further and further from the shore until I am exhausted, until my soul is freed to swim with the dolphins or drift with the tide and wash up on a faraway beach where once I stood beside my lover. Then I will be content for my life to be gone forever and for my soul to become one with the sea and the sky.

But I know that I never will. Life is precious, even when hope is gone.

The Walled Garden 1965–1981

Once my name was Ann Berrington. Now it is Ethel Turner. I was born half a world away, and my earliest memories are enclosed in a walled garden with flowerbeds and roses, apple trees and pear trees, raspberry canes and blackcurrant bushes and soft green lawns. There was even a monkey puzzle tree, tall and intricate, a maze that you felt you could climb until you found your way into the freedom of the sky and could fly away like a lark into the farthest reaches of the heavens. But the leaves were sharp like the scales of a green dragon, too sharp for climbing, so the freedom was forever out of reach.

My mother was as beautiful as a princess, my father as wise and rich as a king, my uncle a magician who could always make us feel happy to be alive, and my older brother James was my knight in shining armour, who would one day transport me to a life in the world beyond the garden walls.

But life is never a fairy tale, and walled gardens can only enclose happiness for a few short childhood years. In every paradise there are dark corners where evil things lurk, patient in the shadows, silently waiting, watching, biding their time.

My father was a financial advisor, and he worked in the city, commuting each day from our village in Surrey, while my mother stayed at home, always there for us, except when she wasn't. Sometimes she got drunk, even during the day, and then we would tiptoe around the house, trying to avoid her wrath.

My uncle Richard came to stay with us at weekends, and I loved him just as much as I loved my father. He was undoubtedly more fun. He took James and me on outings. We went to the zoo, to a castle where you were allowed to climb over the old walls and, joy of joys, he sometimes took us to the seaside, where he would help us to build a sandcastle. We would take home a bucketful of seashells, which we would sort and count and marvel over, until my mother would complain of the smell and the sand on the carpet and would throw them out.

On some Saturday nights there were parties, but James and I were sent up to our quarters on the attic floor, where we had a bedroom each, a playroom and a bathroom. On no account were we to come downstairs. We would listen to the music and the laughter and the voices raised in drunken revelry. We would look out of the windows and see guests running on the lawns, men and women embracing and slipping away into the shadows of the trees. On Sunday mornings we were not allowed outside until my uncle had cleaned up the garden.

Children accept the lives they lead as being normal; James and I were no exception. I never thought to ask the girls at school if their parents had wild parties.

I remember vividly one night when I did go downstairs. James had thrown up on the bathroom floor, and I didn't know what to do. He was sitting on the tiles, hugging his knees, shivering in his pyjamas, too ill to help me decide whether to break the rules and go to my mother for help. I would then have been about seven years old, and James ten.

The party seemed to be over. The noises had stopped, although many of the cars were still in the drive, so I knew at least some of the guests were still there.

I went down to my mother's bedroom and knocked on the door. There was no response, so I went into the room and switched on the light.

She sat up, shielding her eyes from the glare. A man was in bed with her, but he was not my father. Frightened at having disobeyed, I told her James had been sick. She said to go and find my father, he was in his room and he would deal with it. But then she changed her mind. No, no, I was to get Uncle Richard, my father had someone with him. The man murmured something to her, pulled her back down next to him. I switched off the light, closed the door, and went to Uncle Richard's room.

He at least was on his own. He cleaned up the bathroom floor, took us down to the kitchen, and mixed some fizzy stuff for James to drink. Then he carried him back up to bed and took me back to my room, instructing me to fetch him and not bother my mother if James was sick again.

We went to the local village school. The teachers were nice, but the headmistress was awful. She carried her cane with her, often hit children for no good reason, and if anyone answered back when she yelled at them, she would slap them or force them to hold out their hand for six cuts with the cane.

She seemed to particularly pick on James. I will never know why, as he was an intelligent and quiet boy, never in trouble with any of the teachers but always in trouble with the headmistress. To be sure he sometimes had to defend me, as I was harassed by some of the older boys—two in particular—for reasons that I could never fathom. I had never done anything to harm them, and I never answered them back when they called me insulting names—I would never have dared answer anyone back—but perhaps they did it simply to goad James.

They would pull my hair, trip me up—accidentally, of course—when I walked past them, push me out of the circle when I was playing ring o' roses with the other girls. And they would lure me behind the old brick toilet blocks in the playground, telling me stupid stories, which I was gullible enough to believe, about one of my friends having fallen over and needing my help, or James having asked me to talk to him there. As soon as they had me out of sight of the teachers in the playground, they would try to get their hands up my skirt. Eventually I realised I was being tricked. I did try to keep away from them, but they followed me around. Every time they did things to me, James would thrash them and the headmistress would thrash him.

Once when one of them pulled my hair, I got mad and kicked him in the shin. But they were boys and much bigger and stronger than I was. The other boy twisted my arm behind my back and threatened to punch me. James turned up, and punched him, but of course, the headmistress had seen it all. I was caned for kicking a boy, and James was caned for hitting them.

I hated all boys but James and dreamed of revenge on them. Boys were stronger and bigger than girls, even when girls were grown up, but girls were far cleverer, so there must be some way girls could win.

My mother went to the school several times to complain to the headmistress about her hitting James, and she and the headmistress co-existed in a haze of mutual hatred. My mother called her an old maid behind her back, and said she was jealous because she was old and ugly and didn't have a rich husband, while my mother was young and beautiful and did. The headmistress didn't, in fact, have any husband at all.

When I look back now, I can wonder why she was so bitter and twisted. Had she had a lover killed in the War? Had she had a harsh upbringing? That was the nineteen seventies and she behaved as if she was running a school in a workhouse in the eighteen seventies. How had she been allowed to continue for so long without official complaints being raised?

We left that school rather abruptly; there was an altercation.

My brother's teacher was away sick, and the headmistress was taking his class. It was the end of the day, and she had kept the children in after school for five extra minutes, telling them they were all to be absolutely silent for the whole five minutes or she would reset the stopwatch. James told me afterwards it was because one of the boys had answered her back when she had caught him passing a note to a girl.

While I was waiting for him outside the classroom, the two boys, seeing me alone and unprotected, attacked me. One of them grabbed me from behind and threw me to the ground, and his friend pulled down my knickers.

But they had left it too late; the five minutes were now over. The classroom door opened, and James was the first boy out. Within seconds both of my attackers had bloody noses. The headmistress was right behind him, but she didn't see it the way it was. She slapped him across the ear for fighting.

He turned and explained he was defending his sister, while I tried to put my clothes to rights, and two girls helped me to get up. I hardly knew them as they were in James's class, but girls always supported other girls in the war against boys.

The headmistress looked at me with what she would have thought was a withering look, taking in my dishevelled skirt as I pulled up my knickers. I only saw a nasty glare that made me wonder if she was actually a witch.

'Don't you answer back, you stupid boy,' she yelled at James. 'Your sister was exposing herself. She is to blame, not them. She is a total disgrace. Hardly a surprise, since your mother is a whore. Hold out your hands, both of you.'

She raised the cane to strike James, but he had finally had enough. He snatched the cane from her hand, broke it into two pieces beneath his foot, and pushed her away from him. He was tall for his age while she was a small woman, and he knocked her clean over. I felt so proud of him, rescuing me from villains and defying the headmistress.

Then he took me by the arm, we grabbed our blazers and satchels on the way out, and we fled home.

Neither of us said anything that evening. But the following morning at breakfast, after my father had left for the city, James told our mother that he was not going to school that day, and that I wasn't either. It was a Friday, quite late in the summer term.

My mother never liked a fuss. We were allowed to do as we pleased for most of the time, at least when she was sober, apart from the prohibition on coming downstairs during parties.

'Well, I dare say I could send a note on Monday saying you were both sick today. Why don't you want to go to school?'

'There was a fight, and I got into trouble unfairly.'

'But there are always fights at school. Boys always fight.'

James owned up. 'I hit the headmistress.'

'Oh, dear,' she said. But then she brightened up. Perhaps she was proud of him as well. 'I'm sure it will be forgotten by Monday. Why did you hit her?'

But James would say no more.

Later that morning a man arrived at the house; he was the district school inspector. He told my mother there had been a complaint about her son, and James was suspended from school for the moment. But he was a fair man, and he asked us both what had happened.

I told him, as I didn't want James to be in trouble.

'There are two boys who are always bothering me, and James often has to protect me, and Miss Coxley always hits him when he does. Yesterday they attacked me outside the classroom and pulled my knickers down, so James hit them both. Miss Coxley hit him across the head for fighting, and when he said he was only defending me, she said it was my own fault because my mother is a whore. She was going to cane us both, but then James grabbed the cane from her and accidentally pushed her over. What's a whore?'

I can still clearly recall that long moment of deathly silence.

James was, in any case, leaving at the end of term to start at Harton School in September. The school inspector seemed ready to smooth things over when he learnt that, as Harton was exclusive and expensive. After some negotiation—my mother was, after all, still as beautiful as a princess, even if she did sometimes get cross and drunk—he agreed to James having the rest of the term off school, and assured her he would talk to the headmaster of Harton and tell him that James had done nothing to deserve the school suspension. It was totally unjustified.

He suggested I could be placed in a different school, a little further from where we lived but still manageable. It was run by the sisters of the church and only took girls. He would contact them and make the necessary arrangements.

He asked if my mother would like to make a formal complaint. Teachers were allowed to cane pupils but were not allowed to hit them over the head, and James had a bruise where he had been struck. But my mother was never one for anything confrontational, even though she had at times been provoked into going into the school to complain, so she declined.

He reminded James that a man never hits a woman, whatever the provocation.

'Yes, Sir. I'll remember that. Thank you, Sir.'

'Fine young man you have there, Mrs Berrington. He should do well at Harton.'

No one had answered my question about whores.

I enjoyed the three years I spent under the tutelage of the nuns. They were always kind, always just, and the girls were never caned.

School was much better without the cranky headmistress, and there were no boys to pull our hair, trip us up, get in the way when we played ring o' roses in the playground or try to lure us behind the toilet block and get their hands up our skirts.

I learnt by heart great tracts of the Bible. Perhaps not a useful thing to learn, but then neither was geometry. In all my life since school, I have never once needed to calculate the area of a triangle, but I did twice recite the twenty-third psalm by heart.

I loved the stories of the powerful women in the Bible, Jael and Ruth and Delilah, women who made it in a man's world by exploiting their weaknesses. That became my aim in life: to exploit the weaknesses of men.

I missed James, of course, as he now boarded at Harton, but he wrote to me every week, telling me things he had learnt, how he loved cricket, and pranks they had played on one of the masters. I still have all his letters, precious memories of the first love of my life, every word etched into my heart. We had always been close, in spite of our three-year age difference, viewing the outside world as them versus us, and unquestionably loyal to each other.

I went on to Roburn, an exclusive girls' boarding school, when I was eleven. I wished I could be at Harton with James, but Harton only took boys. After a few weeks of homesickness, I loved it there as well. I had friends, girls who were away from their homes as I was, and James still wrote to me. Why had I ever thought I wanted to be at a school where there were boys, even if one of them was James?

I lived for the holidays, when James and I would be together, safely enclosed in the comforting world of the walled garden. It was always good to come home and find him there waiting for me. His school was closer to home than mine, so he was always back before I was.

At times he was a little bossy, and he was always reminding me that boys were better at everything than girls and were much stronger, but I adored him. He was everything a handsome prince should be, and I would have done anything he asked.

Uncle Richard would take us out every weekend in the holidays, always finding us new and interesting things to do, Ferris wheels, lion parks, the ice-rink, mini golf, and every year he would take us to the beach, the highlight of my summer.

On weekdays in the holidays, James and I would play in the garden, as there was little else to do. We were not allowed out by ourselves, even as teenagers. Uncle Richard had put up a swing for us and built us a treehouse, and we could play tennis on warm days and run under sprinklers in our bathers on hot ones. On wet days there were Lego blocks and Meccano sets and model railways, all given to us at Christmas by our uncle, and we built castles with towers, and stations for the trains. To be sure, some of the games were a little babyish by the time we reached our teens, but they were all we had. Children are good at amusing themselves. I had books to read, and by then I kept a diary. I would spend a lot of the evening writing detailed notes about what I had done each day.

In the winter holidays Uncle Richard brought in a Christmas tree, decorated the house, helped us wrap the presents, while my father stayed shut in his study, and my mother spent more and more of her time sitting in front of the television with a gin and tonic in her hand, scarcely even aware of what she was watching.

The parties continued unabated, but not every weekend and mercifully not over Christmas.

When I was almost sixteen, things started to go badly wrong. It was the beginning of the worst year of my life, when my whole safe upper-middle-class world crashed around me.

I was invited to stay for three weeks of the summer holidays with my best friend Angelina, whose parents had an estate in Kent called Mullion Park. I would normally have declined, as I liked to spend the holidays at home with James. But James was going to a camp in Scotland with some other boys who were leaving school that year as he was. In October they would all start at Cambridge.

I was disappointed with James and deeply hurt. He had betrayed me. Why would he want to be with boys he saw all the time at school, instead of spending the holiday with me? I bitterly resented it. I didn't want to be at home on my own with my mother getting cross and drunk all the time. Although even that was better than seeing her sit by herself in a zombie state. Sometimes the television she was supposed to be watching was not even turned on.

I accepted the invitation. I would jolly well have a good time without James.

I went home for the weekend first, as I needed real clothes for the holiday, not just school uniforms, and I travelled to Mullion Park in a taxi on the Monday. It was around thirty miles from where we lived, but my mother was too busy to drive me there. Actually, she was drunk, and I was old enough to realise that both she and I would be safer if I took the taxi.

There were six young people at the house where I was staying: my friend Angelina, who was anything but an angel; her younger sister Elphine, who had more in common with an imp than an elf; their older brother Julian, who was the same age as James but was not a Harton boy; and two of Julian's schoolfriends.

All three of the boys were good looking and friendly. They all gave me a second look when I was introduced. I was getting used by then to men looking at me twice. I looked much older than I was, as I was quite tall, and although I considered myself to be slim, I was not as thin as many teenagers are. I had long black curly hair, frustratingly untameable—cutting it neatly was beyond the skills of any hairdresser—but my skin was pale and my eyes were blue and very large, so I was unusual enough for most people to look at me twice, men and women.

Julian looked a little like James, and he kissed my hand when I was introduced, which seemed very romantic to me then.

His father looked at me twice too, when I met him before dinner, asked who this sweet little blue-eyed Carmen was, and insisted on taking me into the dining room and tucking in my chair when I sat down.

The mother was wary of me after that. Young as I was, I sensed it. She was painted up with bright-red lipstick, bright-red nail varnish, and wore skinny high heels, even indoors. In the right clothes she would have seemed pleasantly plump, like a comfortable story-book farmer's wife, but she wore short tight skirts that showed the tops of her stockings and emphasised her fat thighs, her fat behind and her fat midriff. Everything about her seemed garish and false, even the huge gemstones in her rings and her earrings, and the overbearing perfume that followed her around like a personal cloud, yet still lingered in a room long after she left it. My mother may have been a whore, but she was not a painted-up tart like Angelina's mother.

Angelina's father was always lurking around when I was in the house, calling me his *little Carmen with the big blue eyes*, and touching my bum. For some weird reason the downstairs cloakroom was only for the gentlemen, so if I needed the bathroom I had to go upstairs. He was usually in his study, off the main hallway, and when I came past on my way upstairs, he would come out and talk to me. As I walked up the stairs, he would stand in the hall below. Before long I realised it was to look up my skirt, so I kept further towards the wall. How could a man get a kick out of seeing a girl's knickers? Especially this man, who could see his wife's knickers every time she bent over.

But in spite of this, I did enjoy the first week. The boys were fun, and they bickered among themselves over who would row me on the lake, or play tennis with me, or stand close behind me to help me hold the cue correctly for snooker. These boys were not attacking me but were vying for my favours. This was more like things should be. I learnt how to flirt with all three of them at once. The occasional compliment on their height or strength, an admiring glance in their direction when one of them cracked a joke, an accidental brush of my hand against theirs, asking them easy things so they felt themselves to be clever, and all three of them were my slaves. I was enjoying this holiday.

Angelina was madly jealous, as she liked one of her brother's friends. But Elphine was too young to care about boys and was always playing pranks on them, jumping out from behind furniture in the house or trees in the garden, and hiding their things. It became rather tedious for us all. I realise now it was totally for attention, which I suppose was understandable from a girl of thirteen who was old enough to sense the chemistry between teenage girls and teenage boys but not old enough to be a part of it.

By the end of the first week, I had a complete crush on Julian, with the other two boys now forgotten also-rans. I would get up early to walk in the garden, and he would join me. Once out of sight of the house, he would take my hand, and we would run together across the lawn to a little temple by a lake, where we would sit and talk for a while, before returning to the house for breakfast, which was not served until nine. I found this strange, as by then half the morning was gone. But here I was living, for the first time in my life, in a house that had servants. My mother had a cleaning lady and a gardener in once a week, but they were not live-in.

Julian said he was in love with me, and perhaps both of us really believed he was. The temple had a small room, sheltered from the garden, with a few easy chairs, a sofa and a cane coffee table. For a while it was just an innocent kiss or two, then our hands roaming to investigate mysterious places that differed between boys and girls, but one morning we went a little too far. Well, actually much too far. He had his hand up my skirt, for the first time getting inside my knickers, his fingers warm and oddly slippery and rather thrilling, and he guided my hand to where he wanted it, but this time he unzipped his fly and let me feel his naked dick.

'Just stroke it,' he murmured, and when he groaned with pleasure at the touch of my hand, I realised that this was the power that women had over men.

If things had stopped there, all may have been well, but they didn't. He pulled off my knickers and was on top of me, hard and heavy and insistent, much stronger than I was, so resistance was futile, his body moving in mine as if he was incapable of controlling it, and at last he gasped and stopped, collapsing on top of me.

I was not so naïve that I didn't realise what he had done, but we had learnt at school that a man's dick was supposed to be covered with something before you went the whole way, and there didn't appear to be any sign of that.

'God, that was beautiful,' he murmured. 'I'm sorry if it was a bit quick. Tonight, I'll come to your room when everyone else is asleep, and we can do it properly. I promise it'll feel better for you.'

That was when his mother walked in.

We had lost track of time and were now rather late for breakfast. Had she realised we were somewhere together when neither of us turned up? Had one of the gardeners directed her to the temple, trying his best to hide a snicker? How had she made it across the lawn in those skinny high heels?

She exploded. Her refined accent gradually slipped and so did the politeness of her language. She was sounding more like a cockney fish-wife, swearing at me with words I blushed to listen to and will not transcribe here.

I was a hussy and no wonder, with a whore for a mother. She had seen the way I looked at her husband and her son with those sly eyes of mine, she should have thrown me out the first day I came here. I was to pack my bags and leave, she would complain to my father how I had behaved, and to the school, and ... and ... and ...

There was that *whore* word again, but by now I was old enough to know what it meant. I won't repeat any of the other words she called me and also my mother.

I thought about telling her that at least my mother wasn't a painted-up tart, but I didn't. I would not descend to her level. I would get back at her one day, but for now I would bide my time.

So, I said nothing, retrieved my underwear with as much dignity as I could manage—it is surprisingly difficult to put knickers on elegantly—and walked out of the temple and across to the house while she was still yelling abuse after me. I packed my bags, asked the housekeeper to order a taxi to take me home, and I left the house, with no breakfast and no further word to anyone.

I returned home to Surrey, sore from my encounter, hungry and seething with rage. Her son had seduced me, had practically raped me with no protection at all—he certainly hadn't asked me—and she had the hide to blame me. I could only hope I wasn't pregnant. At least we had been taught how you worked that out.

Uncle Richard was the first to greet me when I returned to the house. It was a Saturday, so he was with us. He knew, of course, that something had gone wrong, as I was supposed to still be at Mullion Park with my friend. I told him what had happened—I was always able to talk to him about practically anything.

I thought I would be in trouble, but he just laughed and asked if I had enjoyed it.

'Not very much,' I confessed.

'Always remember Ann, that giving yourself to a man is a gift for you to give and him to deserve. If you don't want to give it, then either refuse to, or get some payment for it. Men enjoy it more than women do. There are some who would argue with that, but since no one has ever experienced both, we can only go on the evidence we have. Some men enjoy it so much they are prepared to pay for it. Very few women want it that badly. Did he take precautions?'

'I don't think so.'

'I'll give you a packet to keep in your handbag. No decent man would refuse to use one. We'll keep our fingers crossed, but if there are consequences, we'll deal with them.'

I overheard my uncle discussing it with my father that night when they were playing billiards together.

'We could blackmail them. She's not yet sixteen. We could wreck the boy's prospects if it got out.'

It was my father who said it, of course, not my uncle. My uncle was much more honest and straightforward than my father and could never have blackmailed anyone, but I loved them both.

I didn't want Julian's prospects wrecked. I loved him, and I knew he really did love me. Something would happen, and we would be together again one day. Somewhere without his mother.

Meanwhile I consoled myself with thinking of horrible things that could happen to her, like falling in the pond, or tripping over the cat in her ridiculous high heels, or her skirt splitting when she bent over at some exclusive garden party, or finding a cockroach at the bottom of her gin and tonic, preferably one that I had put there.

In September I returned to school. James was still in Scotland with his friends. They were all to start at Cambridge in early October. I had not seen him once for the whole of the summer.

Angelina still wanted to be my friend, although her mother had forbidden her to speak to me. I was expecting to be called to the headmistress's office to explain my behaviour at Mullion Park, but it never happened, so I guess Angelina's mother never snitched on me. It would not have been in her interest to tell anyone that her son had made love to an underage girl, so I was fairly confident I was safe. I also knew by then that there had been no unintended consequences.

Julian sent me a note, enclosed in a letter he sent to his sister, telling me he loved me beyond reason and we would find a way to be together. I never responded; somehow the whole thing had gone sour. I even went off Angelina. She was always very clingy, holding onto my arm with her bony fingers, poking her bony elbow into my side when we walked together, and she constantly pestered me to tell her what it had felt like. She told all the other girls I was no longer a virgin, that I had seduced her brother and her mother had thrown me out of the house. But she was smug that she was the one who was my friend, so she knew all about it, but the other girls didn't.

I found another friend.

Coming of Age 1981–1985

In December of that year, 1981, the first real disaster happened. It was nearly the end of term, and we were all looking forward to Christmas. James was already at home, as the university terms were much shorter than the school ones. It was, quite literally, months since I had seen him. Soon we would be back together.

I was called to the office of the headmistress, and I followed the messenger, wondering what I had done wrong. I could think of nothing. Perhaps Angelina's mother had complained about me after all. Perhaps the headmistress had heard the rumour that I was no longer a virgin, and I would be expelled.

Uncle Richard was with her as well as the school chaplain. My uncle was trying to smudge away tears with his thumb, one of the rare times I had seen a man cry. He held out his arms to me, hugged me while the headmistress told me the news. My mother had fallen down the stairs while she was intoxicated and alone in the house. She was dead.

I don't like to think about that time in my life, and I won't dwell on it more than I have to for my story, but from then on things just went from bad to worse.

Within a few days the police arrived at the house in Surrey, where all of us were staying, sitting huddled together, or wandering aimlessly around the house, unable to think or act rationally, while we planned the funeral and waited for the coroner to release my mother's body.

They marched us all out into the garden and searched the house from cellar to attic. My mother had been dead drunk when she fell down the stairs, but they now knew she had also been high on cocaine.

They never found the supply—I assume my father had disposed of it—but they took him away with them.

The welfare people arrived and wanted to put me in foster care, but my uncle refused to allow them into the house—we had one of those chain latches—and told them to get a court order. They said they would come back tomorrow with a police officer.

That night we fled to my uncle's flat in Kensington, where he lived during the week, and he told me to lie low for the moment and not answer the door if anyone called while he was at work. James stayed at the house in Surrey, with instructions not to tell them where I was.

The three of us spent a miserable Christmas together in the Kensington flat, with James sleeping on the sofa, as there were only two bedrooms. No tree, no presents, no cards, and the decorations in the streets and the shops were a painful reminder that Christmas would never again be the same for any of us.

We cleared out a boxroom in the flat—perhaps once a room for a maid. It was just large enough to fit a single bed for James and a wardrobe with sliding doors, so at least he had somewhere decent to sleep when he stayed with us and could hang up his shirts and jackets.

My father was charged with dealing in cocaine and, after some further investigation, with embezzling money from the clients of his financial advice business. The police couldn't find the missing money or the cocaine. But they offered him a plea deal, a lighter sentence if he pleaded guilty to all charges to save the trouble of a trial by jury, repaid the funds, led them to the supplier of the drugs and told them the names of the men who had been at the parties where the cocaine was supplied.

They were unable to touch the house in Surrey, as it belonged to my mother, who had herself inherited it from her father, so James and I would still have that, but I was unable to return there because of the welfare people. Richard told me there was also some money in my mother's name in a Swiss bank account, but for now we would not be accessing that.

The police had nothing on Uncle Richard. He had his own accounting business, which he ran with a partner, completely independently of my father's firm. James and I were both to deny that he had ever been at any of the parties. Yes, we sometimes saw him on weekends, but it was generally only for him to take me and James on outings. We had never been allowed to come downstairs during the parties, so we had no idea who was there. He told us that he had known about the cocaine, but the theft from the clients was a complete surprise to him. He wondered how my father could have been so foolish, as he made far more from the drugs than he had from cheating his clients.

The last time I ever saw my father was at my mother's funeral. They allowed him to attend, handcuffed to a prison officer, but at least I was able to hug him.

Uncle Richard was executor for my mother's estate, and he managed to get legal guardianship of me while my father was in custody. The welfare people objected, but he had the means to keep me, and the flat had two bedrooms, actually now three, so eventually they left us alone.

I never returned to Roburn School. I doubt that they would have accepted me even if I had wanted to. My uncle managed to get me a place at a small private grammar school near his flat, so I could finish the school year as a day girl and get my O-levels. James returned to Cambridge in January, and Uncle Richard and I went to Surrey on the weekends, James often joining us there. We coped. We had no alternative.

My father died in custody before he could be tried. He had refused the plea deal. They said he had committed suicide, but all three of us knew that he would never have done that. Were there men at the parties who wanted their identity kept secret? Men with the power to dispose of a drug dealer who could expose them? Or was it the men who supplied the drugs to my father who had the contacts to kill a man who was in custody? I will never now know. They could never have convicted him for drug dealing unless one of the men from the parties had come forward, which was unlikely to happen. They had found no drugs in the house, and my mother could have got the cocaine from anyone. He would probably have got away with only a few years for stealing from his clients' accounts, and, since he still had a lot of money stashed somewhere out of reach, which he could access after his release from prison, he would have accepted that. He would never have killed himself.

My uncle wound up my father's estate, with help from the police forensic auditors, and he paid back some of the embezzled funds. But of course the money in the Swiss bank account was not included in the estate. As far as the world was concerned, the money my father made from his firm, and took from the clients, had gone on school fees for James and me, and living expenses. There was no trace of money being transferred offshore. It would have been easier to hide that then. There was also some cash that had been in my father's safe. He had given it to Richard as soon as my mother died, so the police had not found it. The safe had been empty when they had searched the house, apart from some jewellery of my mother's.

After we had buried my father in the grave beside my mother, on a miserable rainy day, the three of us carried on as best we could. James and I owned the house, and there was our father's cash from the safe and some money that had belonged to our mother. James would, of course, stay on at Cambridge with my uncle funding him. I would finish the year at the new school and then decide if I wanted to carry on and study for my A-levels. Gradually we were returning to some kind of normality.

But in April of that year, 1982, during the Easter holiday, the next tragedy occurred, for me the worst one of my whole life.

James was spending the Easter weekend in Scotland with a friend from Cambridge, who drove them both in his small but expensive sports car. On the way back on the Monday evening, there was a pileup on the motorway. Visibility was hampered by fog, the treachery compounded by darkness. They were driving too fast, slammed into the pileup, and both of them were killed.

It was two days before his nineteenth birthday. I sat in my room in the flat in Kensington with the present I had just wrapped for him, a maroon tie with a thin gold stripe that I had found for him and knew he would like. There was a poster on his bedroom wall of a suave film hero who was wearing an identical tie. The film hero was my hero as well, as anything James loved, I loved too.

The last remnants of my magical childhood in the walled garden were gone forever. My knight in shining armour was now but a castle ghost, chained for all eternity in a world where I had no part. Life had no happy endings, and for me it no longer had any meaning at all.

I will skip past how we got through the next few months, just Richard and me, because even now I can't think about it without crying for the two beautiful intelligent young men with their whole lives ahead of them who were both gone in an instant. Their whole futures, bright with the promise of lovers, careers, even children, lost into the shadowy realm of things that might have been but weren't.

I managed to get through my exams, with a lot of help and support from the teachers at the school, but I didn't want to continue studying.

When I was at home in the flat, the school year now finished, my uncle at work, I had no heart to do anything but sit, hugging my knees, rocking to and fro, drowning in my own deep well of depression.

My uncle hired an au pair, a Norwegian girl called Kristen, so I was not by myself when he was at work. She slept in the room that had been James's, did all the housework, took me with her when she did the shopping, and I taught her English, while she taught me a little Norwegian. She did her best to keep me occupied.

Richard had a friend, a lovely man called Amos, who often called at the flat. Amos was older than my uncle by several years, balding, tubby and cheerful, always ready with a joke but never making fun of other people. His equally lovely wife Rebecca, who sometimes came with him to the flat, ran a modelling agency and deportment classes, and she took me in hand.

I didn't want to be a model—and in any case I was not tall or thin enough—but I was persuaded to do the deportment classes, and a makeup class that she also ran. Kristen came with me to the classes, my uncle paying for both of us. Then Rebecca sent us both to learn to do facials and manicures. She took me to her dressmaker's salon where they dolled me up with expensive but casual clothes, and I did facials for some of her friends, who paid her for the services but gave me extravagant tips. She sent us both to classes in massage, and from October of that year I studied to be a physiotherapy assistant. It was a two-year course, giving me a qualification to teach basic yoga, do remedial massage and supervise personal training in a gym. To be a real physiotherapist I would have needed at least some A-levels and a three-year course. But I liked to think of myself as a physiotherapist.

For a while Kristen stayed on. By now she was sleeping with my uncle. I don't know if he paid her for it, if she had some idea he might marry her—he was, after all, single and wealthy—or if she actually did love him. He was a very attractive man, an older version of my brother James. On the rare occasions that we spent a weekend in the house in Surrey, she came with us and did the housework there.

I slept in one of the first-floor rooms in the Surrey house, leaving the attic floor, which James and I had once shared, to the childhood ghosts, their laughter forever locked into the silent spaces of the past.

Eventually, now proficient in English and trained in deportment, facials and massage, Kristen left to return to her family in Norway. For a while we managed alone, but soon another au pair was hired, and from then on, we had a succession of them. I became quite good at helping them with their English. Some of them slept with my uncle, others didn't. He didn't appear to have any preference about the arrangement.

I now owned the house in Surrey and the money from my mother, all still in trust as I was not yet eighteen. There was also the money stashed away in Switzerland that I could eventually access, but for now it was best to leave it untouched and untraceable. Richard thought only a little of it was money my father had stolen from the clients, as much of that had been returned. It was the profit from the cocaine, supplied at the parties to the rich friends. I was not sure I wanted money from drug dealing, but Richard suggested I just accept it as compensation for losing my sad addicted mother. It had all been recreational; the men chose to pay for it, and no one else there had been an addict. My uncle was wealthy, of course, as he accounted money for a living, and it paid well enough that we lacked for nothing.

Richard—I will refer to him as Richard from now on, as I had long ago stopped calling him Uncle—had a much younger partner, Paul, and I got to know him well during the years when I was studying. Paul's father had been Richard's original partner, but he had retired, and his son had taken his place. Paul was fun to have around, and he was my first real boyfriend, although we both understood it could never be a serious relationship. His mother wanted him to marry the daughter of her best friend. Paul told me she was just a kid, boring, ugly, horsey, was only happy when she was egging on hounds to kill foxes, and he hated to be in her company. But he was expected to marry her when she reached eighteen. It seemed archaic to me, like Lady Catherine de Bourgh in *Pride and Prejudice* wanting Mr Darcy to marry her daughter.

I went to films with him, walked in parks with him, partnered him at dances, parties and the engagements and weddings of his friends. There were no drugs at the parties, beyond the occasional whiff of marijuana, and neither Paul nor I ever got drunk or high. One night I went back to his flat after a party, and he asked if I wanted to sleep with him. No strings attached and it would be fun. It was fun, a much better experience than with Julian, and he suggested I go on the Pill, as a second line of defence, and because it made a girl's life easier.

I was never in love with him, and I knew he had other girlfriends at the same time as he dated me, but I went out with him when he asked me and slept with him when I could. I suppose Richard knew, but he never said anything, so I assumed he didn't mind.

One Saturday Paul took me as his partner to the wedding of one of his friends, and his father and mother were there.

'Lovely young lady you have there, son,' his father said, giving me that second look when we were introduced. 'You're Richard's niece, aren't you. He told me you were stunning, and by God he was right.'

'I hope you realise Paul is engaged,' his mother said coldly. 'There's no chance at all of his marrying you.'

I was taken aback by her candour, and it took me a few seconds to think up a response. It was not a good response, but it made me feel better. Afterwards I thought of other things I wished I had said instead but hadn't.

'Yes, of course I do. He told me from the beginning. But as she is not yet old enough to come to these functions, you can't expect him to just mope around at home. I don't want to marry your son or anyone else. I've never yet met any man I could be prevailed upon to marry. I'd rather stay single.'

I was rather proud of my slightly altered quote, although I couldn't actually recall where I had read it. It was probably *Pride and Prejudice*, as that was the last book I had read at school, and the only book we had studied that I had actually enjoyed reading—probably the only one I had actually read. She might think I was well read and bookish. Foolish me. As if she cared anything about me at all. Her only thought was to get rid of a threat to her plans.

'So, there's no one good enough for you, Miss Hoity-Toity. And after what your father did. You've got a nerve.'

I couldn't believe how rude she was to me. How I wished I could think of some clever retort. Paul pulled me away to meet some of his friends, but I saw her glaring at me as I laughed with them over some silly joke one of them had made. Later Paul apologised, telling me his mother was worried that he would find someone else before his fiancée was old enough to be married.

I went home with Paul; his parents had already left, and I knew Richard wouldn't mind. We spent some time on the sofa in his flat, drinking coffee, and I left the mugs in the kitchen sink before we went to bed.

We were woken at around eight the next morning by some-one banging on the door of the flat.

'Coming,' Paul yelled, pulling on his pyjamas as he crossed the bedroom to glance out of the window.

'It's my mother,' he told me. 'Her car is in the street.'

Oh dear.

'Hang on a minute while I find some clothes,' he yelled.

That at least bought us time. I picked up my scattered clothes from the bedroom floor and hid, still naked, in the wardrobe while Paul found his dressing gown, closed the bedroom door and let her in. At least that gave me a moment to sneak to the bathroom, which was accessed off the bedroom, as I was desperate. I crawled back into the wardrobe, wondering if I could get into at least some of my clothes, and realised with horror that I had flushed the loo. Would she have heard it from the lounge and know that there was someone else in the flat? Perhaps he could tell her it was the loo in the flat next door— the sound carried through the pipes. I imagined her storming in here, guessing where I was hiding, opening the wardrobe door, finding me starkers in her son's bedroom. What excuse could I possibly invent? Come on Ann, think! There must be something I could say. I had been so drunk I had passed out on the sofa, and I had slept there for the night. Then this morning he had told me to take a cold shower, and I had hidden when I heard the door bell, in case she thought the wrong thing. That would do.

I heard some mumbled words about a birthday present and Paul remonstrating that his birthday was still two weeks away. He would see her before then.

'Is that girl here?' Well, at least now she was getting to the point.

'What girl?'

'That Berrington trollop. Daughter of that crook Giles and his whore of a wife. The merest glance from a man and she'd drop her knickers.'

'Mum, please mind your language. Ann is my partner's niece and is hardly responsible for the behaviour of her father.'

'Is she here? There are two cups in the sink.'

'She came back for coffee last night, and then I took her home to Richard's flat. It's only a block away.'

'Left her shoes here, did she? Walked home in bare feet?'

I had taken them off while we were snogging on the sofa, so they were still in the lounge. We had overlooked them when I grabbed the scattered clothes from the bedroom floor.

I heard the bedroom door open, and I stayed as still as I could, trying not to laugh, hoping I had picked up all the clothes. I imagined her finding my knickers, but they were safe in here with me, I had been trying to wriggle back into them.

'Yes,' Paul was saying. 'I'm taking them back to her this morning. She wore flats here and brought the heels to change into when we got to the wedding. She left them here by mistake when she changed back to the flats to go home.'

I heard her steps across the bedroom as she checked the bathroom.

It seemed an eternity before she left. I was cramped, cold and trying my best not to giggle.

I heard the outer door close, Paul saying goodbye. There was a pause while he waited to make sure she really had gone. I could see through a crack in the wardrobe door that he was standing by the bedroom window, checking the street below.

He opened the wardrobe and told me it was safe, but I would have to stay here in the flat for a bit because his mother was sitting in her car, parked outside, waiting to see if I emerged from the building.

I dressed, keeping well away from the window, put a shirt of his over my dress to protect it, and we made coffee and toast for our breakfast, Paul checking every so often to see if she was still there. Eventually, she gave up and drove away, and I was able to slip out, still dressed as I had been at the wedding, and return to Richard's flat.

Paul's mother didn't like me, but his father seemed to. He had been Richard's partner in the accountancy business before he retired. After he had met me at the wedding, he sometimes dropped by in the evening to talk to my uncle. They sat with their glasses of port or whisky, and I sometimes sat with them, with a glass of sherry—I was never a fan of gin and tonic, as it made me think of my mother. He was always glad to see me if I joined them, sometimes asking me if I had been anywhere with Paul lately, and making shaded comments about me being part of his family one day. Didn't he know about the rather strange engagement of his son? Or did he just disregard it as a bizarre fantasy on the part of his wife and her friend?

If it had not been for the mysterious young fiancée, I might have married Paul. It would have worked—we were friends as well as lovers—but I was never in love with him because I knew I was not allowed to be. He sometimes asked me to come and live with him in the flat, but I didn't want to be a second-best stopgap while he waited for the real prize.

I had other dates. There were always young men at the parties who liked me enough to ask me out, who knew the arrangement I had with Paul, so did not consider they were encroaching on his girlfriend, and I occasionally accepted.

I came to realise that the initial aim of the young men was to earn enough to have a flat, or at least their own room in a flat, which they could use to take girls back to sleep with them. Some of them, of course, had family-owned flats. They would take you out, then invite you back for coffee, and from there it was just a matter of negotiating whether you would stay the night with them or not. They were generally good about it if you said no, and I usually did. I had known Paul for a long time before I slept with him, and sleeping with someone on a first date always seemed wrong to me.

Sometimes they asked me out again, sometimes not. In the end there were only two I slept with, both of them only once, and neither of them on the first date. It was not fun like it was with Paul, and they were nowhere near as good in bed. It was just the man persuading the woman to allow him access to what he wanted from her. There was no love in it, and any pleasure I felt was fleeting. Neither of them really cared whether I enjoyed it or not, and I felt like I was just a trophy.

The ultimate aim of these young men, when they had tired of conquests, was a match that suited their need for a wife with money or the prospect of inheriting or earning money, or a wife higher up the social scale, or a wife who was beautiful enough to be considered a prize. It made a man feel good to be envied. Most of them were upper-middle class like I was, and the parties gave them a field to select their lifelong partner. The girls had similar ideas, and we did have a few matches and a few weddings among our set. The married ones rarely returned to the parties, as there was no longer any point in it.

But it never seemed to work for me, and I never really felt a part of their social set. I was better off financially than some of the girls, mostly because my money was actually mine rather than my father's, but I was no higher in social status, so my main attraction as a girlfriend was being considered better looking than the average girl there. I liked Paul, and the parties were fun after a drink or two with people you liked to be with, but I didn't find a partner. Being with Paul was safe for both of us.

Looking back, I now believe that I was looking for a man like James. None of the young men were as good looking or as clever as my brother had been, so none of them were the right one. And they were all so completely wrapped up in themselves and what they wanted from life. A girl was just a possession, a status symbol, especially if you found an attractive one that all the other guys wanted.

I finished my course, and Richard and I made the decision to sell the house in Surrey. Neither of us could bear to live there, and we now scarcely even visited it. It was now late in 1984, and I was just nineteen.

One weekend in October Richard drove us down to a little village called Deniton, on the south coast, to see a house, situated, as was the village, on gently sloping land between a length of high cliffs and the seashore.

The house was remote and beautiful, with a wooded garden of twenty acres that bordered the sea, but it was a vast jumble of styles and ages and was in need of repairs and renovation. There were twelve bedrooms, three ancient bathrooms, several large reception rooms and a tower. A magical fairy-tale tower.

The heating system, relying on a boiler and old-fashioned radiators, was no longer functional; there were roof leaks but not catastrophic ones; and the wiring was known to be a little touchy, so the lights would go out unexpectedly for short lengths of time.

It had once been run as a small private hotel by a little old lady, now in her nineties, who was way past being able to look after it or run it profitably. I only ever knew her as Mrs Pearson. Her agent showed us over the house, and she made tea and scones for us all.

She had no surviving children. Her only son had been killed in the Second World War, and her husband had died not long afterwards. The house had been her late husband's family home, but he had no other heirs, so it was now her own. She was sad that her husband's family had died out and the house was falling into a state of gradual decay. She did have a great-nephew, she told us, grandson to her brother, but she had never met him, and since he was her family, not her husband's, he could have no sentimental attachment to the house as a family home. She wanted to sell it before she died so he was not burdened by a huge decaying house with no money to renovate it.

She would retire to a cottage that was once the lodge for the main house and would live there for the remainder of her days. It was on a separate freehold title. Her late husband's aunt had lived there between the Wars, after which ownership had reverted back to her husband and thence to his estate. Mrs Pearson had been running it for many years as a separate holiday let, managed by the estate agent, giving her a small income in addition to her pension, so it was liveable as it was. However, she would use some of the money from the sale of the large house to modernise the cottage and install central heating.

A few days later we made another visit, this time with a builder, who would give us a quote to refurbish the old hotel as Richard wanted. Apart from a few leaks in the roof, the structure was sound, and most rooms were still in good condition beneath ten years of dust and cobwebs.

While the men were discussing the renovations, Mrs Pearson showed me the garden and the path down through the wood to the seashore, past an old icehouse, which had been used to store ice in winter for use in summer to make ice cream. We went through a gate in a high wall, crossed over the footpath and a few coastal plants, and we were on a sandy beach. This was not just visiting the seaside in the summer, this was having the seaside just outside your back garden, living as close to the shore as you can get.

Because the house in Surrey was near London, had eight bedrooms and was situated on an acre of land, the proceeds from selling it would easily cover the cost to buy and renovate the dilapidated hotel. We would set it up as a private retreat for Richard's business clients. I would live in the house during the week, and on weekends Richard would bring clients down to stay. Some weekends would be for men to bring their wives, other weekends for men to meet up with their mistresses or with escorts supplied by Richard. I would give facials and manicures to the wives and massages to the men, we would have a heated indoor swimming pool and a gym that I could supervise, we would refurbish the tennis court, install locks and an intercom on the gate, and we would make money. A lot of money.

I realised then that Richard had encouraged me to study massage and gym instruction because he had something like this in mind from when I left school, but I had enjoyed the course, and I was confident I could run the retreat for his clients.

I remembered the parties in the house in Surrey and made Richard promise there would be no drugs.

He agreed to that. He had, in any case, had nothing to do with the cocaine or the theft of the clients' money. But he did tell me one thing that didn't really surprise me. He had often slept with my mother and was not entirely sure whether I was my father's daughter or his. Even my mother had never known. Later my father had sometimes hired my mother out for sex with some of the guests who came to the parties, and there had been wife swapping, but that was a long time after I was born. Richard had always tried to help my mother overcome her addiction, but he was not her husband, and my father had resented it. There was no way that Richard wanted me anywhere near cocaine.

But before we could sell the house in Surrey, we had to clear everything out of it.

Some of the furniture was sold, and a few pieces would go with us to Deniton, but personal things had to be sorted and disposed of: my parents' clothes, my own childhood clothes, books and toys, but worse, far worse, James's things.

I had not once gone up to the top floor of the house since James had died. The au pairs had done the cleaning. They were always capable and confident young women, but perhaps only capable and confident young women become au pairs, living in a foreign country away from their families. I knew I could never do that. Although in the end I had to.

Our then current au pair boxed up James's clothes and books to send to a charity shop, but she kept his school scarf from Harton for me, rolling it up carefully and sealing it in a plastic zip bag to preserve it from moths.

I still have James's scarf, the only thing I have left that he wore. I keep it with his letters to me and the family photograph album, the last links I have to my first home with the walled garden, the last assurance that the happiness of my childhood, however fleeting, was real.

The Surrey house was sold, the deal was done on the Deniton house, the renovations were set in motion, and Mrs Pearson retired to her little cottage, which we proceeded to wall off from the garden of the main house. Her access was from the lane, with a gate and a parking space, although the cottage had no garage. We installed an intercom with a bell on our main gate, a box for the postman to leave the mail, and a lock that was opened with a code number. There was room for a car on the verge outside the wall, so you could stop safely and open the gate with the code.

I liked Mrs Pearson. When we came down to oversee the alterations, she always came over to talk to us, and she didn't mind that we were changing things. She was glad to finally find a buyer for the house, and we had paid her a fair price for it, so she had enough money to modernise and repair the cottage to a high standard and would lack for nothing in her final years.

She could now afford to run the heating, she no longer had to worry about leaks in the roof, and she had time to go to the activities that the vicar's wife ran in the village, knitting circle and bridge and a yoga class. She had worried for years that the house would fall down around her, she had been sad that she could no longer look after the estate that had been her late husband's family home, and she was genuinely glad it was being given a new life.

I was to have the bedroom in the top of that magical tower, with a bathroom and a small study on the floor below. A safe had been built into a nook below the stairs that led from my study to my tower bedroom, where my mother's jewellery would be stored, along with the cash to pay the cook and the escorts.

An old conservatory was replaced and an indoor pool installed inside the space. We modernised the kitchen, added more bathrooms so that most of the bedrooms were ensuite, set aside rooms for a massage table, gym equipment, a billiard table, and we even installed a dance floor in a corner of the huge lounge, with weird lights set into the floor and a stereo system. We converted an old stable block to garages for the clients' cars, resurfaced the tennis court, and added a lock to the back gate, which led directly onto the beach. Most of the rooms came with furniture, so we had some workmen in to clean it up and refurbish it, and we bought new mattresses for all of the beds.

By late spring in 1985, we were ready for our first guests. Richard, his au pair and I spent a couple of weekends there by ourselves, checking everything was to our liking, and for the first time I slept in my tower room, in an old brass double bed, looking out through the mullioned windows, and listening to the sound of the sea.

Deniton 1985–1987

Our first weekend guests were Paul, Amos and Rebecca, and over dinner I realised for the first time that Amos was actually a partner in this venture with my uncle.

When we were in full swing, the guests would arrive late on Saturday morning, and I would make lunch and afternoon tea for them with the help of Richard's au pair, who would come down on Friday evening with my uncle. A cook from the nearby town would come on Saturday evening to cook the dinner for our guests, and she would return again on Sunday morning to make breakfast. I would make the lunch on Sunday, and the guests would leave in the afternoon. On Monday I would tidy up the house as best I could. On Tuesday a gardener would come to mow the lawns, and a local woman would come to do the cleaning. She would help me make up the beds for the following weekend. I would clean the pool and the gym, as they were both specialist jobs. On Wednesday the laundry service would send a van to pick up the dirty sheets and towels and drop off clean ones.

Amos would look after the bookings and keep track of the guests we had each weekend. Some weekends would be for the men to bring their wives, some for the men to bring their girlfriends or mistresses and some for the men to enjoy the company of escorts, who were supplied from an agency.

I was to be the hostess, assigning rooms and ensuring each room was labelled with its occupant's name, offering massages and manicures, mixing cocktails, arranging the music, checking there were towels for the pool, racquets available for playing tennis, offering a short yoga session before breakfast on Sundays, and supervising the men on the treadmills and rowing machines and weight benches in the gym. I was not expected to sleep with any of the men.

There would be house rules. There was to be no sex outside of bedrooms—although if an escort wanted to give her client a massage on my table, we might overlook a hand job, provided the door was closed and the room was left clean—there were to be no drugs, and no one was to get so drunk that they became disorderly. Respectable day clothing was required at dinner and at breakfast. Anyone swimming on the beach was to be wearing bathers, although nude swimming would be allowed in our pool. The furniture was to be treated with respect and the staff with courtesy. And no one was to make a pass at me; I was not for sale.

During the week I would be here by myself, apart from the cleaning lady on Tuesdays, although Richard offered me a permanent au pair of my own if I wanted company or help running the house. The gate would normally be locked. There was the bell, the intercom and the mail box beside the gatepost, so the postman had no need to come to the house; he would deliver the mail to the box and ring the bell. Richard told me his clients wanted privacy. He did not want reporters wandering in and taking photographs of men with their mistresses.

But for this first weekend Rebecca, the au pair and I looked after the cooking and the dishwashing, while the three men played snooker.

Rebecca and Amos had asked for separate rooms because he snored badly. I assigned a separate room for the au pair, as I did not know if she slept with Richard—some of them did, others didn't. Paul and I had separate rooms, but we spent the night together in his.

He asked me that night if I wanted to marry him. He would tell his mother he was not marrying the daughter of her friend, and would accept the recriminations and the disappointment. He didn't really care about the girl's pedigree or her estate, and she had no money to speak of. She was marrying him for his father's money, not vice versa. He couldn't bear the thought that he would scarcely even see me, now I was living down here and working on weekends when we had previously gone out together. If we were married, we could live together in his flat during the week and both come down here on weekends so I could help Richard and Amos manage the retreat. They could eventually find another hostess to help run their venture.

I said no. I liked him as a friend, and we were compatible as lovers, but I wanted romance, and I knew I was not the only girlfriend he slept with. He told me he would be faithful, and he offered me romance, if that was what I wanted. He would be happy to bring me flowers, take me dancing, whisper love songs to me.

But I still had dreams of a fairy-tale lover who would sweep me off my feet, and I would know, completely and unquestionably, that he was the right man for me. I knew that Paul was not that man and never could be. I was not yet prepared to settle for second best. I was not yet twenty.

Sometimes I wonder if I should have accepted him, faced the rows. His mother may have come round in time. To be sure, my late father was a criminal, but families survived worse scandals than that, and if it didn't matter to Paul, then it shouldn't matter to anyone else. If I had not been wary of falling for him from the start, as he was planning to marry another, could I have loved him enough to marry him? Perhaps.

We make decisions in our lives that forever change our paths going forward, but I no longer regret that one. If I had married him, I would never have met Simon.

The next weekend four retired men and their wives stayed with us, so I had a lot to do. We didn't spell out the house rules to them, as they were unlikely to transgress on any of the points. I made them all sandwiches for lunch, did facials and manicures for all of the women, helped the men on the gym equipment and organised some tennis games. I offered massages, but no one took them up. Perhaps they were all a little shy of being touched by a young woman, although I did explain that they left on their underwear or their swimwear, had a towel over them, and I would never touch them in any personal areas. Richard's au pair helped me where she could and made the afternoon tea for us all.

The cook and her assistant made the dinner on Saturday evening, and the au pair waited at the table then took her meal in the kitchen. The au pairs were always good about things like that, happy to be part of the family when it suited us, or part of the staff when it didn't.

The house had an old-fashioned formal dining room, with a table that seated fourteen, but we called that our boardroom, and we had set up another room to use as a dining room for our guests. Richard wanted more flexibility, and we had more reception rooms that we actually needed.

Our guest dining room had four small tables, each seating four, and this gave us a lot of choice in our seating arrangements. The four tables would seat sixteen, but by pushing tables together, we could seat two lots of six or one lot of ten. We opted for the ten for our retiree group, so all of them were socialising on the one table, with Richard at one end and myself at the other. We could have squeezed the au pair in on a corner, but she was happy to eat in the kitchen.

After the meal she helped the cook and her assistant clear up the dishes and stack them in the dishwasher, while I arranged cocktails and music in the lounge. The guests could choose dancing or watching a film, and they did a little of each. They danced for half an hour, before we all watched a film on the video player—we had a whole cupboard full of films to choose from.

On Sunday morning the cook returned, and a beautiful smell of toast and cooking bacon drifted through the house. Before breakfast the guests were invited to join a half-hour session of simple yoga, and after breakfast I took them on a walk along the path down through our wood to the gate in the wall that led to the shore, telling them stories of smugglers using the path to bring contraband brandy up to the house, and pointing out the old icehouse. I explained how ice was cut in winter and stored deep below the ground for use in the summer to make ice cream. The icehouse story was true, but I had made up the smugglers. Most of these south coast beaches had harboured smugglers, so it had probably really happened.

We walked along the shore, where I pointed out seagulls, the only seabirds I knew the name of.

The cook had gone by the time we returned, but she had left plates of sandwiches for lunch, so I had only to open a few bottles of wine to go with them.

In the afternoon they all packed their things, thanked Richard and me for a lovely weekend, and left to return to their homes.

It all seemed simple enough. Our retreat was exclusive, as only clients of Richard's accounting firm were invited, but they still had to pay to stay with us.

Over dinner that evening the three of us celebrated with a bottle of champagne, and after we had washed the dishes, I taught the au pair a few more English words and gave her a manicure.

The next weekend was completely different, and I had far less to do. Three men, all directors of a large company that Richard audited, arrived with three very glamourous women, all older than I was, and all very proficient in pleasing their men.

They did the massages, they had no need of facials, and they swam in the pool in scanty G-string bikinis, while the three men swam naked. After dinner they danced to music that I arranged for them, the men very free with their hands on the women's bums, but as soon as the cook had left, they played a game they called bunny hunting.

The moon was full—I realised afterwards why this weekend had been chosen—so the garden and the woods had enough light to see your way through the trees. The three women dressed up in skimpy black costumes with a white fluffy tail attached to the skirt, and they set off among the trees. The men, dressed only in black shorts, were given a picnic blanket each and left about ten minutes later to hunt for the girls.

Richard, his au pair and I sat on the terrace, and we laughed until we cried. We just couldn't help it. The men had apparently told their wives they were having a weekend here at our retreat to discuss company business in peace and quiet.

There were faint sounds of laughter from the woods, soft screams and moaning. I hoped that Mrs Pearson couldn't hear it from her cottage, but the house was between the cottage and the wood, and she was old and a little hard of hearing. There were no other close houses, as we owned so much of the surrounding land.

The au pair was fondling Richard, and eventually they retired to his room, leaving me to wait up and ensure all our guests were given a nightcap when they found their way back to the house.

They were not interested in my yoga class the following morning, or going on the walk, or hearing the stories of smugglers, or being shown how to identify a seagull, so I didn't have a lot to do on Sunday either. They did show up for breakfast, but they returned to their rooms with their women for the remainder of the morning.

That weekend was a success as well, although a little different from the first one.

For our third weekend, Richard supplied the girls. They drove down from London in a car owned by one of them. The three men who came that weekend seemed to know each other, even though they arrived separately, and they were each assigned a girl. Again, I didn't have a lot of work to do. At least this group didn't run around semi-naked in the woods. On the Saturday evening, they all watched porn movies together, and I left them to it. I found it revolting. The au pair and I sat in the kitchen, and I told her the English names for all the pots and utensils.

Our fourth weekend was the first time I met Lagan. He was a good-looking man, and was quite obviously impressed with me, but beyond that I didn't take any particular notice of him.

He came with two friends and the same women that the bunny hunters had used, but this time there was no bunny hunting. All three of the men were Italian, but they spoke perfect English. We set up a table for six and left them all to have dinner together, laughing and joking over their meal. The women did a striptease on our dance floor, then retired to the rooms with the men.

I was glad that we were not using the original formal dining room; I imagined the women doing their strip routine on the antique table. A whole lot of Pearson ancestors would turn in their graves.

No two weekends were exactly alike. I liked best the ones with the men and their wives, all very straight and respectable but different couples each time. Some weekends the couples were younger, but they were still couples, although one weekend we did have a group of four couples who wife swapped. Occasionally we had widows or widowers, although Richard tried to match them so there was one of each.

'You're not fleecing these people, are you?' I asked him one Sunday evening when they had all gone home, and we were once more by ourselves. Richard normally returned to London early on Monday morning. He had arranged his work schedule to start that day at ten. Accounting was a flexible profession; ledgers didn't need precise appointments the way that people did.

'No, not at all. They are well-heeled middle-class people, bread-and-butter clients for our firm. They get a holiday here for the weekend for the same price as a cheap production-line resort. It keeps them loyal to us, and it gives us respectability. If there is ever any trouble with the mistresses or the escorts, I have any number of credible witnesses who can testify that what we are running here is entirely above board.'

Although I had more to do, I preferred the weekends with the retired couples to those with the men and their mistresses. In spite of my slightly unconventional upbringing, I saw fidelity as an important part of a relationship. Some of the old men were still romantically in love with their wives, which I always found sweet, although others had a less-than-perfect relationship.

There were husbands who answered questions directed at their wives, and occasionally vice versa, and there were couples who were constantly putting their other half down. Sometimes it was grating to listen to them.

Some of the married couples accepted a massage in their bathers, mostly the men. Sometimes they would chat to me as I worked on them, confide in me, and I came to realise that many of these men never made love to their wives even though they shared a bedroom with them. I suppose it was having a woman touch their skin that made their minds turn to their sex lives, or more usually their lack of any. I never got personal, but sometimes the men reacted to my touch, and I always assured them it was quite usual, I was used to it, I knew how men worked.

One of the widowers, a dear old fellow, asked if I could do a little extra for him. Just a few strokes with my hand beneath the towel was all he wanted. It was years since he had felt the touch of a woman. His late wife had been good at helping him relax when she had been too tired to want him to make love to her, and he really missed it.

Had he heard rumours of what we did at Orchard House from other clients of my uncle? I obliged, leaving the towel in place. I had done this for Paul often enough, and I knew Richard wouldn't mind. The man thanked me, rather humbly, and told me how relaxed it made him feel.

But if a married man asked me for a favour, I would tell him that all the rooms had a bottle of massage oil on the bedside table, and why didn't he tell his wife that just a few strokes of her hand with the oil could make him feel wonderful. No one minded if a little of the oil got onto the sheets. I told them it was a good way for men to relieve stress and live longer lives. They were welcome to take the massage oil home with them, as it was complementary.

We had the bunny hunters again. This time the weather was too cold to be running scantily clad in the woods, so they played musical bedrooms, swapping every time the grandfather clock in the hall struck the hour. I don't know how far into the night they extended, as I went to bed at eleven. They all looked a little bleary eyed when they came down for breakfast.

In the early autumn, Richard invited Paul again and two other young men who worked for their partnership. They arrived, together with a girl, in a rather battered old car. Their names were Scott and Terry, and the girl was Jenny, the girlfriend of Scott. They had all done well at the accounting business that year, and Richard had given them all a free weekend, telling them they could bring their girlfriends if they wanted to. An au pair had come with Richard, and she would help me to cook the meals. It was easy enough with only seven of us in the house.

Jenny was a little nervous, asking me when she arrived if she was to have a separate room, as Scott had assured her she would. She didn't really know him that well. I assigned a separate room to the au pair as well, as I was not sure if this one slept with Richard. I rarely knew their names in advance—he had a succession of them—so unless he asked me to put the girl in the room next to his, I always gave her a bedroom downstairs, well away from the high jinks of the Italians or the bunny hunters, and I just put *au pair* on the label for the door of her room.

All of us spent a glorious Saturday afternoon on the beach, swimming, playing with a beachball and building an enormous sandcastle. I recalled the times that Richard had taken me and James to the seaside, those long years ago, and how happy we had all been then. You can't change the past or bring people back after they are gone, but sometimes something you do will bring back an echo, a memory that can cross the boundaries of time and take you back to a past where life was still touched with childhood wonder, and time was something that could never end for you or rob you of your current joy. Your past is just as much a part of your life as your present is and your future will be.

Jenny and the au pair both helped me cook and serve the dinner, and we watched a video together that evening while the men played snooker. It was a serial of *Pride and Prejudice*. I'm not sure how much of it the au pair understood but she appeared to enjoy it. We managed to get through all five episodes, although we did stay up rather late.

I initially told Paul I wouldn't sleep with him that weekend, as it seemed unfair on the other young men, but I did, of course, although we took care to avoid being observed. I wondered who Paul was now taking out to parties and weddings. There was a down side to being tied up here every weekend.

On Sunday morning, after our yoga session and our egg-and-bacon breakfast, I manicured both girls' nails and gave everyone a massage in their bathers while the others played in the pool. After lunch was tennis.

Although Jenny had officially come with Scott, she seemed to have hit it off with Terry. While the rest of us played tennis, the two of them went for a walk by themselves along the beach, returning hand in hand as we were packing up the racquets and nets, with soft looks between them, the shy attraction of new lovers who were barely out of their teens.

I loved that weekend. Just carefree young people enjoying themselves on a seaside holiday. This was how life should be. How could bunny hunting be more fun than this?

Some of the men brought their own girls, some used Richard's, some brought their wives, but we always ensured there was never any mixing of wives with mistresses.

We had one man who came down by himself, followed not long afterwards by a very high-class woman in a business suit, both of them in very expensive cars that Richard garaged for them so they were out of sight of the lane. There were no other guests that weekend. I didn't ask who they were—we only ever used first names—but I knew that both of them were married to someone else and they wanted somewhere private they could meet. The did discuss business, asking me to set up a table for them outside on the terrace, where they talked for hours, leafing through a great sheaf of papers that one of them had brought. They had asked for separate rooms, although I knew that they both spent the night in his room, as the bed in the lady's room was untouched. They preferred to be left to themselves, so we were as unobtrusive as we possibly could be, arranging them towels and tennis racquets and drinks. They left separately on Sunday afternoon, an hour or so apart.

We hosted some much younger couples, as well as the retirees, although in general their wives were rather snooty compared to the older ones. I offered them facials and mani-cures, but they clearly didn't consider mine would be up to the standard that they normally enjoyed, and they would not let their men anywhere near my massage table.

Lagan was a regular guest, sometimes bringing his two friends, Antonio and Marco, and they always brought their own women. I called them the *tre amici*—the three friends—as they were Italian. I still have no idea what Lagan's real name was. I liked him at the time; he was pleasant and cheerful and entertaining. But now I see him from the perspective of what happened later. I hate him now from the depths of my soul. He was the man whose reputation was more important than a girl's life, more important than my uncle's life, perhaps my father's life as well.

Were they the same clients? Had he been one of the men who paid my father for cocaine and slept with my mother?

He was a dangerously attractive man, tall and slim with thick jet-black hair and a beard, and I called him my Latin lover. He would come up behind me unawares, blow in my ear, kiss my neck, brush his soft beard against my skin, tell me I was the most beautiful woman he had ever set eyes on. He would pay anything I asked for my favours. He would set me up as his mistress in a flat in London, with a limitless credit card and all the diamonds and jewels I wanted. He told me he was a skilful lover, that by the time he thrust into me I would be desperate for him. He could make any woman scream for more.

'Why would you bother, since you would be paying for it? Why would you even care if the woman enjoys it?'

'Because then it is much more pleasurable for the man. Just sleep with me once, you can name your own price, and I promise you'll come back for more.'

I asked Richard later if that was true about it feeling better for the man.

'Absolutely,' he told me. 'But best of all is making love to a woman you really care about, and then it's the most beautiful feeling in the world. You understand then why it's called making love. I loved your mother and she loved me. I will never know why she married my brother and not me. I suppose her parents wanted her to, as he was the elder. I've slept with many women since, but it's just sex for the sake of it. Yes, it feels good, but without love it can never make a man feel satisfied. I always think that the next girl will be better, that one day it will feel like it did with Eloise, but it never does, and I've never loved anyone since. Except you, of course, but that is different; you're my niece. You're all I have left. Everything I do is for you, and everything I own is yours.'

I never agreed to sleep with Lagan, however hard he tried to persuade me to.

Sometimes the three of them came with the bunny hunters' women, but more usually they brought girls with them. Their girls didn't behave like the other women or the escorts that Richard supplied. They were very quiet, spoke no English whatsoever, and never flirted with their men as the other women did. The three men would eat together at one table, laughing and drinking, engrossed in their own Italian conversations, while the three girls sat at a table by themselves, talking in a language that was not English or the French or German I had learnt at school. Richard thought it was Russian, so I thought of them as the Russian girls.

They always looked very young. They didn't dress like the escorts but more like demure schoolgirls. Was this to pander to some fetish of the men? Did they pretend to be innocent virgins?

When I spoke to Richard about it, he assured me that if the girls were from an agency, they looked after checking the ages. There was a vague area. They had to be eighteen if they were paid for sex, sixteen if they weren't. Girls from Eastern Europe often looked much younger than they actually were. He was not paying Lagan's girls, and he didn't know where he got them from, so it was up to Lagan to follow the rules.

At that time I was prepared to be friends with Lagan, although his constant pestering me to sleep with him was sometimes rather trying, and he was occasionally a little free with his hands. He could be excellent company if he wanted to be. He would walk with me on the beach, ask me to play tennis or swim with him. I helped him at the gym and gave him massages, but never with the extra, although he always asked me for it, and occasionally tried to guide my hand to where he wanted it. But he did always treat me with courtesy, and he always thanked me at the end of the weekend.

When he brought the girls, they were never allowed to have manicures or massages, they were simply put in front of the television, watching films they would not have been able to understand—since they couldn't speak English—while the men swam or had massages. But the men took them into their rooms at night.

Christmas came, and I returned to London with Richard and stayed in his flat for the week. But we scarcely celebrated Christmas now beyond exchanging presents. Richard always bought me jewellery, and I bought him socks or aftershave, sometimes a particular book he asked for. Paul always gave me perfume, and I usually gave him an unusual tie.

The weeks passed, winter giving way to spring. I had now seen a whole year of seasons in the woods and on the seashore. Our first full year of owning the retreat was celebrated as a success. On our anniversary weekend we had Richard, his au pair, Rebecca and Amos, and Paul.

It had all gone smoothly. Richard and Amos looked after the bookings. The money came into our business account for the retreat and I wrote cheques for the bills and the costs. Richard took out cash to pay the cook and the escorts, and brought it down with him. He didn't want me taking large amounts of cash from the bank in town, in case someone followed me and tried to steal it. Somehow Amos was paid for arranging the bookings and Rebecca for supplying the girls, but I was never part of that arrangement. The escorts were paid in cash when they arrived, and the cook was paid when she left. Richard never told me how much profit we made, but there was always enough in the account to pay the bills, and he transferred any excess out to the account in Switzerland.

We had guests for around forty of the weekends in our first year; the remainder were Richard and me, usually his current au pair, and sometimes Paul as well. Richard and I came to enjoy the solitude of just the two of us together. We would walk on the beach, or swim in the sea or the pool, or play tennis.

I spent a lot of time in the week by myself, wandering along the cliff path, wandering along the beach, but I was never depressed. I lived in a beautiful house in a beautiful corner of the world, and I came to love it. I did not mind the solitude. But there was a lot to do with the cleaning and the laundry and planning the meals and the shopping. I would phone Richard on Thursday to find out the number of guests we expected. I would then plan the meals, do the shopping and decide if we needed the cook for that weekend. She was retired and just did our meals on weekends when we needed her to, with help from her daughter, so it suited her and it suited us. Richard always paid her in cash.

Paul sometimes came but only on the few weekends when there were no other guests. I was working on weekends when guests were with us, and Paul respected that. I was always pleased to see him, hear news of some of the other young people who had attended the parties, although there were fewer parties now, as some of our old set were married. He said he could never enjoy the parties without me and rarely went to them, instead occasionally staying for the weekend with his future bride and her parents.

As summer approached, we were busy every weekend. The retirees came again, the bunny hunters on their full-moon weekend, and at the end of the summer Richard invited Paul and their two employees again.

Jenny was now the steady girlfriend of Terry, but Scott brought another girl, Claire. I assigned everyone separate rooms but I slept with Paul. There were massages in bathers—I showed the girlfriends how it was done—but there was no nude swimming or anything at all that gave us away as being anything more than a private holiday destination for respectable couples.

The man and the high-class woman, who had wanted the retreat to themselves, came again, spending Saturday afternoon discussing a business deal and Sunday morning swimming in our pool. What they did in between was no one's affair but their own.

In October of that year, 1986, something rather odd happened, but I didn't think about it too much at the time, although I did note it in the diary I still kept. One of the Russian girls who came with the Italian men one Saturday was not there on Sunday morning. Antonio drove in as I was serving breakfast, saying he had dropped her at the station. I asked Richard later what had happened, and he told me there had been a row over what she was being paid and she had gone home.

Sometimes we hosted different men, sometimes different escorts, sometimes different couples, but mostly the same ones as the previous year. Another winter was upon us and another Christmas passed with just Richard and me together.

In early January of 1987, Paul came down for the weekend. We walked along the beach in the cold of winter, the waves crashing angrily on the shore, the seagulls huddling in sheltered spots or being swept backwards as they tried to fly against the wind.

He kissed me as we stood on the beach, told me he missed me dreadfully, asked me again if I would marry him, said he didn't care about his mother. I did waver. I felt isolated here at times, and I missed going out with him. But somehow it never seemed right. To marry him would have been an anticlimax, an admission that I had given up on finding the man who was right for me. In truth I had never felt a part of Paul's world; I had never really enjoyed the parties, or the young men who thought only of themselves. I liked it here, with the walks and the beach and the endless changing moods of the sea. I was twenty-one, young enough to believe I still had years ahead of me to find a mate.

In February he became officially engaged to the horsey girl. She would be eighteen in May, and they would marry in June. He invited me to his engagement party, but I didn't want to attend it. Some weekends he still came to Orchard House, and I still slept with him, but now we both knew it was too late for me to change my mind.

Paul's Wedding 1987

Paul came down to Deniton on the weekend before his wedding in June of 1987. Over dinner he discussed the accounting business with Richard—he was never a partner in the retreat business, as that was only Richard and Amos.

He would not come here for a weekend again. He was making an unstated pact with the horsey girl. He would be faithful and obedient, and he would share—and help fund—the large house and estate that she would one day inherit. Her father was a member of the House of Lords, but was nearly broke. Paul had made it from being upper-middle class, as I was, to being upper class. His father was paying for it. It was what Paul wanted, and he admitted the girl was not that bad. She did as she was told, and he didn't mind a few horses around the estate, provided they were never allowed indoors. He would not risk losing it all by any indiscretion.

I laughed and told him I wouldn't sleep with him that night, but of course I did. We lay side by side for what we both knew would be the last time. He told me he would give it all up for me if I would have him. He would leave her waiting at the church with his dragon of a mother throwing a tantrum when his best man gave her the news that he would not be turning up after all. We could escape to Italy. He had enough money for that, and so did I. We could leave tomorrow. He would phone his mother from Italy and call the whole thing off a day or two ahead of the planned wedding, as he didn't really want to abandon the poor child at the altar. She didn't really like him much anyway; she would be relieved to get out of marrying him and would soon find someone else.

I'm not sure what he would have done if I had agreed; I knew he was only asking me because he knew I wouldn't.

But I told him that this was our last time, and I expected him to behave properly towards me at his wedding, and towards his wife when he was married.

'I'll put a pillowcase over her head, turn off the lights, and pretend she's you. I might be able to get it up for long enough to do my duty.'

I told him that was a repulsive thing to say, but he just laughed and made love to me again, and we pretended to plan the things we would do and the places we would visit when we lived together in Italy. We would make love between rows of grapevines on a grassy hillside on a warm and lazy summer afternoon, surrounded by the gentle sound of bees and the soft scent of wild violets.

Richard and I were both invited to the wedding, which was to be held on the following Saturday morning. I spent that week with Richard in London. Both the cleaning lady and the gardener knew the code to open the gate, and the cleaning lady had the key to the house, so I could spend the week away without too much disruption. If I was not there in the week, I would simply cancel the laundry pickup, as we had enough sheets to last for a fortnight. We had often done this before when I went up to London to shop.

Rebecca's dressmaker friend Vera found me a beautiful silk dress to wear, light and airy and blue as the sky, the skirt with layer after layer of lace and gathers, and pearl buttons all the way up the front. I was given a wide-brimmed white hat with blue ribbons and flowers, a matching blue silk clutch bag and elegant blue high heels. I felt as if I belonged at an Edwardian-era garden party, playing croquet on a green English lawn on a beautiful summer day, with no care in the world, at a time when Britain was rejoicing in a new world of motor cars and the overthrow of bustles and strict Victorian morals. A time when the First World War was still but a faint and harmless cloud just emerging on the horizon.

'Can we find a husband for her?' the dressmaker asked Rebecca, bringing me back to earth, as they both looked me over.

'There will be plenty there for her to choose from,' Rebecca acknowledged, 'and none of the other girls will hold a candle to her. But they would need to overlook her father's crimes, and I'm not sure if Richard would like losing her.'

I assumed Richard paid for the clothes; I was never asked to.

The Saturday was fine and warm. Richard and I took our assigned seats in a beautiful gothic church. We were close to the front on the groom's side, and I was next to the aisle. Paul was standing at the front with his best man as we waited for the bride. I sensed that he knew I was only a couple of yards away from him, but he studiously avoided looking my way. I was curious to see what the ugly horsey girl looked like. Surely, every girl looked beautiful on her wedding day.

I could see Paul's mother in her seat in the second row, and when she looked around, impatient for the arrival of the bride, she was barely able to contain the joy that kept breaking out into a smug and self-satisfied grin.

There were whispers from the back. The mother of the bride—much younger and prettier than I had expected—was escorted to her seat, the music started, and the bride came down the aisle on the arm of a handsome old gentleman with a wonderful moustache. Thankfully, he was not one of our week-end guests.

Even through the wisp of her veil, I could see that she was stunningly and exquisitely beautiful. She was blonde, blue eyed, with a complexion that some girls would kill for, and her face was childlike and perfectly angelic. She was small and delicate, like a dainty story-book princess. Her four little bridesmaids, all blonde and sweet like she was, made me think of Flower Fairies.

How could that man have ever referred to her as ugly? How could he have ever risked losing her by sleeping with me? How could any man, offered such a prize, not be madly in love with her?

I could never be jealous of her because I was never in love with him, but I was angry with him for having talked about her behind her back as if he did not value her at all, when he should have considered himself the luckiest man in the world.

She was nice as well. I spoke to her after the luncheon, which was held in a large marquee on the lawn of their enormous house. She was friendly and polite, although a little timid, innocently telling me that Paul often mentioned his friend Ann, and she had been looking forward to meeting me. I wondered if she would be so friendly if she knew I had slept with her new husband only a week before. But I knew he would treat her well, and he would be a kind and gentle first-time lover if they had not yet gone that far. She was scarcely eighteen, and he was twenty-seven. In the end it had been his choice to marry her. I had refused him, but she was not the only alternative.

Her father came over to join us, giving me that second assessing glance, asking his daughter who this fine gal was. He actually kissed my hand, brushing it with that magnificent moustache, told me I had beautiful eyes, then put his arm around my waist.

I hoped his wife wasn't watching, but then I thought he probably did this with all of his daughter's friends and his wife would be used to it. She wasn't a painted-up tart like the mother of Julian but a really beautiful and high-bred woman with perfect manners, who had allowed herself to grow old gracefully. Not that she was old, probably still less than forty, a good twenty years younger than her husband. But when you are twenty-one, as I was then, anyone over thirty seems old. She was talking to a very attractive younger man, no older than Paul, the backs of their hands accidentally brushing together, a slight link of their little fingers, a quick glance exchanged between them, and instinct told me they were lovers. Perhaps her poor husband had to take what solace he could from touching the waists of his daughter's friends. I wished I could give him a nice warm massage and perhaps a little extra to help him relax.

There was a vain and self-focused young man who took advantage of any chance he had to talk to me, but I had not the slightest interest in his narcissist conversation beyond the minimum required for good manners. He handed me his card, and I politely put it in my blue silk clutch bag. He was the Honourable Percival Murphy. He told me his father was an earl, but he was the third son, worse luck. He worked as a stockbroker, but he complained that his father never gave him any money, and how unfair it was that he had nothing to live on, while his oldest brother would get everything. There was no fate worse than being a younger son.

Didn't he earn money in his job as a stockbroker? Perhaps he would rather have never been born at all? But I didn't say either of those things, of course. He had made self-obsession and victimhood into an art form. Did he think I was well off, and he might get out of his dreadful predicament by marrying money? But these were upper-class people, and the amount I had would be pocket money to them. I did not feel part of their world.

But I had to be polite and say something, so I changed the subject and asked if he was a friend of Paul or a friend of the bride—the bride won, their mothers were cousins—and I was grateful when Paul's mother came up to gloat—not in words, of course—that she had finally achieved her heart's desire to have her son married into the aristocracy. But my joy at being rescued from the inane conversation of the Honourable Percival was short lived.

'Have you found someone good enough for you yet, Miss Berrington?' she asked me. 'Or is it just that no one has ever asked you?'

Couldn't she be nice to me, when I had done the right thing and not accepted her son? She knew I had only said it for a joke at the time, to appease her because Paul was taking me out. She had made me think of Lady Catherine De Bourgh.

'I have had offers. At least three of them from your son. He was almost good enough, but not quite, and I didn't want him to upset your plans. Only a week ago, while we were in bed together in my room at Deniton, he begged me to change my mind and run off with him. He said he would leave his child bride waiting at the church with his dragon of a mother having hysterics when his best man arrived without him. So, I told him he must think of you and how upset you would be. And of course, I could never marry a man who was sleeping with an old flame only a week before he was to marry someone else. How could you ever trust such a man? How would his poor little wife feel if she knew?'

Oh, revenge is sweet, and this was real revenge, not the imagined revenge I usually had to be content with. But I knew

I should never have said it, I was ashamed that I had given way to petty spite, and I hope she never repeated it to Paul. It put us both in a bad light. When I thought about it later, I realised that it was no revenge at all. She had won the prize she craved, however close she had come to having it snatched from her grasp. She had no need to grovel at my feet and thank me for saving her dream.

Her jaw dropped, and she looked at me in absolute horror. As she stormed off, I saw a smirk on the face of the luckless younger son. I had forgotten that he was there listening, and he was second cousin to the bride. What had I done?

'Please don't repeat that to anyone,' I asked him. 'I don't want the bride to hear it. It isn't actually true. I just wanted to annoy her. I once went out with Paul, and she was very rude to me, telling me he would never marry me, as he was already spoken for.'

He looked a little perplexed—he clearly didn't understand the intricacies of cattiness between ladies—but I allowed him to change the subject to one more congenial to himself, and ramble on for a while about how good a shot he was, and how he was looking forward to the glorious twelfth. I knew he would already have forgotten what I had said to Paul's mother. He asked me if I enjoyed shooting, so I admitted I didn't. He looked crestfallen and asked what I did like. What about cricket? He was playing in an old boys' match at his old school next weekend. I could come and watch him play. When I greeted this idea with less than the expected enthusiasm, he asked if I would like to go out to dinner with him one day in the week. I told him I lived too far away, in Deniton, on the south coast.

'Perhaps I could come down one weekend? Could you put me up?'

Was he thinking he might sleep in my bed with me, as Paul had?

I was rescued by the father of the bride, now my favourite old gentleman, who wanted to introduce his daughter's pretty friend to some of the other chaps. I gave my young admirer a smile and allowed my old admirer to take me away to meet his friends, his arm around my waist and mine around his. I no longer cared what his wife would think.

'You're Berrington's daughter, aren't you? Paul's business partner,' he said, but I did not correct him.

Inevitably one of the chaps I was to meet was one of the guests who availed himself of Richard's escorts, but I pretended not to recognise him and was very polite to his wife, who suddenly appeared at his side when she saw me with the group of men. I saw a few of our other clients that afternoon—Paul was in partnership with Richard, and our Orchard House visitors were mainly their accountancy clients—but I carefully avoided them when I could, and pretended not to recognise them when I couldn't.

At least my bunny hunters were not among the guests. I could not have kept a straight face if I had been obliged to make small talk with their wives. I recalled one of them once telling me that his wife refused to have sex with him but threatened to take him to the cleaners if he filed for divorce. But I had never heard his wife's side of it, so I reserved my judgement. Perhaps the real truth was that she had refused to play bunny hunting with him in their garden. I could never blame her for that.

There were a lot of men who wanted to talk to me that afternoon, a lot of men who gave me that second glance when I was introduced to them. Yes, my dress was a little low cut, but it was my face they looked at, not my decolletage. A couple of others were immediately rescued by their wives, wary of where their husbands were straying. There were other young single men, but they all seemed to have the same self-focus as the earl's youngest son.

A couple of women actually brought their sons up to be introduced, and I wondered if there were other impoverished estates that needed the help of a marriage with even a little money attached. My uncle was wealthy, although not hideously so, and I was clearly his heir. But these young men were like the rest. After a few minutes I knew everything there was to know about them, but not one of them even asked what I did for a living. Well, perhaps that was not actually a bad thing, but they could have asked what music I liked, or what my favourite colour was, or what books I liked to read.

There was a brass ensemble and dancing. It was always good to dance up close with an attractive young man, and I did enjoy it, partnered by my earl's son, who was a surprisingly good dancer, and later by some of the other young men, but not by Paul.

When our dance had finished, the earl's son and I were approached by a photographer and a journalist who were covering the wedding for the social column. They appeared to know who he was, but they had to ask my name. I was not comfortable with being in the newspaper, in case they associated my name with my poor disgraced father, and I hesitated. I had a wicked thought that I might tell them I was Lady Ann Berrington, but I would never have dared.

'This is Ann,' the young man had already answered for me, and I knew then that he would be the sort of husband who would always answer when his wife was asked a question. We had a few of those at the retreat. I always enjoyed talking to those wives when I did their manicures and their husbands were not there to answer for them.

They asked who had created my dress, and I told them Vera Gilmore. I was pleased that she might get a mention in the social pages although I later knew she often did.

There was a break in the dancing, and I returned to my uncle. Paul's father was with him.

'You look lovely today, Ann,' he said to me.

He put his arm round me, as the bride's father had done, so I put mine around his waist, hoping that Paul's mother was watching us as he smiled down into my eyes. This was better revenge.

'I always hoped that you and Paul would make a match, but I'm happy with my sweet little daughter-in-law, although it cost me a pretty penny to bring it off. It has made my wife happy. There is nothing more conducive to a man's comfort than a happy wife.'

I could see the happy wife making her way towards us, looking grim, so I gave him a sweet smile and excused myself, slipping away to rejoin the dancers in the marquee. I always enjoyed dancing, especially when it was the type of dancing where men held women close to them, murmuring compliments.

It was finally time for the bride and groom to leave for their honeymoon; they were flying out that evening to Italy. So that was where the idea had come from, I thought, but I behaved impeccably. I couldn't bring myself to kiss the bride; I touched her dainty little hand, and wished them both happiness. I couldn't say anything else to Paul while they were standing together, but then for a moment her attention was taken by someone else.

'Don't forget to think of me when you make love in the vineyard.' I whispered, and he laughed.

It was done. Paul was no longer mine and could never again be mine. I had made my decision in January on that cold winter beach. Last week's proposal had been far too late for me to change my mind. We had both known that.

I did get my picture in the social pages but under false pretences. The Honourable Percival Murphy with his sister Lady Ann Murphy in a dress by Vera Gilmore.

I puzzled about it until Richard told me that Percival did have a sister Ann, so the journalist had assumed that was who I was. It was my only incursion into the upper class, but not the only time I borrowed someone else's name.

Richard also told me that there had been a good deal of money changing hands to secure the marriage of the impoverished peer's daughter to Paul, who had family money over and above what he made as an accountant, and had wanted to worm his way up a class or two.

We spent what was left of that weekend in Richard's flat, but I returned alone to Deniton on the Monday morning, as I needed to be there for the cleaning and the laundry. I had already missed the previous week while I was fitted for the dress for the wedding, and the pool could not go for more than two weeks without cleaning.

I knew I would miss Paul, and I did miss him. I fell back into depression, but now there was no Kristen to pull me out of it. I had to do that myself, and I did try.

During the week I was alone with my thoughts, and it was not good for me. I would wander down to the beach, wander down to the village to post letters. But they were only bills; I had no friends to write to. Sometimes I would wander through the churchyard, reading the names of long dead village worthies, and working out their ages from the years they had been born and had died. I found the graves of Mrs Pearson's husband and son, and Susan Pearson, the aunt who had lived in the cottage between the Wars. She had been born in 1865 and had died in 1939.

Occasionally I spoke to the vicar or the vicar's wife. She had once told me her name, but I had forgotten it. She was just the vicar's wife. I knew the vicar was called Reverend Ralph, but that was his Christian name, so she was not Mrs Ralph. She was a solid woman, always dressed in a tweed skirt and a twinset, with flat lace-up shoes, thick stockings, and a pearl necklace. She had an air of being a distressed gentlewoman, once used to a certain way of life that she could no longer afford, but resigned to it and quite at ease with her place in the world. The vicar was older and smaller than she was, and rather vague but sweet.

Mrs Pearson was often in her garden, and I would always chat with her over the wall if I saw her when I went to fetch the mail. Sometimes she would pull up a carrot, wash it under the garden tap, and give it to me to eat, as if she was giving a treat to a child. I always ate the carrot, of course, although I was not overly fond of raw carrot, and there were occasionally still a few grains of sand on them.

She would tell me gossip from the village, but I barely followed it; I could never remember all the names of the people she spoke of, and as I could not even put faces to those names, I scarcely took it all in. Mrs Gobbleboot's son was marrying Mrs Crankshaft's daughter, who was obviously in the family way. Mrs Bluemelon's dog had got out one night and killed one of Farmer Featherduster's lambs.

Mrs Pearson didn't seem to realise that I had no idea who any of these people were. But she was a least another human soul in this remote corner of the world, and I always liked her refreshing cheerfulness and her contentment with her life. Perhaps when you are old it is easier to think about the small problems faced by people in a village than the large problems faced by those in the wider world.

On some days I rambled alone along the path on the top of the cliffs, looking out over the English Channel, always busy with shipping, and I would think about the crew on the ships, the men far from their homes, and wonder what the cargoes were, where they were going and where they were from.

The weekends dragged without Paul. He had not come all that often, but now he never came at all. It was all getting rather tedious, the same men, the same girls, the same drunken horseplay, the same silken murmurs of the men and the giggles of the girls in their rooms in the night. The same men asking me, for the umpteenth time, how much money it would take to persuade me to sleep with them, even though they knew that asking me was against the house rules.

We had the retirees again that summer—I always loved hosting them—but we didn't invite Richard's employees that year, since Paul did not want to come with his wife. I was glad, as I knew I would be very hard hit, watching them together. Richard paid his young men a bonus instead.

Was this always to be my life? I was now twenty-two. Would the years just slip past me, leaving me trapped here in a place that was beautiful but so isolated, with never any chance of meeting someone I could love? Would there never be a handsome prince who would rescue me from my lonely life and sweep me off my feet and into my happy ever after?

Occasionally I went up to London for the week with Richard, stayed in the flat, went with Rebecca to be fitted with new clothes, yet more designer dresses to wear while I hosted lecherous old men in my seaside resort—men who couldn't have cared what I wore, as they always looked at me as if they were imagining what I would look like naked.

The clothes were not all bespoke and specially made for me—in fact very few of them were—most of them were just Vera's label, clothes she designed and made for sale in high-end boutiques. Richard had given me a credit card. He looked after paying it off; I was just to buy anything I wanted.

The vicar's wife asked me if I had anything for a jumble sale she was planning. She always appeared from nowhere when I walked to the village to post a letter or to shop. Was she always in the street? Or did she spend all her time at the window of the vicarage, looking out for me to come by?

I found some of the designer clothes that I no longer wore and took a box of them down to the vicarage. I had been rather overconfident of my strength, and the box was damned heavy by the time I reached her door.

I saw the notice outside the post office for the date of the jumble sale, a Saturday morning, of course, but by chance we had no guests that weekend, so Richard allowed me to go.

When the sale opened at nine, my dresses were hanging neatly on wire hangers on a rack that had pride of place in the clothing section, with a notice saying *Designer dresses £2 all size 10*. Within minutes they were gone.

I wandered for a while among the tables laden with heaps of things. Some of the things, like books, tools, toys, clothes and framed pictures, were sorted onto their own tables. But other tables were full of random things: pots and pans, purses, handbags, tennis racquets, tape recorders, radios, clocks, half-finished craft items, even a violin that was missing a string.

Some things were still good, some broken or so old that they should have been discarded years ago.

There were two women fighting over a battered frying pan, the vicar's wife attempting to arbitrate between them. I spied another one under a stack of pots and retrieved it, offering it to one of the women, who eagerly snatched it from my hand, leaving the first woman with the original prize. The vicar's wife and I laughed together as the women continued on, now once again friends.

'Thank you for that, Miss Berrington. Sometimes rational thought goes out of the window at jumble sales. It is always wise to keep things in perspective. I see your clothes have all been sold; it was good of you to donate them. Most of our items are ten pence, but I put a couple of pounds on your dresses. I knew they would sell for that.'

'I'm glad they are getting a new home. Why would they fight over an old frying pan?'

'It happens every year. People think they are getting something for practically nothing, and sometimes that does bring out the worst in people.'

'What do you do with things that aren't sold? Some of these things don't look very useful.'

'I always put out everything that people donate because some of them look for their things when they get here, just to make sure I haven't binned them. They like to feel their donations are appreciated. At the end we pack up anything unsold, and later I go through and discard the useless stuff, just keeping a few things that might sell at the next sale. But most of it does sell. Older people are often happy to buy things that need mending.'

The frying pan had been rather sticky, with a layer of baked-on oil that had defied any attempt of the previous owner to wash it off, so I asked the vicar's wife to direct me to the cloakroom.

The toilets were outside at the back of the village hall, brick buildings that made me think of my first school and the boys who had lured me behind the toilet blocks to investigate what lay beneath my skirt. James had come to my rescue, as he always did. But now there was no James, and it all seemed such a long time ago. Yet for a moment I felt he was somewhere close to me, still there to love and protect me, wanting me to keep going forward and live my life for us both.

Luckily there was soap—there had never been any soap in the school toilets. I could not have washed the grease off without it, but even with soap, it was stubborn.

Mrs Pearson was manning the second-hand book stall, helping a small boy who had asked her if there were any train books. I helped him search while Mrs Pearson served another customer, and we found half a dozen of them. He didn't have quite enough money, and I offered to make up the shortfall, but Mrs Pearson said it didn't matter.

'Jumble sales are not about the money,' she told me. 'They are just a social event, and an opportunity to recycle things from people who don't want them to those who do. Some of the ladies here live on very little, and they are glad of a chance to buy a few new things at a small price.'

I bought a copy of *Pride and Prejudice* and handed her my ten pence. She assured me I would like the book—it was one of her favourites.

We had read it at school, and back then we had all thought Mr Darcy was so romantic and sexy. But now I thought he was just an impossible dream. My Mr Darcy had married the girl his mother had chosen for him; that was not supposed to happen; my story had gone wrong.

Once when I was in London, I phoned the unhappy but honourable Percival Murphy—I still had his card—and he took me out to dinner. He told me his sister had been furious at the social column putting my picture instead of hers and having the wrong designer's name for her dress. But he spent the remainder of the time talking about himself. His old boys' team had won the cricket match; he told me how many runs he had made, how many of the opposing team he had bowled out and caught out—I thought there were only eleven in a team but I swear his numbers added to more than that—and he had bagged heaps of grouse in August on his friend's moors in Scotland.

I enjoyed the meal, and I enjoyed dancing with him. He was a good dancer. It was just a matter of turning off from listening to what he said, and enjoying the music and the closeness of a man's body to mine.

He invited me back to his flat in Mayfair for coffee. Unfortunately, he had to share a room there with his brother Alphonse, the second son, but Alphonse did sleep very soundly. Some girls didn't mind but others didn't fancy it. The eldest son, of course, had a room of his own, so bringing back a girl was easy for him.

Was this the real source of his grievance against his privileged first-born brother? Spending the night in a single bed with a man who was constantly either showing off or whingeing was not appealing, particularly with his brother feigning sleep in the same room. When I showed no enthusiasm, he asked if we could go to my place.

I told him my uncle would be there, as it was his flat. Richard would not have minded, of course, but by this time I was so bored with Percival's constant self-focused drivel, that all I wanted was to get away from him.

'What say you come down to our place in Kent for the week-end? Mater never minds me bringing a girl, provided they don't swear. My sister might not be keen though; she's out for your blood over that silly photo. I can't imagine why she got so upset about it. It was me they were photographing, and no one would care what girl I was with.'

Did this man ever stop thinking the world revolved around him?

'I work at weekends.'

'Do you? How very odd. Would you like us to get a room at a hotel for the rest of tonight?'

'I'm not sure I want to turn up at a hotel at midnight in a dinner dress and with no luggage.'

'Well, I suppose not. Back of the car?'

I declined, and he finally stopped talking. He had run out of ideas.

I didn't think I could face the prospect of going out with him again. When he dropped me at Richard's flat, he asked me to phone him again next time I was in town and perhaps we could work out something. If he had more notice, he could book us a hotel. We could arrive looking like normal travellers, have dinner there, dance for a while, then spend the night in a room. I promised I would contact him—with my fingers crossed behind my back.

The Icehouse 1988

We went through another winter and into another spring. Paul never came again although Amos often did, sometimes with Rebecca. He was always kind to me. I think he realised how depressed I was becoming. We walked on the beach, watched films together, I got to know how he liked his drinks mixed, and I always gave him a massage when he came. If he was on his own, I sometimes gave him the extra beneath the towel. He told me Rebecca would be fine with it. They never slept together.

Richard asked me one evening if I would sleep with Amos, but he stressed that it was for me to choose. It was a gift for me to give if I felt he deserved it. He had been in love with me for a long time. He had asked for Richard's permission, but there was no money changing hands.

I suppose Amos knew I had regularly slept with Paul before he married. But this was different. His wife was my friend. I knew he sometimes slept with one of the escorts, when he was down here without Rebecca, and I would never have said anything to her. Richard said Rebecca knew what he got up to, and I remembered they had slept in separate rooms.

He and I had known each other well for a long time. I liked his company, and I knew he cared about me. He was always cheerful and often amusing. He had pulled me out of despondency on a few occasions, encouraging me to cheer up, and telling me the latest joke he had heard. They were always very good jokes. I knew that he really had fallen in love with me, and I was so starved for company my own age that I was at least a little in love with him. I told Richard I would agree to it.

I knew how to make men feel good, and I made sure he felt good. I gave him a massage, teasing him with just a little of the extra. I sat close to him all evening, leaning against his shoulder and fondling his thigh, with a glass of sherry to help me keep my nerve, while he and Richard sipped their whisky and talked business together. There were only the three of us in the house. I had asked Richard not to bring a girl, even the au pair, as I didn't want anyone snitching to Rebecca. Afterwards Richard and I were both very glad that we were otherwise alone. Around ten o'clock, I told Amos to go up to bed and I would join him shortly.

When I slipped into bed beside him, he pulled me close to him, told me I was beautiful, that ever since he had first seen me, he had wanted to make love to me. Rebecca knew he was in love with me, and she didn't mind, she understood him. He had never cared for any of the other girls, they were just lust, but with me it was different. This was how a man showed his love for a woman, and he wanted me to enjoy it if I could. But he said he didn't mind if I couldn't; it was enough for him just to have me there with him.

I took off my pyjamas and let him make love to me, his body heavy over mine. I wanted him to be happy, so I pretended to enjoy it. It was only a small thing for me to do, and he would never know I was faking. He moved rapidly, getting more and more out of breath, and I was a little nervous that he was overdoing it. He climaxed, catching his breath in great gasps, then he collapsed on top of me.

'Can you roll off a bit,' I whispered. 'You are rather heavy and I can hardly breathe.' He was no taller than I was, but he was rather overweight, and I felt suffocated.

He rolled off me, gave a few more rasping breaths, and was silent. Had he fallen asleep? Paul had often fallen asleep after we had made love. I lay beside him for a while, wondering if he would snore, as Rebecca had once told me he did. He was soundly asleep, so he wouldn't know if I was there beside him or not. If he did snore, I could go back to my room, now I had given him what he wanted. But I stayed beside him and dozed for a while, as it was now quite late, nearly eleven, and the glass of sherry had made me relaxed and sleepy. I rarely drank in the evenings. My mother had been an alcoholic, so I was always careful not to let that happen to me.

I was suddenly awake with a jolt. I had realised through a haze of sleep that I couldn't hear him breathing, and it took me several moments of frozen fear before I understood what had happened. I felt his limp wrist for a pulse, desperately trying to find a place where I could feel that comforting heartbeat, but there was nothing. I turned on the lamp. He was absolutely still, his eyes closed but his mouth open.

I had learnt CPR when I had studied physiotherapy. I pushed him over onto his back and pressed on his chest, but I knew it was hopeless. I had been dozing for a while, and it was now far too late. Even if I called an ambulance, I knew there was nothing they could do to bring back someone who had been dead for well over an hour.

I stood up, found the pyjamas I had earlier discarded on the floor, and went to Richard's room. It was a little after midnight, but he was still awake, reading a book by the light of the bedside lamp.

I was so shaken I couldn't even explain what had happened; I could only show him. He followed me to Amos's room. He knew, as I did, that he was dead and beyond help.

He took me downstairs and made coffee for us both; we had to think what to do.

We could call an ambulance, but it would be fairly clear what had been happening by the state of the bedclothes. I told Richard I didn't want his wife to have to face the embarrassment of her husband dying while making love to another woman, and Richard didn't want any prying into what we did at Orchard House.

We went back up. We discussed simply moving the body into another room, where there would be no trace of me having been with him, but he was a heavy man, so we rejected that idea.

Richard cleaned him up so all evidence of what had happened was gone, and we got him back into pyjamas, finding it surprisingly difficult to dress a dead body. We managed to change the sheets on the bed while he still lay there, rolling him to one side then to the other.

We laid him on his back with one arm over his chest, to make it look as if he had clutched at his heart, and covered him with the bedclothes. By then we were both out of breath and sweating.

What to do with the soiled sheets? I took them downstairs and put them through the washing machine, then left them tumbling in the dryer. First thing in the morning we would take them out and put them on an unmade bed in one of the smaller rooms that we never used for guests. We could never fold and press them the way the laundry did.

I knew that neither of us would sleep, but we had to go back to bed so we were at least rested by the morning. We would then call an ambulance and say we had found him dead when he did not come down to breakfast.

I slept with Richard in his room, both of us in pyjamas and with a sheet between us. He was my uncle, possibly even my real father, and we never crossed the line. We loved each other far too deeply for that. But to be together was comforting, to have someone else there when the night was so long and the worry so deep.

It all went as we had planned. The police came, but it was all just routine. He had died from a heart attack in his sleep. Best way to go, their doctor told us, and quite a common way to die. They checked his wallet and, rather miraculously, found an appointment card for his doctor, so they phoned him, and he confirmed that Amos's heart had been weak. Their doctor signed the death certificate, and the mortuary would confirm it. In the end it was all so simple. We gave them the contact details for Rebecca, but Richard phoned her to tell her what had happened.

When they had taken the body, we locked up the house and returned to London for the week. I didn't want to stay in the house by myself.

I saw Rebecca at Amos's funeral. She hugged me, said she was sorry that Amos had died in my house and hoped that the shock had not been too much for me. Oh, how guilty I felt, but how I loved her for her concern.

Life slowly returned to normal. Summer was again upon us, when the retired couples came for their holidays, now their fourth year. I knew them all by now, and I was always glad to have them, rather than the men with their mistresses or the ones who asked for escorts. They were always very courteous to me, although they all knew by now what a seagull was, and I never had anything new or exciting to show them. Perhaps I should learn the names of some other birds.

Richard now looked after the bookings, although Rebecca occasionally came down with him for the weekend as well as his au pair. The escorts he supplied were from her agency. I still sometimes spent the week in London, where Rebecca and Vera found me yet more new clothes.

We had the bunny hunters again. The moon was right for their game, but the weather turned against them, so they took over the lounge, and their women did a striptease on the dance floor. Richard, his latest au pair and I sat in the kitchen, watching the television there, Richard occasionally checking if they needed more whisky and looking after the music, as I was reluctant to go into the room.

Lagan came with his two friends and their small fair-haired girls, who spoke no English but looked at me with their troubled sidelong glances, almost as if they were wondering if I could be trusted. They were meek and docile, not like the girls that Rebecca sent, who were all over their assigned men, laughing and flirting with them. It bothered me.

Lagan pestered me, as he always did, to sell him my favours, telling me he would give me pleasure like nothing I had ever before experienced, guiding my hand to his crotch when I gave him a massage, as if he hoped that if I felt his dick, I would want to fall into bed with him. I didn't. Not that there was anything wrong with his dick.

I asked Richard again if the girls that Lagan and his other Latin-looking friends brought with them were old enough.

'Those Russian girls always look much younger than they really are. I'm not supplying them, so it's up to him. They are paid to act like reluctant virgins. That's what he told me. He keeps offering me money for you, crazy amounts, but I always tell him you're not for sale. I know you don't like him, but he helps bankroll this place. A lot of our money comes from him and his friends.'

Were they the same girls each time? They all looked the same, but I never knew their names, they kept to themselves, and it was a couple of months between the times Lagan brought them here. I wasn't sure. I recalled that once one of them had left and caught the train back to London, but that never happened again.

The other men came for their weekends with the escorts from Rebecca, men who told their wives they were on a business weekend. How could they get more pleasure from sex with someone they didn't even know, than with the woman they had loved enough to marry? I had at least liked Paul, I could have loved him if he had given me the chance to, and our lovemaking had been fun, because it was given freely and the joy was shared. We were friends. Even with Amos, I had been prepared to give him his pleasure as a gift. But the couple of other lovers I had slept with, now several years ago, had been a hollow experience, sleeping with a man just for a few moments of carnal pleasure. Their pleasure, as I was not sure I had felt any at all. I knew that if I really loved a man, and he loved me, it would be a much better experience. Caring for the man you were making love with was part of the enjoyment.

I asked Richard why these men would pay so much for a girl they hardly knew instead of just making love to their wives. Were the girls that good?

'Their wives don't want to sleep with them. It suits both parties.'

'But can't the wives just give them a hand job? Even that would be better than sleeping with girls they care nothing for.'

He shrugged. 'Who knows what goes on between husbands and their wives? Men like to think they are good at what they do, and can be put off sex for life if they are made to feel inadequate when they make love to a woman. Sometimes the men feel rejected if their wives no longer want them, and they worry they can't perform any more, so our girls are trained to reassure them that they can. It makes them feel good about themselves. Some of the marriages are arranged, like Paul's, and the wives don't care about their husbands' infidelities and have lovers of their own. And it's better for the men if they use escorts for their pleasure, rather than chasing after some girl from their office, who expects love in return, and risking ending up in a messy divorce. The escorts are discreet; it's part of their job. The men pay well, we provide the venue, and we make money.'

'Why do we need all this money? Surely, you earn enough for us to live on without this, and I could get a job.'

'Don't you like it here, Ann?'

'I feel very isolated at times.'

'Come back to London with me for the week. I wish you had married Paul. The arrangement he had with that girl was crazy. He loved you, he even told me so, and he would have married you, but you wouldn't have him. So he agreed to please his mother and save the girl's family from financial ruin, possibly at the expense of his own family's financial ruin. Those large estates eat money.'

I did spend the week in London, but this time I didn't go to be fitted for clothes I didn't need from Vera. I shopped on the high street and bought some jeans, tee-shirts and jumpers, flat sandals and hiking boots. I was fed up with walking in skirts and shoes with heels, even low heels. Now I could go further, and I could scramble over rocks and logs with less risk of slipping.

But I sometimes wished I had someone to share my solitary walks.

Most weekends, whether we had guests or not, Richard would bring his au pair with him. His current au pair was a small fair-haired girl from northern Europe, perhaps it was Finland, I could never afterwards recall. She had been around much longer than the au pairs normally stayed. I couldn't pronounce her full name; Richard just called her Lottie, so I did too. Her English was scarcely existent, but she was always cheerful, chattering away in her own language even though she knew I could not understand her, and she was happy to help with the cooking and stacking the dishwasher. I did try to teach her a few English words when she helped me in the kitchen, and we laughed together when she didn't understand what I was saying. She and Richard would spend the whole evening in his room, with him laughing and her squealing in pleasure. I kept away, of course, staying in the lounge watching a video, or reading in bed in my tower room.

But one night he came to my room in a state, as I had once come to his when Amos had died. I followed him to his room, dreading what I would find. The girl was lying limp on the bed, dressed only in a black G-string, with whips and ropes on the bed around her and Richard's black silk tie around her neck.

'Get an ambulance,' I yelled at him, knowing it was too late. She appeared to be dead, but I did what I could to revive her.

'It was just a game,' he kept telling me, making no move to go down to the phone. 'She likes me to strangle her while I make love to her—to pretend I am raping her—but we both fell asleep while she still had the tie around her neck. God, Ann, what can I do?'

We needed to think, as we had needed to think about Amos. I knew the ambulance team could do nothing and my uncle would be arrested for murdering her. This was like Amos but not like Amos. Amos had died of natural causes, but this girl clearly hadn't. Whatever had possessed them to play such a stupid dangerous game? I felt trapped in a nightmare.

He was shaking and crying, and I knew I had to work this out myself. There was no way we were ever going to make this look like an accident.

'Richard, calm down and listen. Does anyone else know she's here? Did you arrange it through Rebecca?'

'She used to be one of Rebecca's girls but she's been living in the flat with me the last few months, and I pay her directly.'

'Will anyone miss her?'

But Richard had no idea. She was just a girl who would look after the housekeeping in his flat and do sex and bondage. She liked him to pretend to strangle her, to pretend he was raping her. It was just for fun. He kept repeating the same things, over and over. I had to come up with something.

There were only the three of us in the house. I recalled the old icehouse in the wood, built into the slope of the hill as the land fell away towards the sea. I passed the door to it when I walked down to the gate to the beach, and I pointed it out to my guests when I took them for their Sunday morning walk. The gardener never went near there; he only mowed the lawns close to the house and tended the flowerbeds. Tomorrow at first light we would see if there was enough space in it for a body. Then we would wrap her in a rug, place her inside, relock the door and pile earth and leaves around it, so it blended once more with the bank and the soil. We had no Plan B.

I dressed her, so at least she could be buried with some dignity, and covered her with a sheet for the night. We took her handbag with her purse and her passport down to the kitchen.

It was autumn, and the gardener often burnt piles of leaves in a spot by the sheds. We would burn her things with the leaves tomorrow.

Richard slept in my room, as the girl was still in his. He was once more shaking and crying, and I realised that he really had liked her, was at least partly in love with her. I stroked his face and his hair, comforted him as best I could, and I managed at last to calm him down. Neither of us slept, but we could do nothing in the darkness. We had to get through the long weary night without losing our nerve. I remembered lying beside him like this when Amos died, but this was much more serious. Richard would be jailed if the girl was found, and I would be an accessory after the fact and could be charged as well. Hiding what had happened was now our only choice. He had helped me with Amos. I knew I had to help him.

We crept out at the first chilly light of dawn. There was no one to see us, as we owned a lot of the land along the beach, and we were quite remote. It was lightly raining, but perhaps that would actually help us. I found a spade in the garden shed, and we located the icehouse. It took Richard a while to dig the earth and leaves away from the door so we could open it. There was an old rusty lock, but it was already broken. The door was jammed, so Richard wrenched it open with the spade.

A narrow steep staircase headed downwards, but we did not descend it. The stench of damp rotting earth was overpowering, and I could not have gone into that dark space if my life had depended on it. But we wouldn't need to. We could just slide the girl down the stairs far enough to close the door.

We collected the body, now wrapped in a rug, and Richard lifted her into a wheelbarrow. I could hear a small squeak in the wheel as we took her down the path, but there was no one about and no other sounds but the morning cries of the gulls, waking to another day of soaring into the wind and catching fish from the sea.

Sliding her down the stairs was easy for Richard. He was a tall strong man, while she was a small and light-weight girl. We closed the broken door as best we could, and Richard heaped the soil back up against it to suffocate the smell of a body rotting, covering it all with leaves so you could no longer even see that there was a door there. It looked like a mound on the hillside, an old barrow, or just the remains of the base of a fallen tree.

We stood for a moment of sheer relief, surveying our handiwork, wet from the rain. We could at least say a prayer for her, even if we were denying her a Christian burial. I stood near the mound and recited the Lord's prayer and the twenty-third psalm, which I knew by heart from my time at the convent school. Richard joined in with the prayer but not the psalm.

We returned the spade and the wheelbarrow to the shed, washing them both at the garden tap. Then we put her things on the pile of leaves, collected some newspapers from the house, and burnt her passport and her handbag. When they were consumed, I raked out the ashes, found the unburnt metal rings and clips from the bag, and put them in the dustbin. We heaped some more fallen leaves onto the pile, ready for the next bonfire.

It was done. But now we were both criminals, while everything we had done before this had been legal. Not always moral and ethical, but legal.

I made the breakfast, but neither of us could eat it. In a few short hours things had gone so horribly wrong. I knew that both of us would now live the rest of our lives in fear of the girl being found. To my eternal shame I did not then think about the girl's family or friends. I didn't even know her real name. I had never been good at names. She was just one of the au pairs, nameless like the escorts, the girls who came here to sleep with rich and powerful men, selling their bodies for more money that they could ever earn in a regular job. I only thanked my stars that she was out of sight, and we could go on as before. At least for now.

The weeks passed and nothing happened. If anyone had reported her missing, they had not connected her with Orchard House. Some of the girls were illegal immigrants, wanting to stay anonymous, others were girls who were homeless and friendless and glad to be earning a decent price for the use of their bodies by men who cared nothing for their souls. Rebecca was good to her girls and made sure they had somewhere to live and were over eighteen. This girl had once worked for her, before Richard had hired her as his au pair, but she no longer did. Rebecca would not miss her, and if she noticed the girl was no longer with Richard, he would tell her she had returned to her home country.

I had recurring dreams that something happened and the girl was found by a walker or a stray dog, or by a tree falling and exposing the ground where she was buried. Sometimes there was a demonic figure standing over her grave, holding her in his arms, still wrapped in the rug. I would wake in a panic, gradually realise I was dreaming, then wonder if we had buried a girl at all. Surely, that was just a dream as well.

But then I would walk down the path to the sea, look over to the place where the icehouse door had once been visible, and know that the girl was real, even if her discovery had been part of a nightmare. Oh, how I longed to one day walk down that path and find the icehouse looking the way it used to be.

Sometimes I felt too afraid to sleep, lest she haunt me yet again.

Richard never again brought a girl for himself. We managed without an au pair.

We still hosted the occasional weekend with the men and the escorts, but they rarely went along the path through the woods, and when they did, they were intent on reaching the beach. They had never been interested in hearing tales of smugglers and icehouses.

The bunny hunters never played their game in the woods in the colder months; they had to content themselves with musical rooms or striptease. We knew that we would need to find an excuse in the summer why they could not play it at all, lest they stumble on the buried girl.

The retirees and their wives only came in the summer. I had always pointed out the icehouse on our walks down the path to the beach, but if I no longer mentioned it, they would assume that it was because I had told them about it already. I hoped none of them would notice that you could no longer see the door.

We would cope; it was all going to be all right. The dreams gradually faded.

A Funeral 1989

Life went on as normal, time passing too quickly as time always does. I was twenty-three, and it was the spring of 1989, nearly summer. Nothing had been said about the girl we had buried last autumn. There were no enquiries, no one had reported her missing, and we were starting to feel ourselves safe.

Yet every time I walked down the path to the beach, I would look across to where the door of the icehouse could once be seen in the bank, imagining her ghost standing there, reproaching me. But what could I have done? I had been unable to save her life, but at least I had saved my uncle from going to prison for an accident. She had been a willing participant in their stupid dangerous game.

Richard had toned down our business with Amos gone. There were fewer weekend guests and fewer guest weekends.

Paul never came again, of course, after he married the horsey girl, who had turned out to be beautiful. But perhaps no woman is beautiful when she is served up as the only choice. I felt for her much more than I felt for him. She had grown up knowing she would have an arranged marriage only a week or two after her eighteenth birthday, to preserve the lifestyle of her family. It might have been acceptable a hundred years ago, when it may have been more commonplace, but in this day and age it was unforgivable. Paul had deliberately bought his way into her way of life, giving a lifeline to her father, who was, according to Richard, nearly bankrupt, ruined by the estate tax when his own father had died. Although Paul's mother had wanted it, in the end it had been his choice. At least Paul was good looking and easy going, and he appeared to be willing to make a go of it. Surely, if they really hadn't liked each other, they would have called it off.

Often Richard would come back by himself for the weekend, and the two of us would swim in the pool, walk along the beach, play tennis or sit on the terrace for long afternoons when he would tell me things about my parents that I had never known. Both he and my father had been in love with my mother, all those years ago. She had been beautiful but rather fragile, emotionally as well as physically. She had been forced to choose between them, and she had chosen the elder, but she had slept with both of them, and my father hadn't minded.

My father's lucrative job managing money for rich clients had never been enough for him. He had wanted more and more, and he had set up the parties for clients and supplied them with cocaine because he could make serious money from that. He had supplied girls as well to men who wanted them, including hiring out his own wife. There had been rows, with my father always reducing my mother to a crying wreck. She had become more and more disillusioned and had started to drink in the week when she was alone in the house. Richard had been concerned for her, but my father became angry if he tried to interfere. He had several times asked her if she would leave with him, but my father had threatened that he would expose her as a drug addict and she would lose custody of me and James.

'I loved her beyond words, but I had to watch him destroy her, when I would have traded my soul for the right to make her happy again. I will carry the guilt with me to my grave, that I could never do anything to save her from my brother. Sometimes I wish I had murdered him, just to set her free.'

His stories always seemed hard for me to reconcile with the close-knit family I remembered, all of us together in the walled garden, in our own world where nothing mattered but the five of us, including Richard, who was there on the weekends. He had played with James and me and made us laugh, and he had taken us on outings. My father had never taken us anywhere. But in spite of her cross words and her addiction, I knew my mother had loved us, eternally and unconditionally, and she would never have left us even when her own life was so miserable and oppressed.

During the week I was left by myself in the house by the sea, and I rambled alone on the cliff paths, wondered sometimes whether this would always be my life, whether I would grow old here with the gulls and the sea and the wind and the solitude. Every evening I would fill in the diary, noting what I had done that day, what guests were staying with us, anything that made one day different from the others, lest the days all merged into an endless blur of lost and lonely years.

I wondered why Richard had set this place up. He had a perfectly good business running his accountancy firm; he and Paul made a good living from it. I could have stayed in his flat, working in a gym, and we would have wanted for nothing. Why was it so important to make money that we had to stash away in Switzerland and may never even use?

Each day I would get the mail from the box when the postman rang the bell, walking along the drive to the gate then back to the house with the letters. On Tuesdays the gardener would come to mow the lawns and tend the flowers, and the cleaning lady would come to tidy the house. I would help her change the sheets on any of the beds that had been used on the weekend, ready for the laundry van which arrived after lunch on Wednesday. The van man would ring the bell, and I would walk out to the gate and unlock it for him to drive in. On Friday afternoons I would drive into town to do the grocery shopping, as by then we would know how many guests to expect on the weekend.

The gardener only worked on the front garden and close to the house at the back. He never ventured into the wood, so the disturbance around the icehouse had never been noticed. Autumn leaves had covered the earth that we had piled up above the entrance, and they had rotted into soil; spring flowers now grew over the mound, and there was no trace left of where the door to the icehouse had been.

One Wednesday in May the bell for the linen van rang much earlier than usual. I had already brought in the mail for the morning, so it was not the postman. It was scarcely past twelve; the van didn't normally come until two, and we never had any other visitors during the week. I picked up the intercom phone and asked who was there.

The vicar's wife answered, sounding a little nervous at this new-fangled way to communicate. I could almost see her jump at hearing my voice when there was no one there.

'Miss Berrington, I called on Mrs Pearson because she didn't come to bridge this morning. I phoned her, but it rang out. I am worried about her. I came to see if she was feeling unwell, but when I rang her bell, she didn't answer. I'm worried she may have fallen and be unable to answer the door. Have you seen her today?'

I asked her to wait while I came out to the gate. I unlocked it with the code so I could get out into the lane, then closed it again, in case she had any thoughts that I might ask her into the house.

We rang the doorbell of the cottage, but there was no response. The front door was locked. The back door was also locked. We tried calling but the house was silent. I knew in my heart that something was wrong, and so did the vicar's wife.

When she was not at the village activities, Mrs Pearson was always out in her garden in the mornings if the weather was fine, tending her vegetables or trimming her hedges and rose bushes. And if she was at home and everything was as it should be, the doors would not be locked at this time of day.

I found a spare key under a plant pot in the front porch—a lucky guess—and I unlocked the door, still calling her name. I could sense that the vicar's wife didn't want to intrude in someone else's house, but I knew we had no choice. If Mrs Pearson had fallen and broken an ankle, she would never object to us coming in unannounced.

But I knew we would find her dead. She was very old by now, well into her late nineties, for all that she was still spritely and quick-witted.

Everything was eerily silent. There was no one downstairs, so we went up to the bedrooms.

She was lying peacefully against the white sheets in a white lace nightgown that could have come straight from the set of a Dickens film. I felt the fragile dry skin of her wrist, but there was no pulse. Her hand was already stiff. She had died in the night.

At least she had been found quite soon after she had died. I remembered horror stories of bodies left to rot in their homes for months before they were found. I knew it would have taken me several days at least to realise she was no longer in her garden when I came for the mail, as on some of the days she was in the village enjoying the activities that the vicar's wife organised.

I guided the vicar's wife down the stairs to where the phone was. I called the emergency number, and they said they would send an ambulance and the police. I tried not to flinch at the mention of the police, but this was not my house, and the ice-house was on the other side of our garden, hundreds of yards away.

We then phoned the vicar, who came almost at once, as we were a scant half mile from the vicarage. He comforted his wife—she had known Mrs Pearson for over thirty years—then went upstairs to say a prayer for the soul of the dead woman.

The policewomen who attended asked if I had any contact details for the next of kin. I recalled that Mrs Pearson had mentioned she had a great-nephew, her only surviving relative, the grandson of her brother. I offered to give them the contact details for her solicitor, who had handled the sale of the house. He was based in the local town, and he may have her will and contact details for her heirs.

I returned to the house, found the contract and wrote down the details. One of the policewomen had offered to come to the house with me, but I kept calm and declined, without giving any excuse. Even without the girl in the ice-house, I didn't want anyone in the house who might be curious about what we did there.

The policewomen seemed confident they could trace the great-nephew. They would arrange for the mortuary to collect Mrs Pearson's body, would wait with her until the van arrived, and would lock the house when they left.

The vicar asked if I would like to return to the vicarage with them and have some tea, but I declined as the laundry van was now due.

A few days passed, and I thought very little about my dead neighbour. She was old, and old people die. I wished my parents and my brother had lived so long and died so peacefully.

I passed the vicar's wife in the village street when I went out to post some letters, and she asked if I would be coming to the funeral on the following Friday. The police had traced the great-nephew, and he would be attending with his mother. He was a school teacher. The ladies from the village would all bring something for the afternoon tea to be held at the village hall after the burial. She thought it would be good for me to join them and meet the new owners of the cottage, although she expected they would be selling it, as they lived somewhere near London. I didn't need to bring anything; there was always plenty to eat at these functions.

Since I didn't have a lot to do in the week, I decided to go. I had always liked Mrs Pearson. She had always had a cheery word for me if she was in the garden when I passed her house, as well as the occasional somewhat unwelcome carrot. She had lost her whole family as I had, but she had come to terms with it, and she had treated life as if it was a precious blessing.

I did the shopping on Thursday afternoon so I was free on Friday. I already knew the weekend would be only Richard and me.

I pulled my unruly black curls back into a passable bun, put on my best black suit—made for me by Vera for the funeral of Amos—with a dainty black hat and high-heeled shoes, and I walked to the church.

I was a little early. The great-nephew, his back to me, was talking to the vicar at the church door, while his mother was with the vicar's wife, who called me over to join them. The lady's name was Mrs Davis. I was introduced as her late aunt's neighbour, Miss Berrington, whose uncle owned the big house next to her cottage, and the vicar's wife explained that I had been with her when we found Mrs Pearson.

Mrs Davis reminded me a little of the mother of my friend Angelina, who had shouted obscenities at me when she had found me having sex with her son, but I was very polite, of course, telling her how sorry I was about her aunt and how much I had liked her.

She seemed a little taken aback when I spoke, and she gave me a second look as most people did, taking in my unusual looks, my smart black suit and my Roburn accent. I had immediately picked her accent as fake, as too studiously refined, as I once had with the accent of Angelina's mother. She was wearing far too many rings, and she was over made up, as Angelina's mother had been, with dark-red lipstick, bright-pink rouge and a red rinse through her hair that looked unnatural and did nothing to disguise the grey. If you want to cover grey, you do it with blonde or brown, not red. Did these women who were way past their shag-by date really think a bit of dark-red lipstick and bright-ginger hair would make them look sexy?

Rebecca had once told me that women should age gracefully, that mature complexions were still beautiful when they weren't tarted up with garish makeup. All that was needed was a light foundation and a touch of face powder. That was part of what I did with the facials. I restored older women to their natural beauty and gave them the confidence to wear their age with pride, not try to disguise it.

But at least Mrs Davis wasn't bursting out of a mini-skirt. She was dressed in a very smart black midi-length suit and was slender and upright. If she had been less painted up, she might have looked elegant. In spite of her excessive makeup, I could never have thought her a tart.

'We never actually met her,' she admitted. 'She was apparently the aunt of my late husband, but until a few days ago we had no idea she even existed. My son appears to be her only heir, but it is only a little cottage apparently—we haven't seen it yet—and he is hardly likely to want to live there, so I imagine we will sell it.'

'Do you have grandchildren?' the vicar's wife asked her. 'They might like to holiday here. Children always love the seaside, and our beach here is sandy and safe for them.'

Was she trying to ascertain if the son was married, thinking that a girl alone as I was might like the company of an unmarried man next door?

'No, my son is not married yet.' That forlorn little word *yet*, indicating hope was not over. 'He has never met the right girl. He is a teacher at Harton, where he went to school, and he lives at the school for most of the time. Do you know Harton School, Miss Berrington?'

Was she showing off to me because she thought I came from a rich family who owned a large house and she wanted me to know she was my equal?

I could still never hear anything that reminded me of James with perfect equanimity.

'My brother went to school there,' I told her, but then wished I hadn't, as I usually liked to keep my life private from the people in the village.

'Where did you go to school, Miss Berrington?'

I told her Roburn, and she seemed impressed, until I asked if that was her old school.

'No, it was too far from where we lived. Does your brother live here as well? Perhaps my son would remember him.'

She looked at me again, and I suddenly had the strange idea that she was assessing me. I saw her glance down at my hands. Was she checking if I was wearing an engagement ring? Was she wondering if I might be the elusive right girl for her middle-aged yet-unmarried nerd of a son, and was probing to find if I was the heiress to the large house next door to the cottage that her son would soon own, or if my brother would get it all. It was, of course, mine already, but I was not telling her that.

'Sadly, Mrs Davis, my brother was killed, along with his friend, in a car accident, about seven years ago, not long after they left Harton and started their first year at Cambridge.' I honestly saw her expression brighten up when she learnt that there was no competition for my uncle's imagined millions.

'Oh, you poor child,' the vicar's wife intervened, laying a gentle hand on my arm. 'You have never told us that. I am so sorry. It must have been a great shock for you and for your parents.' At least she was a lady with no pretensions to being more than a little genteel, and I knew she genuinely was sorry. She really did care. In that moment I loved the vicar's wife.

The vicar brought Mr Davis over to join us, excused himself as he needed to greet some mourners who were arriving, and I looked at the son properly for the first time.

He was not middle-aged—he looked thirty at the most—and he was definitely not a nerd. He had straight dark brown hair, which fell over his forehead in a rather endearing cowlick, high cheekbones, beautiful brown eyes, a beautiful smile and a neat beard, trimmed into a slight point beneath his chin. I found myself feeling glad he wasn't married, but then I chided myself for being so silly. If a man as good looking and strongly built as he was hadn't been snared by a girl by now, he would have to be gay.

He gave me that second, searching look, as most men did when they realised how unusual I looked, but then for a moment his eyes held mine, and I knew that I would like him, in spite of his rather silly mother. He reminded me of James; the same height, but perhaps a little heavier as James had still been a boy; the same cowlick in otherwise straight hair, although James's hair had been black like mine; the same way of looking at you as if you both shared a secret, some magical knowledge that both of you understood but no one else did.

The vicar had introduced him as Mr Davis, but he held out his hand to me and said his name was Simon. I felt slightly shaky at the warmth of his hand against mine and the quick surprised glance he gave me as our fingers touched. Had he felt my hand shake?

But we had no time for even the briefest of conversations. His mother was still trying to pry information from me.

'Did you go to university, Miss Berrington? My son went to Cambridge. Perhaps you did too.'

'No, I left school when I was sixteen.'

'Oh.' It was clear that she was not sure what to make of that. 'Did you spend a year in Switzerland?'

I looked at her blankly for a moment, unsure what she meant, but then I realised, Swiss finishing school. Did they even still exist in this day and age?

'No, it was too far from where we lived.'

I saw the vicar's wife glance at me with the ghost of a smile, appreciating the jibe that the mother would have totally missed.

She asked if I would like to say a few words about my neighbour during the service. She wanted to keep things as informal as she could and give everyone a chance to speak. I declined at first, as I hardly knew Mrs Pearson, although I had liked her. When she persisted, reminding me that the dead woman had no relatives she had known at her funeral, only friends, I asked if I might read the twenty-third psalm. She seemed to like that idea. Having finally got the pagan and secretive occupant of the grand house into her church, she was going to show me off.

She encouraged me to sit with Mrs Davis and her son when we went into the church. I had never actually been in the church before, but I had only a short time to think how lovely it was before the hearse arrived. The vicar asked Mr Davis if he would like to help carry in the coffin, so he left us for a while.

Several of the village ladies spoke of their lifelong friend, hymns were sung and texts were read. I did feel sad that all she had left were friends, dear though they would have been to her, that the only relative she had at her funeral was a great-nephew who had not even known she existed until after she had died.

I recited my psalm, my head raised proudly to look out over the heads of the congregation, my voice soaring heavenward to the ancient beams and rafters of the ceiling, as I knew it by heart and had no need of the printed card that the vicar had handed to me.

The Lord is my shepherd; I shall not want. He maketh me to lie down in green pastures: he leadeth me beside the still waters. He restoreth my soul: he lea- deth me in the paths of righteousness for his name's sake. Yea, though I walk through the valley of the shadow of death, I will fear no evil: for thou art with me; thy rod and thy staff they comfort me. Thou pre- parest a table before me in the presence of mine enemies: thou anointest my head with oil; my cup runneth over. Surely goodness and mercy shall follow me all the days of my life: and I will dwell in the house of the Lord for ever.

The sunlight through the stained glass filled the whole church with a glow of heaven, filtering through the dust and the shad- ows, and I felt very close to the soul of the woman in the coffin below me. I did not look at Simon for fear I would falter, but I felt his eyes on me, and I hoped he was thinking I looked like an angel.

I could see the vicar's wife smiling rather smugly at her success, clearly pleased with my faultless performance, and Mrs Davis looked self-satisfied when I returned to sit beside her son.

'That was beautiful,' he whispered as the next reader stepped up for their text. 'You know it by heart, don't you?'

Mr Davis had also been invited to read a passage from the Bible—he read his from the book—and afterwards he spoke a few words, telling us he was sad that he had never known his aunt but he was grateful and touched to see that she had so many loving friends during her life, and he said how lucky she was to have lived her life in this beautiful corner of the world.

To me he looked like a Greek god. I had wanted him to think I looked like an angel, but angels are not usually considered to be sexy. Perhaps he could think of me as Venus, but no, she was Roman, not Greek. Aphrodite, that was it—but not in a church, of course.

There was the burial, the committal, the handfuls of earth on the coffin. I didn't join in with that, as I didn't want to get my manicured nails dirty. There were a lot of flowers. Perhaps I should have brought a bunch from her garden; I hadn't thought of it. But I could easily bring some in a week or so, when today's flowers would be dead and brown. She would appreciate having her own flowers then, instead of everyone else's dead ones.

We all had tea in the village hall, standing up. Coffee was only a cheap brand of powdered instant, so I chose a cup of tea. It was very strong, and the Deniton ladies had clearly never heard of tea strainers, but at least it was from a pot and not instant powdered tea. A small girl handed me a plate with a cream-laden cupcake, and I found myself trying to juggle the cup and saucer in one hand and the plate with the cake in the other. There was nowhere to put anything down. How was I supposed to eat the cake? I found a tiny space on the edge of the table, which was covered with enough plates of food to feed an army—no wonder the vicar's wife had said I needn't bring anything—put down the teacup and concentrated on the cake. There was no sign of any cake forks, and I was not sure I could eat it without getting cream on my nose, but at least there were some paper table napkins.

The vicar's wife rescued me, handing me a teaspoon.

'Not the best thing for this type of function,' she admitted. 'But Janice made them herself, and she's a sweet girl. You're an honoured guest, Miss Berrington.'

I was also a bit of a novelty, it seemed, as some of the ladies, and most of the men, came up to talk to me, many of them starting the conversation by complimenting me on how well I had read that beautiful psalm.

I was starting to realise it had been a mistake for me to come, as Richard liked us always to keep to ourselves. I tried to keep the conversation general and didn't answer questions about the house or what I did with my time there.

One of the ladies was wearing a dress that I had donated to the jumble sale. She looked remarkably good in it, so I was glad it had found a new home. I didn't mention it to her, of course, but I imagine she knew, through the vicar's wife, that the designer clothes at the sale had come from me. She had paid two pounds for it, while I had paid two hundred.

I sensed that Simon Davis was stealing glances at me the whole time, even when he was conversing with other people. He had a sandwich, a more sensible choice, as there was no chance of getting cream on his beard. Not that I would have minded licking it off for him. Had he seen my antics with the cake?

I finally managed to drink my over-strong tea, still patiently waiting for me on the corner of the table, but it was by now rather cold.

The vicar's wife approached me again, took me to meet Mrs Boyce, who played the organ, but as she was talking to Simon and his mother, I realised it was an attempt to involve us once more in the same conversation.

'Mrs Pearson was the previous owner of Orchard House, where Miss Berrington now lives,' she told them, after she had introduced me to Mrs Boyce, who was then completely left out of the rest of the conversation. 'She ran it as a private hotel, but it became too much for her, so Miss Berrington's uncle bought it and renovated it, about four years ago. It is a vast house, and it was in a terrible state. When I last visited her there, she spent most of her time in the kitchen, as she could only afford to heat one room, and there were leaks in the roof. She told me she had decided to sell it and just keep the lodge. She was much happier after she moved to her cottage.'

'Do you still run it as a hotel?' Simon asked me. 'If you do, we might perhaps stay there when we return to sort out the cottage.'

'No, I'm sorry, we don't.'

'Do you and your uncle live there by yourselves?' the mother asked me.

None of your damned business, I thought, but I answered the question. Perhaps they were wondering why my uncle was not at the funeral with me.

'My uncle comes down at weekends. During the week he lives and works in London. He is an accountant.'

It wouldn't hurt for the village to know we were perfectly respectable.

'Are you there all by yourself during the week?' Simon asked, and I knew he was being kind rather than curious, concerned perhaps that I might not like being alone in a vast house.

'Most of the time. But I don't mind. I have always liked my own company.'

'And your parents?' the mother persisted. 'Do they never visit?'

I wanted to scream at her that they were both dead, but I didn't. I said nothing. I had already said too much when I had told them about James.

Both the vicar's wife and Mrs Davis were clearly burning with curiosity, trying to get me to tell them—without directly posing the questions—why we needed such a large house when most of the time I was the only one there, and if I lived with my uncle because I was an orphan.

I was tired, my high heels were becoming uncomfortable with standing for so long, and although I was savouring every moment of being with this very attractive man, I wanted to go home. The earlier mention of Harton, and the upset of being at a funeral, even of someone unrelated to me, were making it more and more difficult for me to make small talk with people I scarcely knew.

'Is the cottage far from here?' the mother asked me. 'We understand you live next door.'

'It is about half a mile away. I could show you if you like. I would like to go home shortly, and you could both walk back with me.'

'May I drive you home?' Simon asked. 'You look rather tired.'

I looked at him, and I suddenly had tears in my eyes. Here was a man who actually cared enough to see I was reaching the end of my tolerance, a man who had noticed that I knew the psalm by heart, a man who would never ask the price of a night in bed with me.

'Thank you but I can manage the walk. If you would like to come with me, I will show you where the cottage is situated. Otherwise, I may see you again when you come to fix it up for sale. It has been a pleasure meeting you both.'

I turned away from them all and left the hall before the tears fell on my immaculate black suit.

He followed me, but so did his mother. I tried to hide that I was dabbing at my eyes with my inadequate lace handkerchief, and they were polite enough not to notice. It was, after all, a funeral, and mourners were allowed to cry. I tried talking about the trees that lined the lane leading from the village past the two houses.

'I think they are oaks,' I told them. 'There are sometimes acorns on the road.'

I stole a sideways glance at him and saw his face light up in a smile.

'They are indeed oaks, Miss Berrington. You can tell that by the shape of the leaf. You don't need to find an acorn. Didn't you learn to recognise trees at your school?'

'Perhaps we did learn about oaks. We didn't have any in our garden when I was a child. I can recognise a monkey puzzle. We had one of those, but it had sharp scales so I couldn't climb it. I found that very frustrating.'

Oh, that beautiful smile. Was he imagining me climbing a tree in my tight black suit and my skinny high heels, sitting in the top branches like some strange black bat, with my stockings in shreds? I think I was in love with him even before we reached the cottage. I suddenly found myself imagining him on my massage bench, the muscles in those strong shoulders hard beneath my hands, then giving him the little extra ... no, no, Ann, stop thinking that; this is a decent man. Instead, I wondered what his beard would feel like pressed against my cheek while we ...

'Are you feeling better now, Miss Berrington?' his mother said kindly. 'You looked a little shaky for a while.'

That's what your son does to me, I thought. Oh, please let him fall in love with the cottage and want to keep it.

I looked at her and realised I had misjudged her. Whatever her motive, she was prepared to be kind to me. Had she seen the looks I gave Simon and the way he had looked at me when we first met? Was she hoping that this rather serious young man had finally met a girl he was interested in. That was how I read it. But of course, it was all an illusion. If she knew my background, she would shun me and keep her son from my clutches. Yet

I found myself wishing I could give her a facial, tell her that she didn't need to make herself look like a painted ostrich.

'You asked about my parents,' I said. 'They both died only a few months before my brother did. I find it hard to be reminded.'

'I am so sorry, my dear. I had no wish to upset you. The vicar's wife told me you were with her when she found Mrs Pearson. It would have been very distressing for you.'

'She was a lovely lady. She always had a cheerful word for me, and she gave me carrots that she grew in the garden. I don't actually like raw carrots, and sometimes they were gritty, but I always ate them so she wasn't offended. Although she had lost all of her family, as I have, she always seemed so happy to be alive. But she was very old, and she looked so peaceful lying there. I wished the people I had loved had been fortunate enough to live as long as she did and die as contentedly.'

He stopped me in the lane, a strong hand encircling my wrist, turned to stand facing me, took a clean white handkerchief from his jacket pocket, shook it free from its folds, and gave it to me to wipe my eyes.

How I wished he would hug me, let me bury my face against his shoulder, hold me while I cried for all of the dead souls that fettered my life.

'Will you be all right alone in your house after this?' he asked me, still holding my wrist.

I was not sure what he had in mind as an alternative, but I knew he was simply concerned. I looked at him, and he withdrew his hand, a little embarrassed that he was still touching me.

'I'll be okay. I just find funerals a bit upsetting. It's Friday, so my uncle will be back tonight, and we don't have any guests this weekend.'

Oh, dear, I had blundered. I had said we lived alone and were not a hotel, but he didn't pick me up on it.

We had reached the cottage. It was locked, of course, and the key was no longer under the flower pot—the police had taken it—but I showed them the extent of the garden, the view to the sea, and the public footpath that led from the lane, alongside the boundary wall of both our gardens, down to the beach. The walls were all about four feet high, so you could easily see over them but not easily climb over them.

'That's a seagull,' I told him, pointing out one that flew past us and down towards the beach. 'We have a lot of them here.'

I saw that he was trying not to laugh at me, so I turned away from him, knowing I was about to cry again. He had laughed at me about the oak tree, and now he was laughing about the seagull.

'Yes, Miss Berrington, it is indeed a seagull, although its correct name is herring gull. They are sometimes considered a nuisance, and their behaviour does sometimes leave something to be desired, but they are actually a beautiful bird, with that clean grey foliage and the graceful way they soar in flight. Perhaps you feel that too.'

I looked up at him, unsure whether he was mocking me, or trying to make me feel better.

'They are the only seabird I know. I do know robins and blackbirds, but they occur everywhere. Seagulls are mostly near the sea.'

'My son is an expert on birds, Miss Berrington,' his mother told me. Was she proud of this, or was she trying to put me in my place for imagining he wouldn't know what a seagull was.

For a moment all three of us stood in silence, looking through the trees to the English Channel, listening to the waves on the beach and the cry of the gulls, a moment of peace enfolding us.

'This is such a beautiful place,' he said. 'It must be wonderful to live here.'

'It is,' I agreed. 'I can swim in the sea in the summer and walk on the beach every day of the year. There are paths through the woods and along the cliffs, and you can walk for hours without seeing anyone. Perhaps you might like to keep the cottage and come here sometimes. We have a lot of different birds here, but I don't know the names. You might find them interesting.'

Perhaps I sounded wistful. I wanted to see him again. I saw him glance at me, as if the idea of keeping the cottage was taking hold of his mind, but he did not reply, so I continued.

'It is only a very small cottage, but if you are the only heir, you should also get the money that we paid for the house, which was a quite substantial sum. Much more than it would have cost for Mrs Pearson to renovate the cottage, so there should be some of it left. The house was very run down, and we spent more than the same again modernising it, but we both love it. I once showed Mrs Pearson over the house after it was renovated, and she told me that she had never regretted selling it to us. It was her husband's family home, where he had been born and lived all his life, so it had been hard for her to part with it. Her son was killed in the War.'

'We are confident the cottage will belong to my son,' his mother said. 'But we don't yet know how much the estate is worth. This was all a surprise to us, and so far, we have only been told there is a cottage. So that is interesting news.'

They offered to stay at my house with me until my uncle returned, but I assured them I would be fine. I left them in the lane outside my gate, opening it with the code then closing it behind me. I did not look back until I reached my door, but when I did, they were both still standing there. I waved my hand before I went inside.

I looked in the mirror in the entrance hall, hoping my makeup had not run with the tears, and was horrified at the streaks of black mascara beneath my eyes. Perhaps he hadn't noticed. Men never look closely at things like that. I still had his handkerchief in my hand, and to this day I keep it in a box with his letters and those from James. A memento of the day we first met.

I was already in love with him.

Simon 1989

It was July before I saw him again, a full eight weeks later. I had thought about him every single day, wondering if he would come back or simply put the cottage up for sale. Every day when I collected the mail, I would give a nervous glance along the lane, looking for the *For Sale* sign on his cottage that I dreaded.

It was a Monday. We had hosted a few men and some escorts over the weekend, and I had roughly tidied the house as I normally did, ready for the cleaning lady who would come tomorrow. I heard the bell for the postman and walked to the gate.

Simon was standing in his garden near my gate, close to the wall dividing his land from mine. He would have seen me walking along the drive towards him, as I was in the sun, but I had not seen him in the shadow of the trees. Had he seen the postman, heard the bell, and hoped I would come to the gate for the mail?

I collected my letters from the box, saw him by the garden wall, and stopped to talk to him.

'Good morning, Miss Berrington. It is a pleasure to see you again.'

'You came back,' I said, rather lamely. That was obvious, of course, but I could scarcely string two words together.

117

I was so happy he was here and even happier that his mother didn't appear to be with him. 'Are you keeping the cottage?'

I looked up at him, remembering how kind his eyes were. I was actually quite shaky, my heart beating rapidly, thoughts jumbling themselves together in my mind. I so desperately wanted him to say yes.

'For the moment. I work at a school, and I live there during the term, but I thought I might come here in the holidays. I would enjoy swimming and rambling, and a bit of solitude is rather nice when you spend most of your life among rowdy boys.'

'What do you teach?' I wanted to keep him here talking. I wanted to know everything about him.

'Science and maths. Not your best subjects, I gather.'

'I did get the oak tree right, and the seagull.'

'Yes, of course you did.' Was he laughing at me? I didn't want him to think I was dumb.

'I am a qualified physiotherapy assistant,' I told him. I wanted to tell him I was a physiotherapist, but I decided to be honest.

'But you don't work at the moment?'

'I look after the house for my uncle. On the weekends he sometimes brings clients here. We are a retreat. They can swim in our pool or in the sea and play tennis, and I do massages for them and help them train on the gym equipment. Some of them have very important and stressful jobs, and they can relax here with us. It is all very private. Usually their wives come with them, and I do facials and massages for them as well, but the wives don't usually want to train in our gym.'

Well, now he knew. Would he accept it all at face value? Or would he realise that we actually ran a retreat where men could hook up with escorts? Was he wondering how much of the men I massaged? Should I let him know the massages were quite respectable? Suppose he was here one weekend when the bunny-hunting game was in progress. He wouldn't be hard of hearing.

But I remembered we had to ensure that the bunny hunters were never invited here in suitable weather again. We didn't want anyone in the woods near the icehouse door. They would have to play their game of musical rooms instead. He wouldn't hear that from his house.

He seemed to accept it all, however, and if his curiosity was piqued, he didn't show it.

'But you are free during the week?'

'Most days. On Tuesdays I help the cleaning lady keep the house up to standard, on Wednesday afternoons I need to be here for the laundry van, and on Friday afternoons I drive into town and do the shopping. But the other days I am free to do as I like. I swim in the sea or walk on the beach or along the cliffs.'

'Would you show me some of the paths? I could teach you the names of the trees and the birds in exchange.'

'Yes, of course. Is your mother here as well?'

'No. I asked her if she would like to come down with me, and she said she might join me for a few days if I was able to get the cottage to a liveable state. It is actually in a far better state than we imagined. We were not even sure how many bedrooms there were. I usually stay with my mother during the holidays, as she lives near Harton.'

'Is your father still alive?' I knew as soon as I said it that it was a mistake. I vaguely recalled Mrs Davis had mentioned her late husband, and if his father had still been alive, he would be the heir, not Simon.

'He died when I was a teenager, but I hardly knew him, as he no longer lived with my mother and was never very interested in me. He was many years older than she was, and they didn't get on, so they lived apart. My mother can be very difficult to live with at times.'

'She was kind to me when she came here.'

'She seems to like you. She told me she thought you were the most beautiful girl she had ever seen, and she was concerned that you were in the house by yourself when you were so easily upset. She asked me to check that you are okay. She rarely likes people—she is always finding fault—but that is just the way she is.'

I was not sure how to reply to this; it seemed an odd thing for him to say to me. Was he making a pass at me by repeating his mother's words? Or was he just so naïve that he didn't realise she was trying to get him interested in me because I appeared to her to be well off and eligible, and he had looked at me a second time when we first met? He looked at least five years older than me, and if I were his mother, I might have been worried that he was not safely married by now.

I had a wicked desire to ask him if he thought I was the most beautiful girl that he had ever seen, or whether it was only his mother who was taken with me.

'I am trying to find out about my great-aunt,' he continued, when he realised that I was not going to respond. 'I have been looking through her things to see what she liked to read, and whether she had any photos. I am wondering what I should do with all her clothes. It is such a pity that I didn't know about her before she died. I could have come here to see her and learnt something about her life. The sad thing is that she knew about me. She even knew my name; it was written in her will.

I am hoping you will tell me what you know of her. Will you come inside and have coffee with me? Perhaps this afternoon you could show me some of the paths.'

'I need to look after the mail and tidy the house,' I told him. 'But I am happy to walk with you later. I'll come and find you at one o'clock, and we can walk along the cliffs to the town. We can have coffee there and walk back.'

'That sounds perfect. Thank you, Miss Berrington.'

'My name is Ann. We can ask the vicar's wife about the clothes. I know she will help you. She collects things for her jumble sales. I gave her some clothes that I no longer wore.'

I remember that afternoon as one of the happiest I have ever spent in my life. We walked along the cliff path to the town, about three miles away. He told me the names of some of the trees and easy ways to remember them. But it wasn't just tree names that he knew, it was flowers as well. I could recognise stinging nettles and buttercups and daisies, I knew that grass was grass, and I could recognise roses, of course, although they were garden flowers. But he knew the names of everything, the Latin names as well as the common ones, even for the different types of grasses.

We had coffee at a beachside café. I told him the little I knew of Mrs Pearson. Her son had been conscripted, as most young men were, at the beginning of the Second World War, and he had been killed in 1944; his name was on the war memorial in the village. Her husband had died in 1950; I knew that from the gravestones in the church yard. She had once told me that she remembered Queen Victoria, who had died when Mrs Pearson was about ten. She had wanted to sell the house before she died, so her heirs were not burdened with the maintenance costs. As Simon was her relative, not her husband's, he would have no family connection with the house. I recalled that she played bridge and belonged to the knitting circle and that she enjoyed gardening. But beyond that I knew very little of my neighbour.

It was one of those occasional days in summer when the sea was as calm as glass. There were boats for hire on the beach, and he rowed me out over the water, his arms strong on the oars, and I thought again how beautiful he was, how much I would enjoy the feel of those stretched muscles beneath my hands. This was just ecstasy, romantic ecstasy, being rowed by a man over the clear water, so clear that we could look down to rocks and seaweed, and we even saw a few little fishes, darting past our boat.

He was asking me about my life, but I told him as little as I could. One day he would find out all of it and would no longer be my friend. But today it was just him and me, together in a boat, with the sunshine and the pale line of the horizon between the clear blue of the sky and the glass blue of the sea, the surface broken only by the gentle ripples from our boat. He showed me how to work the oars, his hands covering mine, and my life had never felt so beautiful.

I was happy for us to just be together with silence between us. He didn't invent things to say just to fill the void, and he was one of the few young men I had met who was not continually talking about himself.

Later he bought us both an ice-cream, and we walked back to Deniton along the beach. You could only do that when the tide was very low, but you still had to scramble over rocks in places, and return a couple of times to the path along the shore. He took my hand to help me on the rocks, and we found seashells washed into the spaces between them.

He knew the names of all the seashells as well. I knew there were different types, of course, but I only knew them as the flat triangle ones shaped like a woman's maidenhair and the very long pointy ones that looked like a man's ... stop that, Ann!

He was having dinner at the pub in the village, so I joined him. Afterwards we walked back home along the lane while there was still some lingering daylight left, and he offered to walk down to the house with me, but I insisted he left me at the gate. I passed through and closed it, turned for a moment and looked at him, the bars of the gate between us.

'Thank you for a wonderful afternoon. I'll wait here until I see you go inside. Do you sleep up in the tower?'

'Yes.'

'Like Rapunzel, a prisoner of your wicked uncle?'

I knew he was joking, but I froze in my tracks because in a way it was true. Richard kept me here in this isolated house, where the only men I met were either married and old, or married and unfaithful.

'Rapunzel didn't have a wicked uncle. It was sorceress who imprisoned her. And my uncle isn't wicked; he is very kind to me. He is the only family I have left, and I love him like he was my father.'

I turned from him and walked back to the house without once looking back. It was all just a dream, and he had suddenly woken me from it. Here was the most wonderful man I had ever met, a man who treated me as if he cared about me, cared who I was and what I thought, but he could never be my lover. He lived in a safe world, and I envied him for it, but I could never spoil his life by wanting him to share his safety with my shady past. If a teacher at a school like Harton wanted to marry a girl like me, he might lose the job that he loved. There could be no hint of scandal.

I didn't want him to know that I was—well let's face it—only one step better than a whore. I didn't want him to know that my mother had been an alcoholic and a drug addict, that my father had been arrested for drug dealing and stealing from clients, that my uncle and I ran what was really just a high-class brothel. Sooner or later, he would find out. His mother would remember something she had read in the newspaper seven years ago. Or she would mention to a friend that her son had met a Miss Berrington, and the friend would tell her that a Giles Berrington had stolen money from one of her friends, a client of his, and he had died before he could be tried. There were drugs involved too, and the mother had been an alcoholic and had been high on cocaine when she fell down the stairs and died. It had all been in the papers. Perhaps his mother even knew Julian's mother and would know that I had … no, not that. Julian had made love to a girl who was under-age. No mother would be silly enough to admit that, even to her best friend, however spiteful she was feeling.

That night before I went to sleep, I opened the curtains and stood at the window in the darkness of my bedroom, looking over towards the cottage. I could see a light in an upstairs window. Was he thinking of me, thinking what a wonderful day we had spent together? I switched the light back on in my room so he would see it. Then I sat in bed for a while, reading *Pride and Prejudice*, imagining Mr Darcy looking just like Simon Davis, until I was too tired to stay awake any longer.

The next day was Tuesday, when the cleaning lady came. Simon was by the wall again when I went for the mail.

He apologised for what he had said about my uncle, and said he had only been trying to amuse me.

'That's okay. I can't come out with you today because it's cleaning day. The cleaning lady does the house, but I clean the pool and the gym. If you go down to the village and knock on the door of the vicarage, the vicar's wife may be able to come and help you sort the clothes. Their house is next to the church.'

'Will you walk with me on Wednesday?'

'It would have to be the morning, as I need to be here at two for the laundry van.'

'Would you like to have dinner with me again tonight? What time does the cleaning lady leave?'

'About four. But this time you must let me pay for the meal. Is that okay?'

'If that is the condition for having your company, then yes, I agree to that.'

We had dinner at the pub again, and afterwards we walked down to the beach in the stillness of the evening. He told me the names of some of the flowers that grew beside the gate to my garden, sea thrift and sea bindweed, its flowers now closed for the evening but its leaves unmistakable. For a while we stood silently together, looking out over the softly lapping water as the light gradually faded, and I knew that all I wanted in my life was to be with him. He had been sent to me by fate, and there had to be a way.

On Wednesday morning we walked inland, along a path that crossed fields. He had his camera with him, and he would occasionally stop and photograph a bird. It was his hobby, he told me. He had been all over Britain photographing birds, and now had a photo of almost every species that occurred here. The best photos were taken from a bird hide, as you could get much closer to the birds and support the camera on a tripod.

We reached a village, the end of our walk, and found a tea-shop where we could have our morning coffee.

He told me he had been educated at Harton, had gone on to Cambridge and then had returned to the school as a science teacher. Nothing unusual, just a boring conventional life, but he loved his job.

Yet I envied him. I wished I could have had a normal life. I still resisted telling him much about myself, even when he asked questions. Why had I left school?

I mumbled something about my parents having died and it was a very expensive school.

For a long time I looked at him and he looked at me. I knew he was perplexed, unable to understand why I was reticent to talk about my past.

'Were you expelled?' he asked at last.

'Not exactly, but I don't know if they would have allowed me back.'

'Whyever not? Surely your uncle could have managed the fees. He had the money to buy the house from my great-aunt.'

I said nothing. How could I tell him my mother had been a cocaine addict and my father a drug dealer?

'Why are you hiding your past?' he asked me, but his eyes were kind. His eyes were always kind. Yet he made me feel like a child caught in an act of disobedience, trying to find excuses that would make things right again. He had that air of quiet authority that all successful teachers have. I swear there were times when I only just stopped myself from calling him *Sir*.

'I didn't want to go back. I was upset at losing my whole family, so my uncle found me a small privately-run school, close to his flat in London, where I didn't need to board, and

I finished my O-levels there. Then I trained as a physiotherapy assistant.'

Would that stop him from asking questions? I hoped it might.

I will never know what it cost my uncle to have that school accept me. They had been unbelievably kind to me, had negotiated with the examiners to have my records from Roburn considered along with my exam papers, and their help and support had got me through the worst months of my life. Whatever he had paid had been worth it to me.

'Where did you learn to quote the psalms? You really did know that by heart, didn't you? You didn't once look at the card.'

'I know most of them by heart, not just the twenty-third. I spent three years at a small primary school run by nuns. I loved it there because there were no boys.'

'Don't you like boys?' he asked, amused.

'I didn't then because they hassled me. I did when I got older because then they were nice to me and were competing for my attention. I always loved my brother.'

'Don't you get lonely, living in that big house by yourself during the week? I was concerned that you seemed rather depressed when we first met you. Do you have friends here?'

'I was upset about the funeral. But I am sometimes a little depressed, although I usually manage to talk myself out of it, and sometimes I am a little lonely.' It seemed so easy for me to tell him that. 'Most of the men who come to our retreat are old and married, and I never meet anyone else. I did once have a boyfriend, but I didn't want to marry him, so he married someone else. I like solitude. You once told me you do as well.'

'Yes, I do. I like to get away from the boys at times, and I like to get away from my mother at times as well, as she never stops talking. But with you I can have it both ways. You keep me company, but you don't natter on about trivial things, so I still have the solitude to think.'

Well, at least he was honest and open, and I knew what he meant. I liked his company too.

'Did you know my brother James Berrington at school?' I asked him. 'He left in 1981.'

'I was at Cambridge then. I'm sorry but I don't remember him. Boys tend to only know those in their own year. Now I'm a teacher, I need to know the names of all of them.'

I knew he really was sorry that he had disappointed me.

'And do you know them all?'

'Yes, absolutely. It's part of my job.'

As we walked back towards Deniton, he asked me if I remembered the names of the trees he had taught me on Monday, and I got most of them right. If he could remember the name of every boy in the school, I was sure I could manage to learn a few tree names.

He didn't ask me about my past life again. He accepted that I didn't want to talk about it, so he left it alone, just occasionally picking up on little things I let slip.

The vicar's wife was coming to help him sort the clothes that afternoon, and he hoped I might join them when I had looked after the laundry.

I had scarcely noticed the interior of the cottage on the day we had found Mrs Pearson, but that afternoon I had leisure to look around me. It had been completely renovated before she moved in, and even the furniture was new. Although that was hardly surprising, as the existing furniture would have been battered by years of holidaymakers. The wardrobes were built in, the kitchen and bathroom were modern, and a new cloakroom had been added downstairs.

There was a photograph of Mrs Pearson's son on the wall, along with her wedding photo and also a photo of the aunt who had owned the cottage between the Wars. Simon would leave them all there. Although the aunt had not been a blood relative of his, she was part of the history of the cottage.

The vicar's wife seemed pleased to see me and was glad of my help. She had ceased her prying questions about my life here and my uncle. Had they discussed me while they were there by themselves sorting the clothes? Had he suggested that they should just allow me to be secretive about my life? Perhaps he had told her my parents were dead.

She had brought a man's scarf with her, beautifully knitted in shades of blue. Mrs Pearson had been working on it for the knitting circle, and the vicar's wife had finished it. They made gifts for an old people's home, as well as layettes for new babies and jumpers for the local children. The ladies from the knitting circle had thought Simon might like something his great-aunt had made.

She told us she had known Mrs Pearson since she herself had first come to live here when she married the vicar thirty years ago. Mrs Pearson was by then a widow, so the vicar's wife knew nothing of Mr Pearson or his family. Mrs Pearson had run the house as a small hotel, open only in the summer months, although the cottage had been available as a holiday let for most of the year. She had barely made enough to live on, but she was always a cheerful soul and was well loved in the village.

We packed some dresses from the wardrobe into one box, and cardigans and twinsets into another. Mrs Pearson had very few clothes. There were none of Simon's things in here, so I assumed he was sleeping in the other bedroom.

There were a couple of the Dickens-era nightdresses in a drawer, brand new with their original labels. The vicar's wife offered them to me if I could use them. They would not have fitted her, of course, as she was quite solid, while Mrs Pearson had been small and slender. I doubt that they would have fitted me, either.

'Thank you but I never wear nightdresses.'

She looked at me in shock, her jaw dropping, and I saw Simon try to cover a smile with his hand.

'I prefer pyjamas,' I hastily added, and he actually laughed. The vicar's wife looked at us both, but said nothing, as she set the new nightdresses aside from the used ones, which she was packing into a third box.

I opened the next drawer and hastily shut it again. It was full of Dickens-era bloomers, and I had glimpsed a label; some of those were new as well. I imagined having to tell her I never wore bloomers. In front of him. Both of us would explode.

'Perhaps Mr Davis could take the two full boxes downstairs,' I suggested, 'and put the kettle on for tea while we finish up here.'

He flashed me a smile and took down the first box.

The vicar's wife didn't stay for tea with us, as she needed to return to the vicarage to make tea for the vicar. Was she deliberately leaving us alone together? In league with his mother perhaps? But she was a dear soul, and I won't laugh at her expense.

Simon told her he would put the boxes in his car and drive them down to the vicarage later in the afternoon. He would leave them on the porch. He thanked her for her help.

'Why did you call me *Mr Davis*?' he asked, when she had gone and we were sitting in his kitchen, drinking coffee and eating chocolate biscuits, a CD with jazz music playing quietly in the background.

'I didn't want her to know we were friends already.'

'You really are a very private sort of girl, aren't you?'

'Yes, I suppose so. Actually, I was panicking, and I wanted you to go downstairs before I exploded with laughing. The next drawer had some very old-fashioned bloomers, some new with labels, and I didn't want to have to tell her I never wear bloomers.'

We both collapsed into laughter.

'Tonight when I look out for your bedroom light, I'll be able to think of you in pyjamas,' he said, when we both finally stopped laughing.

'Behave yourself. I assure you they are very respectable pyjamas. Definitely not skimpy black lace, and don't you dare think of me without my bloomers.'

I hadn't meant us to be joking over what I wore to bed, or what I wore beneath my skirt. I had wanted us to be friends before we were lovers, but I liked to hear him laugh. Even then I hoped we would one day be lovers.

'Will you stay all summer?' I asked him, desperate to change the subject.

'Yes, why not? We still have lots of directions to walk, and I haven't gone for a swim yet. But I suppose I should spend some time with my mother. She does like me to go home sometimes.'

'Perhaps you could go and see her at weekends, when I am working and can't walk with you.'

'Is that every weekend? Then perhaps I will.'

With Mrs Pearson's room cleaned out, Simon intended to move into it, as it was larger than the spare room where he was currently sleeping, and had a queen-size bed instead of two singles. I vacuumed the floor and the cupboards for him, we made up the bed with clean sheets from the airing cupboard, and I helped him move his clothes.

Late that afternoon we took the boxes down to the vicarage in his car, spoke with the vicar, left some roses we had cut from his garden for Mrs Pearson, and bought a frozen pizza from the village shop to cook for our dinner that evening, along with a punnet of strawberries.

There were some carrots and tomatoes in the garden, planted more than two months ago by his great-aunt and now ready to eat, so we included some with the meal. He had the jazz playing quietly in the background again, but he did ask me if I minded. I didn't, and that was the beginning of my lifelong love of quiet background jazz.

We spent Thursday morning visiting an open garden a few miles from Deniton, and in the afternoon we swam in the sea. It just seemed natural for us to be together.

He was so beautiful in his bathers. They were not the brief sort that men wear for swimming races—nowadays called budgie smugglers—but more like shorts. But I could still enjoy watching the sunlight glistening on his wet skin, the muscles rippling as he moved, the male hair below his navel denser and darker until it disappeared from view. I didn't need his bathers to be tight to imagine ... stop that, Ann!

But I was hoping he was thinking the same thing about me. I had chosen a one-piece swimsuit, as modest as I could find. I felt too shy to swim with him in a bikini.

On Friday morning we walked in a wood, and he photo-graphed birds again while I held the camera case and waited beside him in absolute stillness. In the afternoon I needed to shop, and he returned to Harton to spend the weekend with his mother.

When Richard came home on Friday evening, I told him that Mrs Pearson's great-nephew had moved into the cottage and would be staying there all summer. We had gone for a walk together, and Simon was teaching me the names of the trees.

Richard asked me not to bring him into the house, preferably not even in the grounds. What we did here was private.

It was summer, when we had the retirees visiting our retreat on most of the weekends. But now I knew it all by rote, so I had plenty of time that weekend to think about my new neighbour as I organised the racquets for tennis, the towels for the pool.

How ugly the old men were compared to Simon. But I knew I was being unfair. No one chooses to grow old.

Summer 1989

Oh, those precious days we had that summer, walking, swimming, just the two of us and no one else in the world. He kept his distance, and I didn't try to seduce him, as I understood that he was a little shy of me. I let him set the pace, sometimes touching me, rather timidly, if he helped me over a rock or a stile, but usually just walking beside me, sometimes talking, sometimes in shared silence, communicating without words. I hoped that one day soon we would be lovers, and that was enough for me.

Yet I wanted to put off the time because then I must tell him that this could never be for real, that I was not the girl he believed I was, that I could never spoil his prospects of a decent normal life by allowing him to share it with me. I should have told him that from the start, not allowed the two of us to get closer and closer until we almost thought as one. He still told me the names of the trees and the flowers, the birds and the seashells and even the stars when we stood on the beach at night.

Every minute of every day that I could be with him, I was with him. We had long ago stopped having dinner at the pub. Now I cooked it for us in his kitchen every day from Monday to Thursday, but on the weekends he had to fend for himself. He spent them with his mother, leaving after lunch on Friday while I did the shopping.

I would tear myself away at the end of each evening that I spent with him, lock the gate between us, return to my bedroom in the tower, look over to his lighted window and blow him a silent kiss goodnight. Then I would dream of having him beside me in the night, dream of him making love to me with the stars above us and the sea whispering a lullaby.

He never mentioned Rapunzel again, but he did once tell me he liked to go to sleep thinking I was in the tower that he could see from his window, and that he thought of me as an elf princess, someone too perfect to be real.

But the summer was slipping away, day after precious day, week after precious week, and soon he would be gone, back to the school where he taught. I didn't want to think about it. I wanted that summer to last forever.

One Thursday, when I went to the gate to get the mail and saw him waiting for me, as he usually did, he had a letter in his hand. Every day I dreaded that because I was worried it would be his mother writing to tell him she had found out I was unfit to even be a friend to him. She would have phoned, of course, not written, but fear is not always rational.

It was from his mother. It was a birthday card. I hadn't known it was his birthday, and I had nothing for him. I didn't even know how old he was.

'Twenty-nine,' he told me when I asked. I told him I was almost twenty-four; my birthday was in three more weeks.

And then I remembered the present I had bought for James for his nineteenth birthday, the maroon tie with the gold stripe, still sitting in my drawer with James's letters. I took the mail back to the house and returned with the wrapped tie, handed it to him to open, told him I had once bought it for James, and explained about the poster and the film hero.

He hesitated, asked me if I was sure, so I told him that there was really nothing of James in it for me because he had not lived long enough to wear it. I had never known what to do with it, as I could never bring myself to throw it out. If he could use it, I would be grateful for it to go to a good home. He untied the ribbon that surrounded it, loosened the tape that held the paper, took the tie from its wrapping and unrolled it from its seven-year sleep.

He let me tie it for him, his collar warm beneath my touch, my fingers shaking when they brushed against his beard, his eyes on mine. It is such an intimate thing to fasten a tie for a man, to help him dress and face the world looking neat and cared for.

It took me a couple of attempts to get the length perfect, with the top of the triangular section just in line with the top of his belt and the short end tucked neatly into the loop. We had been taught at deportment how a tie should be done so we could have our husbands perfectly dressed.

'The length has to be right. If it's too long it can catch in your zipper, or worse, and if it's too short it looks as if your trousers are falling down,' I told him, and he gave me a wicked smile. Oh, how I wished his trousers would fall down, or I could unzip his ... stop that, Ann!

'It's just a tie,' I said, 'and quite ordinary, except that it would have meant something to James, but if you wear it you can think of me.'

'I think of you all the time,' he said, as I smoothed the tie against his shirt, stopping when my hand reached his belt, wondering how he would respond if I slid my hand further down. I felt he was tense, reacting to my touch, so I kept my eyes on his face, while he looked at me hesitantly. I knew he wanted me as much as I wanted him, but he was always so shy, so timid, when he touched me or I touched him. I wanted him to know it was all right for him to want me, but I wanted it to be his choice to take it further. I was unused to men who didn't want to take me to bed the first time they took me out. I recalled Richard once telling me that a bad experience with a woman could make a man feel inadequate. Had Simon once had a girlfriend who had humiliated him? Or was he simply unused to girls?

'Hardly surprising, since I'm here all the time,' I replied, one part of me wanting him to lose control and make love to me, another part of me wanting him to keep his distance so I was not tempted into letting him. 'You were supposed to be enjoying solitude away from the boys.'

'I am enjoying solitude. You are a part of the solitude. What are we doing today?'

'Building a sandcastle on the beach, and this afternoon we can walk along the cliff path. Tonight we'll go out to dinner in town to celebrate your birthday.'

That was a magical day. We built our sandcastle, not yet as acknowledged lovers but almost there, and I remembered the castles James and I had built with Richard when we were children. And yes, I did dream of future sandcastles, of Richard with us, and children that Simon and I might one day have, all together here on the beach. This man was my destiny, and things had to work out right.

We sat side by side on the sand in our jeans, loosely hugging our bent knees, closer than we had ever sat before, our bare feet touching, silent because we had no need of words, and when I put my arm through his and leaned against him, he did not shy away but leaned his cheek against my way-ward hair.

Our castle stood for a while, surrounded by our footprints, bravely facing the incoming tide, with a prince and a princess sharing the joy of their love within its walls, until it was swept away by a rogue wave into the eternity of the sea, leaving only memories that themselves would one day fade into the realm of myths and ghosts and things that might have been.

In the afternoon we trod a faint path in the woods near the cliffs, rounded a bend, and saw a red fox, not four yards from us. For an eternal life-changing moment the fox looked at us, and we looked at the fox, Simon's hand reaching out to hold my wrist to warn me to keep still. Eventually the fox slunk away, and he slid his fingers down until they were twin-ing with mine. We were alone on the path with the trees and the sky and the faraway whisper of the waves on the shore. His other hand was gentle on my cheek, I closed my eyes and leaned towards him, his lips met mine, and the passion was unleashed. He crushed me against him and kissed me until we were both out of breath.

'I love you,' he whispered. 'God how I love you. I want life always to be just you and me.'

I knew it could never be, but I wanted to savour every moment that I had before he knew the truth about my life and we would part forever.

As we walked back to the cottage hand in hand, we stopped every few minutes to kiss again.

We had dinner together in a hotel in town to celebrate his birthday, formal but not dinner-suit formal, so he wore a jacket with the tie, and I wore a little black dress with sheer black tights and black strappy high heels. I had gone back to the house to change.

The restaurant was dimly lit, and the waitress found us a quiet corner. I scarcely even noticed what I ate; I just wanted to sit there and look into his eyes, watch every slight expression that touched his face. They had a dance floor, and we danced close together, his body pressed hard against mine, my arms around his neck, his face against my hair, the passion between us barely contained.

When we returned to the cottage, we made coffee and sat for a while on the sofa with the jazz soft in the background. I could have just slid my hand along his thigh, let him know what I wanted, I could have offered him a massage, but I wanted any advance to come from him. I would never deliberately try to seduce a man, and I knew that a shy man like him would feel more self-assured if I let him take the lead.

He had his arm around me, and I leaned back against his shoulder, his face close to my hair, my hand on his knee but no higher. He touched my cheek, turning my face towards his.

'Would you stay with me tonight?' he asked me. 'I can't make love to you, because I don't have what we need, but I would just like to sleep with you beside me. I could lend you some pyjamas of mine—we could turn up the cuffs. It's torture when you go home. I think of you sleeping in that tower and wish you were here with me. I always go down to the beach at daybreak—I walk past your house and think of you still asleep—and I stand on the beach and watch the sun rise. Tomorrow morning you could come with me, if you are happy getting up that early.'

I was not sure if I should just let him take the initiative, sleep with him tonight without going the whole way, then let him organise what we needed for tomorrow. Hadn't he even thought that we might do this sometime this holiday? Whatever we did, I wanted him to feel good about it. But tomorrow was Friday, so we would have to wait until Monday night. Eventually he would find out how I really lived, and then he would no longer want me. That could happen over the weekend. Someone may already have told his mother about me. I was by now crazy for him, and I was not even sure that I could sleep with him without us going the whole way.

Should I tell him I had what we needed in my clutch bag? I knew he would be a little shocked, but he could hardly expect me to be a virgin at twenty-three. I had always carried a pack with me since Richard had first suggested it when I was seduced by Julian. But I had a better idea.

I asked if he would mind if I went back to the house first, to get some jeans I could change into in the morning so I wasn't seen on the beach at daybreak in an evening dress. And I told him that I had what was needed; we supplied them to guests as all good hotels did.

I was also on the Pill, but I didn't tell him that. Even though I no longer slept with Paul or anyone else, it did make a girl's life easier. In any case, AIDS was by then a consideration, so precautions were not just about contraception.

He came back to the house with me; it was dark by now and I was glad of the company. I took him up to my room, as I didn't want him wandering around the house unsupervised. He joked about having finally got inside the citadel.

I found a duffle bag and packed jeans, a shirt, a jumper and my sandals, and he suggested I bring my pyjamas. I didn't tell him I had no intention of wearing them when we were upstairs in his bed. I took him into the storeroom off the kitchen and found what he needed. He carried my bag as we returned to the cottage.

That night we slept together in his room upstairs, our bodies and our souls merging into one, and I felt, for the first time in my life, the joy of making love with someone you truly cared for with all your heart and all your soul. Every love song in the world now had meaning for me. Every touch of his skin against mine, his beard against my cheek, held us together in a world where there were only the two of us and the soft whisper of the sea. Nothing else mattered because nothing else was real.

He would buy a house for us near Harton, he had enough money for that, so we could still keep the cottage. He didn't need to live at the school to work there. We could be married by Christmas, the two of us together for all time.

Here was the happy ending I had waited all my life for, my handsome prince who would sweep me off my feet, a love that was all-consuming, that I could never doubt was my destiny. Oh, how I wished it could be true, but I couldn't disillusion him, not when we were here together and, for the first time in my life, I felt complete.

He said he would talk to my uncle, he had still not yet met him, but I told him not to speak of other people because tonight there was only us.

At dawn we walked together along the beach, barefoot and with the cuffs of our jeans rolled up, and we stood on the fringe where the cold sand met the colder water, letting it swirl over our feet, the soft grey light enveloping us, the cry of the gulls as they woke to a new day, the chill breath of the wind on our faces, the sound of the waves on the shore, here long before we were and still here long after we are gone.

I made our breakfast and we rambled along the cliff path, my hand in his, until it was time to return for lunch.

'How did you reach twenty-nine without being spoken for?' I asked him, as we ate our meal, the ubiquitous jazz faint in the background, not loud enough to cover the murmur of the sea.

'I was waiting for you. That first day we met, you seemed so fragile and vulnerable that I wanted to look after you. You stood in the lane, trying not to cry, and I wanted to hug you, tell you I would keep you safe and make you happy again. For days afterwards you were all I could think of. I have never known many girls, and never any I really liked. My mother was always parading young women in front of me, trying to persuade me of their merits, but none of them were right for me. They all hated jazz, and they never stopped talking, generally about horses and dogs, but a lot of it was just criticising other girls. The last thing a bird enthusiast wants is a dog with him on a walk. And all they ever wanted was to go to parties and get tipsy, while I like a quiet life, just walking and birdwatching, like you and I do together. I could only imagine marriage with any of them as being doomed like my parents' marriage was, with my mother talking incessantly about nothing and my father unable to stand it beyond the first few years. They never actually divorced, and he occasionally came back and stayed overnight, but it was not my idea of being happy. I think my mother was hoping I had finally fallen for a girl when we first met you. She couldn't stop talking about you as we drove home, saying how beautiful you were, and how quiet, and trying to get me to admit I was taken with you. But I could ask the same of you. You are well off and beautiful. I'm not your first lover, and I can't be your first offer. You told me you had a boyfriend who married someone else.'

Was it so obvious he was not my first lover? I remembered telling him I had once had a boyfriend. Was I his first lover? He had at least known what to do. I would never ask him that because it didn't matter. If he had lovers before me, they were no longer part of his life.

'I haven't had many of either,' I told him. 'I have never wanted to marry anyone else because I was waiting for you. You're the only one I ever loved, even for a moment.'

But today was Friday. I had to do the shopping for the weekend and be back at the house before Richard came home. There were guests every weekend in summer.

We still had one more week left of his holidays, just one more precious week.

We stood at the gate, reluctant to separate even just for a weekend, knowing that it would be Monday before we would meet again.

'Does your uncle have some sort of hold over you?' he asked me.

'I work for him on the weekends, that's all.'

'But he leaves you here all week by yourself.'

'Sometimes I spend the week at his flat in London. But not since you came, as I wanted to be here with you.'

'Would you leave him for me? Please say you'll marry me. You haven't yet said it.'

I didn't answer. How could I answer? It wasn't that simple. I slipped through the gate, closed it, touched his hand one last time through the bars, said I would talk to my uncle and see what could be done, that I would see him on Monday, and I walked back to the house, the way blurred by my tears. How could I possibly marry him? It would ruin him. The school where he worked would ask him to resign, to save the scandal of one of their teachers marrying a girl whose father was a criminal, arrested for drug trafficking and stealing from his clients. And if the girl in the icehouse was found, I could go to prison.

I wavered between despair that our love could never work and hope that it might. He would overlook my past. I was not responsible for the sins of my father, and I had never had sex with any client for money. I would tell Richard he needed to find a new hostess. Surely, he realised that one day I would meet someone I cared for, and I would want to leave. And the girl might never be found.

I spent that weekend scarcely able to concentrate on our guests. They were the last group of retired couples for the summer. Perhaps this would be the last year we would offer this. I wanted us to close down so I could marry my lover, but of course I said nothing. When we walked on Sunday morning, I was able to point out other birds as well as seagulls and tell them the names of the plants that grew on the margin where the sand of the beach merged into the vegetation outside of the garden wall—the sea thrift and the sea bindweed, its shy pink flowers now open. Simon knew their Latin names, of course, but I was happy with the common names, and so were my highly-impressed retirees.

I no longer pointed out the icehouse or told them the stories of the smugglers, hoping they would think it was because I had told them all that already.

On Monday when I went for the mail, Simon was waiting for me, and it was so good to be back with him. We walked along the beach in the morning, hand in hand because now we were lovers, not just friends, scarcely even speaking, as we didn't need words to share the joy of being together.

In the afternoon we swam in the sea, then slipped inside the back gate of my garden, found a soft spot on the leaves beneath the trees—well away from the icehouse—set down a towel, and made love in the open air, with birdsong around us and the soft hum of bees. It was just too long to wait until the night. For a while we lay side by side, my hand in his, and we dozed in the shade of the trees, enfolded in the warmth of summer.

Eventually we returned to the beach, walked along the path that ran outside the garden wall and back to his cottage, where we had wine with our dinner and spent our second night sleeping together, lost in a world where only the two of us mattered.

On Tuesday I had the cleaning to do, but I spent Tuesday night with him.

On Wednesday morning we walked inland to the village tea shop we had visited that first week. I needed to open the gate for the laundry van at two, so I let Simon come to the house with me while I handed over the bag with the dirty sheets and towels. We walked back to the gate to close it when the van had driven out, and took the clean linen inside. I no longer cared that Richard had asked me not to bring him to the house. There was no one else here, and the house was mine.

I gave Simon a massage, something my fingers had wanted to do since the first day I saw him. No extras, of course, as I didn't want him to think that was part of what I normally did.

'You missed a bit,' he said, when I told him it was finished.

'I don't do those bits.'

'Not even for me?' he said, laughing.

How easily we had slipped into intimacy, how natural it felt to be talking like this with him. I gave him the extra, my fingers now expert in giving men the relaxation they craved, but I only went part of the way. I led him upstairs to my room in the tower, and we made love on my bed, joking that he had overcome the wicked uncle and reached the princess in the tower.

'You're not just a princess,' he said, 'but an elf princess, mysterious and ethereal, too beautiful to be real, and I worry that one day you will simply disappear.'

Afterwards we swam naked together in the pool, before we returned to the cottage for dinner. It was less than a week since the first time we had kissed.

Thursday was the last complete day we would have together until half-term, seven weeks away. We walked to the town again, sat at the beachfront café with our coffee, hired a boat, bought ice creams and walked back. But this time we were doing all this as lovers, with the timeless romance of sharing a beautiful day, wishing it could all last forever, treasuring the memory of every moment, looking forward to ending our day making love, surrounded by the velvet darkness of the night and the whisper of the sea.

That night was our last together. We planned our future, but even then I knew it was only a dream. We would marry and live together in a house near Harton. I would work as a beautician, or assist in a gym, while he worked at the school. And we would spend every night together for the rest of our lives. I could leave here and join him any time I wanted, as his mother had a spare room where I could stay until we were married and had a place of our own.

Tomorrow afternoon he would pack his things and leave, spend the weekend with his mother, then return to living at the school. He would write to me every week, and he would come down at half term. It was obviously pointless him coming here at weekends, as I worked then. He would phone me on Wednesday evenings, and I gave him the number, asking him to promise never to phone on a weekend. I told him I would look after the cottage for him, and my gardener could mow his lawn. At half term we could plan a wedding and look at some houses for sale near Harton.

I pushed aside the thoughts that tried to intrude into my mind and spoil our night of dreams. One of his mother's friends, asking her if I was the daughter of Giles Berrington, the fraudster whose wife had been a cocaine addict, telling her the uncle was not much better, telling her the husband of a friend was a client of Richard Berrington and he had said that some of the clients spent weekends at a retreat on the south coast, consorting with escorts. Not her friend's own husband, of course, he would never do that, but he had heard it from another client who did avail himself of the service.

But tonight those thoughts were banished, thrust back into the dark pool of doubts where they belonged. Tonight was the joy of giving pleasure to a man I loved, the joy of knowing that he and I were one soul. Who cared that tomorrow we would be parted? Tonight, we were together. I lay awake, listening to the soft sound of his breathing as he slept beside me, knowing that this was all I ever wanted but fearing deep in my heart that it could never be.

On Friday morning we stood on the beach at dawn as we now did every morning, then had breakfast in the cottage, holding on to every precious moment before we had to part. I helped him pack his things, the jazz CDs, the camera, the scarf that Mrs Pearson had knitted, the tie I had given him, the canisters with the undeveloped film for the photos he had taken over the summer—some of them of birds, some of them of me, one I had taken of him that he had promised to send to me. He only trusted a professional photo laboratory in Harton town to process them. So in the end I never saw any of the photos from that summer, and I never had the one of Simon, for he never sent it to me.

After lunch we said our goodbyes, and I returned to the house then drove out to the shops. But he was loading his bags into his car when I stopped on the verge to close the gate behind me, and of course we kissed again, in full view of anyone who was passing in the lane.

'Can't you just leave here and come with me?' he asked. 'How can I bear seven weeks away from you? I worry that when I return here, I will find my elf princess is gone, the house is just a ruin under a tangle of thorns, and this whole summer was but a dream.'

'The time will pass,' I said. 'I will ask my uncle if we can just wind this place up; then at half-term I may be free to return with you.'

I waved as I drove away along the lane. When I returned with the shopping, his car was gone and his gate was closed.

I was swamped with a feeling of emptiness, a fear that he had gone from my life forever. My beautiful fairy-tale summer was over, and the doubts swirled around me. There were evil things lurking, biding their time, in this paradise too. The sad ghost of a girl who was buried deep in the cold dark earth. How could I ever have a happy ending while she lay unloved and unclaimed?

That evening, while Richard and I were watching a film, close together on the sofa, Richard with a glass of whisky in his hand—he was drinking more and more and was sometimes noticeably drunk—I told him I was thinking about getting married and leaving here. Perhaps it was time we closed our retreat and he returned to just being an accountant. He earned enough from that.

'Not to Lagan? Has he offered you marriage? Don't trust him. He's already gone through four wives. He married rich old women, outlived them, and got their money. I'm not letting him get his hands on yours.'

'No, not Lagan. Simon. The school teacher who lives next door. I told you I was spending time with him. You asked me not to bring him to the house. Have you forgotten?'

'But you can't marry a school teacher. You can't be serious. Life would be completely boring for you, and it wouldn't last six months. You could have anyone. Didn't you have some earl's son in love with you?'

'I am serious. We could close down the retreat and sell the house. Simon and I would live in a house near Harton School, where he works. It's where James went to school. It's much closer to London. If you were living in the flat, I could still see you every weekend if you wanted, like we do now.'

'Does he know what you do? How your mother died? That your father was a drug dealer?'

'Not yet.'

'Well, if he's a decent man he will overlook all that, but we'd need to keep it all fairly quiet. The school where he works might not be keen on one of their teachers being married to someone with a past like yours. There's the girl, of course, but if they ever find her, I would take full responsibility for that and tell them you knew nothing about it. You had still been asleep in your room when I buried her. I could easily have done it on my own. I am so sorry now that I got you involved in that. When are you planning on leaving?'

'He is back at the school next week, but he is coming here at half-term. He wants to meet you, and I told him I would arrange it when he returns here. Are you okay with me accepting him then?'

'Well, you haven't known him for long, and I would want to know he is not just after your money. He inherited the money we paid for this house, and he would get the house back if he marries you. Funny how things can work out. I've given you all the profit from the retreat, and most of what I make, as well. I've been transferring it to your mother's account in Switzerland. I'd want it all arranged so if you split up, he wouldn't get half of it. But marry him if you want to; we'll arrange the details around the money. Everything I have is yours, and everything I do is for you. You're all I've got, and I want you to be happy.'

Blackmail 1989

In the end Simon and I had only those six weeks as friends, with five beautiful days and nights together as lovers, then a few precious love letters, before the whole dream was swept away like the castles in the sand.

Richard accepted that we might be closing down. We had a couple more guest weekends, which had already been booked, and Lagan came down with his friends and his girls. I was tired of his slick flirting, his constant breathing down my neck while he asked if I had changed my mind about sleeping with him, tired of him always wanting massages and following me when I went down to the beach.

I was becoming concerned at how much Richard was drinking, but I knew he was stressed about the girl. He had never been the same since the night we had buried her, now almost a year ago, and he had never once since brought a girl here for himself. We never spoke of her, except for that one evening when I told him I wanted to leave. He had said he would take full responsibility if she was found and I would bear no blame, so Simon would only have to overlook my father's indiscretions. If we kept quiet the school was unlikely to know. They would only know me as Ann Davis, not as Ann Berrington.

I knew Richard was also stressed about losing me, but I kept reassuring him that I would still see him, and he would no longer have this house to worry about. Why did we need all this money? We had everything we wanted, and the excess was just being stashed away in a bank account. We may never use any of it. It was not worth the work or the stress to run this place when we had no need of the money.

I suggested that if he really wanted us to keep Orchard House, we could leave the house with a caretaker in residence, and all come here for weekends and holidays together, perhaps occasionally inviting Paul and his wife, or Rebecca. Not Lagan, I thought, but I didn't say that. He was Richard's friend, but I didn't want him anywhere near Simon.

Simon remembered my birthday and sent me a card in late September along with a pocket guide to British birds. He had placed a small bookmark at the picture of a herring gull, with a note on it in his neat hand.

Seagulls are now my favourite bird. I love you, Ann.

I was counting down the days until we were together again, resolving that I would tell him everything, except for the death of Amos and the fate of the au pair, and if he still wanted me, I would leave here and live with him. He had telephoned me every Wednesday evening at eight as he had promised, but we never had a lot to say to each other. For lovers like us, for whom sharing silence was as good as conversation, talking on the phone just didn't work.

It was a Friday, with only a couple of weeks left until half term.

I went out to the mailbox, eager for a letter from Simon but knowing it was unlikely, as one had arrived only yesterday.

There was the account for the laundry and a letter for my uncle. That in itself was unusual, as most of his mail went to his flat in London. The mail here was almost always bills and occasionally letters for me.

It was typed and simply addressed to *Richard, Orchard House, Deniton.* Had one of his girls fallen for him and written him a love letter?

It was anything but. When he came down from London that evening, I gave it to him to read while I cooked the meal. I saw him look at the envelope, turn it over in his hand, but there was no return address.

I handed him a knife to open it. I saw his hand shake as he read it, but he did not share it with me. He was straight away on the phone in the hall.

He scarcely ate anything, and I knew he was worried, badly worried. I asked what the letter was about, as that appeared to be the source of the problem.

'Lagan will be here first thing tomorrow,' he told me, evading my question. 'We'll sort it out.'

We sat quietly watching television after dinner, his arm around me and my head on his shoulder as we often sat when we were alone. There was never anything improper between us, but he often hugged me, and I gave him the occasional massage but without the extra. We never crossed the boundaries.

When the program finished, he took the letter from his shirt pocket and silently handed it to me to read.

It was a blackmail note, neatly typed. The sender claimed that she had been raped by a man known as Lagan in Richard's house when she was fifteen years old. She now knew his real name. She also knew that a girl had disappeared at Orchard House, and she thought the police might be interested in that. She wanted money, of course, a lot of money. A million pounds from Richard and another million from Lagan, paid into an account she had set up at a bank in Switzerland. She gave the account number. They had six days. After that she would go to the press, who would pay her well for her story, then to the police.

'She means the Russian girl, not the au pair. And if they find Lottie, we will tell them you knew nothing about it. Understand?'

I dimly recalled that one of the Russian girls had left early. One of the men had driven her to the station. This was better than the police knowing about the au pair, but it was worrying.

'What happened to the Russian girl?'

He only shrugged and said he didn't know. She was Lagan's girl, not his. Antonio had taken her to the station and bought her ticket, but she had never arrived back at her home in London. Nothing to do with him.

I knew he was lying to me and he did know.

'You told me none of them were underage.' The seriousness of this was slowly dawning on me. The press would have a feeding frenzy, and both men could be jailed. Certainly Lagan could; I was not sure about my uncle. Probably only for a year or two, but prison was prison, and reputations are hard won and easily shredded. But if the police came here, they would discover the girl that Richard and I had buried. This was really serious. They would easily find her if they searched the grounds for the missing Russian girl. And had my uncle been involved in that girl's disappearance?

'Rebecca never sent any girls who were less than eighteen. It is the lawful age for prostitution, and it was always her policy. They were not strictly prostitutes but escorts, and what they did with the men was their own affair. But Rebecca kept to the rules, and she always said that by eighteen they were old

enough to make the choice for themselves. But Lagan sometimes brought his own girls. Their age was none of my business.'

'Richard, is what we do legal?'

'If the girls are over eighteen, then yes. They could pick me
up for living off the earnings of prostitution, perhaps, but the
escort agency sends the girls, and what they do here is their
own choice. We simply provide the rooms and the service and
supply a companion for the men if they want one. They won't
touch Rebecca because she plays by the rules, and the police
know her girls are checked for age and tested regularly. Our
enemies are the press, not the police, and this girl knows that.
What the men who come here need is absolute privacy, and so
far, we have managed that.'

I carefully copied the words of the blackmail note into my
journal so we had a record of it and of the bank account
numbers.

We got very little sleep, and once more we shared his
room. I knew he was desperately worried, even if what we did
was within the law. Except for the dead girl in the icehouse.
If the police were investigating a missing Russian girl, Lottie
would be found.

Lagan and Rebecca arrived together in his sports car
around mid-morning. He had a letter as well. I made us all
coffee, found some crackers and cheese, and we sat on the
terrace while we discussed what to do, with the gentle sound
of the waves on the beach, and the bright sunlight glinting on
the sea beyond the trees.

'She can't be one of my girls, unless she's lying,' Rebecca
said. 'I check their passports before I allow them to work
for me.'

'She would be one of mine,' Lagan admitted. 'I like them
young. I do them no harm. A Russian woman gets them for

me. I pay her a lot more for virgins, but that is a win-win. It's such a turn-on for me if a girl has no idea what I am going to do to her and is lying there naked, crying and scared. Then I train them up, teach them how to please a man, and how to enjoy it themselves when they do, and then they like their job more. I don't know where she gets them from. If she sends out underage girls, then she is the one the police should be charging, not me.'

I felt like I was going to throw up. This man was the devil incarnate, and I was so glad I had never slept with him. If we got through this and carried on with our lives, I would ask Richard never to invite him here again. This was, after all, my house. Had he forced himself on young girls here, under my roof, unbeknownst to me? Had Richard known? The girls had sometimes seemed very young, but none of them had ever complained or looked upset or screamed in the night. Although Lagan was always in a room far away from my tower, so I would not have heard them if they had. And they were unlikely to complain to me, as I would have seemed to them to be part of the arrangement, and most of them spoke little English. Some of them had looked at me with troubled eyes, but they were just girls; we had heaps of girls here, and it was their choice to sleep with the men and accept the rewards.

'Are we going to pay her off?' Richard asked. 'And why are we involving Rebecca in this? It wasn't her girl.'

'No, we're not paying her. If we give her two million, in six months she will want another two. In the note she sent to me, she also asked for a couple of thousand pounds so she had enough to get out of the country. I was to put it in an envelope addressed just to Lily and give it to the old Russian madam I use for my girls. I don't recall a Lily, so I assume that is not the name she used when I trained her, but the Russian woman will know who she is, and I'll get it out of her. She's the one supplying them, so she's the one who should be charged. We'll give the girl the two thousand, but then we'll find a way to persuade her to keep quiet. And if we can't arrange that, we'll brazen it out, say the girl made the whole thing up. Rebecca is here because I want to get Ann out of this, and I wasn't sure she would trust me enough to leave here with me. Rebecca is good at getting people new names and new places to live. She worked during the War smuggling people to Britain from Germany, and she still sometimes arranges new identities. It will only be temporary, while we sort this out. Ann will have a new name and a job in Australia. She can stay there until it is safe to come back. I am not taking no for an answer on this. We need to protect her. Have you got any cash here that we can give to the girl?'

Richard took a bundle of banknotes from the safe, counted out two thousand pounds in crisp new notes for Lagan, and gave the rest to me. I gave it no thought at the time. Cash was untraceable.

I asked him if he wanted me to leave, told him I would prefer to stay here with him, he had done nothing wrong.

'Go with them,' he urged me. 'That way whatever happens you are not involved in it. You can come back when this blows over. All I want is for you to be safe and happy.'

I knew he was worried that if the police came here looking for the Russian girl, they may find the girl we had buried. He never expected any real trouble from the blackmailer. If the girl went to the press or the police, the worst he could lose was his reputation, but he was now old enough and wealthy enough to simply retire from view. He had never hired out any underage girls. It was Lagan who had the most to lose.

I went back to London with Lagan and Rebecca, cramped in the back seat of the sports car with my clothes, my brother's scarf, Simon's handkerchief, my parents' photo albums, the bird book and my diaries—all in a suitcase in the boot—and the remaining contents of Richard's safe in a bag on the seat beside me, with my mother's jewellery and my letters from James and Simon. I was to give the cash to Paul to bank for me, and I was to trust him absolutely. Richard would telephone him as soon as we had left. Paul would arrange to transfer money to a bank account in my new name in my new country, and he would give me the number of the Swiss bank account where my mother's money was stashed. Paul had nothing to do with the activities at Orchard House. The police could have nothing on him.

I never saw my uncle again.

I stayed for a few days with the dressmaker Vera in her luxurious flat in the West End. I helped her in her salon so I was not left by myself in the flat while she worked. I liked her and was glad to be useful. She told me if I was ever able to return from my life abroad, she would be happy to employ me and could easily find me a rich husband.

Paul brought me my new passport and birth certificate, my ticket to Australia—tourist class as they considered that would look less conspicuous—some cash, both British and Australian, and my bank account numbers. I was now Ethel Turner. My new credit card would be waiting for me at the Perth branch of the bank. If I showed them my passport, they would give me the card. He had transferred some money to the Australian account—enough for me to live on for at least a couple of years. The Swiss bank account that had been my mother's had been set up so that either Ann or Ethel could now access it if I ever needed more. It all looked genuine enough.

I asked if Ethel was a real person.

'She died from leukaemia when she was nine, so the birth certificate is real. Her birthday is only a few days different from yours. Remember always to use your new name and your new birthdate. If things blow over, you can come back and be Ann again. We will write and let you know when we think it's safe. I don't know how this is going to end. I don't believe what you and Richard did at the retreat was illegal, and the girl was not one of Rebecca's, so it may all work out okay. Richard said you have a boyfriend. If you have an address for him, I will drop him a line and tell him you have left England for your own safety and will contact him when you are able to return.'

What else could I do but agree to that? I wrote a short note to Simon, saying I loved him with all my soul but I had to leave England as a precaution, as there was some trouble with one of the men who had stayed at our retreat. I said we had done nothing wrong there and I was hoping that one day soon I would return. I asked him to make no attempt to trace me. Paul said that all sounded okay and he would enclose my note in his letter.

At that stage the police were not even involved, but I sensed that this was not going to end with a blackmailer being persuaded to keep her mouth shut. Not when Lagan had so much to lose. Hosting a few men and escorts at a retreat was not actually illegal, but raping a girl of fifteen was. And what had happened to the Russian girl who disappeared?

I signed over power of attorney to Paul so if I could never return, he could look after my British bank account and sell my house. I trusted him, and I know he never cheated me.

He said that if worse came to worse, he would take over Richard's share of the accounting business and change it to be in his own name. He would pay Richard out and send the money to me. He was clearly planning for that eventuality. Was it just a precaution, or did he really think my uncle would go to prison? Paul knew nothing of the girl we had buried. At this stage we were simply in damage control. I wondered if Paul was silently thanking his stars that I had never agreed to marry him.

That afternoon I took a taxi to Heathrow Airport, paid the driver in cash, and took my seat on a flight out of England, wondering where Simon was, what he would think when he found me gone, whether I would ever see him or England again.

How could they charge Richard just because some avaricious girl had tried to blackmail him over something that he had no part in? None of his girls had been less than eighteen. But I didn't trust Lagan. Could he make my uncle a scapegoat to save his own skin? And I couldn't get out of my mind the thought of those young girls, coming to a new country as au pairs, being handed over to Lagan and raped for his own sick pleasure. God, how I hated him.

Perth 1989–1991

After twenty-four hours with no sleep, and a couple of stops in crowded foreign airports, I arrived in my new country. The customs people looked at my passport and made sure I understood that I was on a work visa, sponsored by a Mrs Marek, and I was to work for her for at least three months before applying for any other job. If I stayed here working for two years, and kept out of any sort of trouble, I could then apply for citizenship.

Vera had told me I was to take a taxi to Hillside Private Hotel in Bishop Street in the city, where I would work as a receptionist at the hotel in the evenings. The owner Mrs Marek was a friend of both her and Rebecca, and she would help me to find my feet.

Mrs Marek was very good to me. The night I arrived she stayed up to welcome me, and she made me supper, even though it was well past midnight. She had herself escaped as a child from Poland with her parents during the War, with Rebecca's help, and she was glad to repay her by helping me.

I would man the desk in the evenings, five nights a week, from six until midnight, with occasional later times if guests were arriving, as I had, on late flights, although there was a watchman who sat at the desk from midnight to morning. I would have a small bedroom to myself, and she would pay me a wage as well as giving me board and lodgings. I would be unable to work in massage or gym instruction, as my qualifications were in my old name, but she would help me to study for another career if I wanted to. I was allowed to study in Australia, but I would need to pay my own way at tech school or university, as I was not a citizen.

The work was easy enough. I quickly realised that she also ran an escort service as Rebecca had, as there were half a dozen girls who regularly had dinner and shared rooms with some of our gentlemen guests. But she didn't expect me to be an escort, and I was grateful for that.

The escort business was only a small part of what we did. We were an exclusive private hotel. From the beginning Mrs Marek and I both knew that we had a mutually beneficial relationship. She provided me with support and a home in an unfamiliar country, and I provided her with a high-class receptionist from England, who spoke passable schoolbook French and German, and who could be relied on to be absolutely professional and courteous to her guests, some of them business men from Britain and Europe, others from Sydney or Melbourne, Singapore, Tokyo or New York. I no longer had bespoke clothes, but I could afford designer clothes, and I always looked well dressed. The hours were flexible, as Mrs Marek would attend the desk any evening that I wanted to go out, and I was happy to work all seven evenings if I had nowhere particular to go.

Our hotel was in a quiet shady street at the top end of the city, close to an extensive park with green lawns, lakes, glorious flowers and natural bushland. After breakfast I would walk in the park, and later each morning I would walk through clean streets, past shop windows and the train station, to the state library. There I would look at the newspapers from England, searching for news of my uncle and news of a body being found in a disused icehouse in the garden of a house on the south coast.

It was not long before I found the headlines. My uncle's photo was on the front page.

I dreaded to read the story, and it was far, far worse than I could possibly have imagined. Accountant Richard Berrington had been charged with hiring a hitman to murder a prostitute. The girl had blackmailed him over hiring her out for sex with his clients, at a retreat he owned on the south coast, when she was underage. The retreat was owned by his niece, the daughter of Giles Berrington, an alleged conman, who had been charged with theft and drug dealing in 1981 but had died before he could be tried. There was a photograph of the murdered girl, but I did not recognise her as one of the girls Lagan had brought to the retreat, although there were so many of them, and they were there for such a short length of time, that I could not be sure. Another photo showed Orchard House from the lane, with the locked gates. And they had dredged up the photo taken at Paul's wedding of me with the Honourable Percival. They only showed my half of the photo and had corrected their mistake and captioned it as *Ann Berrington.*

There was nothing about Lagan, although I didn't know his real name, and nothing about a body being found at Orchard House. Richard was being held in custody, pending a trial in three months' time. He was applying for bail. The police, meanwhile, were looking for the clients of the retreat.

I went to the cloakroom and threw up.

For a while afterwards I just sat in the library, feeling numb and faint. Eventually I went outside and bought a bottle of water from a kiosk at the railway station, sat on a park bench in the open air for another hour, then returned to the library.

I recalled reading an article a few days previously about a girl's body being found in an old canal somewhere near London, so I went back through the rack of papers and there was the story. I had never connected it with my uncle. He would never have murdered the girl. I remembered how upset he was when the other girl had died by accident. Somehow Lagan must have framed him.

Simon would have read the papers, realised why I had left. I felt his pain because it was also mine. His mother would have read them too, and also the vicar's wife. The beautiful high-class girl who lived in the big house with her uncle was an illusion. My uncle had been running a whorehouse with underage girls, I was clearly part of it, and, even worse, he had arranged for a girl to be murdered. I could never hold my head up in Deniton again. Even if he was vindicated, the smut would stick.

But by the time I returned to the hotel, I had recovered enough to eat my lunch with Mrs Marek and pretend that nothing had happened to shake me. I asked her if she could recommend a hairdresser, and she sent me to her friend Mrs Bukowski, whose salon was only a block away.

The hairdresser was a small cheerful woman, much like Mrs Marek. She knew who I was, as Mrs Marek had phoned and asked her to try to fit me in. I wanted her to cut my hair and straighten it, hoping that anyone here who had seen the photograph in the British newspaper would not then connect it with me. She was happy to give me a new shorter style, but she protested against straightening my hair. It would not work, and it would make my hair dry and frizzy. Just cutting it would make me look different.

Mrs Bukowski did an excellent job, and I liked the new look; my wayward hair was finally tamed.

A note came to Mrs Marek for me, through Vera, from Paul. The police had contacted him to ask if he knew where I was. I was the owner of the house, and they wanted to talk to me. He had told them he knew I had gone abroad but he didn't know my new address. He advised me to just lie low for the moment and not contact anyone. He had spoken to Richard and his lawyer. Richard had been framed for the murder of a girl who had blackmailed him and one of his clients. He was hopeful that it could be sorted out, and he wanted me to stay out of it, for my own safety. Someone else who was involved had threatened Richard that he would harm me if Richard gave the police his name. As far as Paul was aware, the only people who knew both my new name and my new address were Rebecca and Vera, and they were endeavouring to keep it that way.

I remembered that Paul had never been at Orchard House when Lagan was there. He knew nothing of what had really happened.

Had they also found the girl in the icehouse? Did they believe it was me running the retreat and employing the escorts? Did Lagan know who and where I was? Had he helped Rebecca set up my new identity? Did he know about Simon?

Days and weeks went by with no further news.

I helped more and more with the running of the hotel, organising the pay for the girls who did the housework and the cooking, and helping Mrs Marek with the accounting as well as the bookings. There was always light music in the background at the hotel—it was surprisingly soothing—and she allowed me to add a few jazz CDs to the mix that we played. She treated me almost as family.

One of the gentlemen clients of Mrs Marek's escort service was a lecturer at the local university, quite close by, on the other side of the vast green park. We called him Mr Appleby, but I later learnt that was not his real name. I suppose Mrs Marek had told him at least some part of my story. Perhaps he just liked the way I looked; some men did. He had asked if I was available for the escort service but was polite enough to apologise when I said no. He had noticed when I had cut my hair, telling me he liked my new hairstyle; it emphasised the beauty of my face, showed off my huge eyes and gave me an elfin quality. He always chatted to me while he waited for the escort to arrive, and I was often working on the books at the desk, although I would always stop what I was doing to talk to him.

One evening in December he asked if I was trained in accounting, so I told him my uncle had been an accountant but I had only studied physiotherapy. I couldn't use my qualifications here; I was intending to study for something else once I had found my feet.

He asked me if I was on witness protection. He had seen my photograph in a British newspaper, only a few days after he had first seen me here. It was before I had cut my hair.

I was immediately tense; I had hoped the photograph would have gone unnoticed in this corner of the world.

'Not officially, but I can never return. I did nothing wrong and neither did my uncle. I would be grateful for your silence.' I looked at him, hoping he was not going to try to blackmail me into sleeping with him, but he didn't.

'Of course, my dear. It was never in the papers here. I always read the British ones for the company news.'

The next time he came, he asked if I would like to study accounting at the university where he taught. He offered to help me with the applications and the paperwork. I hesitated at first; I didn't want to feel obligated to him. He seemed to understand that, however, and assured me there were no strings attached to the offer. He genuinely wanted to help me.

I invented some A-levels, said the certificates for them had been destroyed in a house fire, I easily passed their mature-age entry test, and I was accepted. Ethel Turner would one day have a degree in accounting.

Christmas came, and we spent a quiet day, with only two British businessmen there for that evening's dinner. We had few guests over the holiday, and the others were spending the day with their extended families or with business acquaintances. Mrs Bukowski came to spend the evening with Mrs Marek.

The two businessmen sat together at dinner and asked Mrs Marek if she would allow me to join them. They talked of the contrast in the weather from leaving a British winter to coming here to an Australian summer, and told me where they lived in Britain, trying to include me in their conversation. They knew from my accent that I was from England, so I told them I had been brought up in Surrey and had gone to Roburn School. I had come here for a working holiday and had decided to study at the university here.

At least they stopped me from thinking of how this Christmas might have been so different. If things had gone as they were supposed to, Simon and I would be married by now, living in a house of our own and inviting his mother and Richard to have Christmas dinner with us.

In late January Rebecca sent me a note, along with one from Paul, enclosed in a letter sent by Vera to Mrs Marek.

She told me that the girl had been murdered by a hitman, her body dumped in an old canal. It had been days before her flatmate had come forward and had identified her, but just by chance they had picked up the same hitman on another job where the police had laid a trap for him, and the flatmate had identified him as the client who had called to collect her friend for a date. When they caught him, they had searched his flat, and some of the banknotes they found had been traced to a withdrawal that Richard had made from the account for our retreat at the bank branch near to his office. Cash was traceable; banknotes had numbers, and large withdrawals were recorded. Richard always took cash out in large chunks to pay the cook and the girls. The hitman had agreed to a plea deal, and had given Richard's name as the man who had hired him to murder the girl.

I reached the second paragraph of the letter, and what was left of my world fell apart.

Richard had been granted bail, but had mysteriously died from an overdose of a prescription sedative before he could be tried. The police were calling it a suicide. Rebecca had now realised that Lagan had sent me away because I was the only credible witness to what had gone on during those weekends, the only one who could tell the police that he had himself brought the girls to the retreat and that Richard had given the cash to him. She didn't think he knew where I was, as she herself had arranged the new identity. She had not given him my new name, as she had never trusted him, but she begged me never to return. He was a dangerous man.

She thanked me for what I had done for Amos, and said I was never to feel any guilt over the way he had died. He had been her brother, not her husband. They had escaped from Nazi Germany with faked identities as husband and wife, and she had spent the remaining War years working for an agency that smuggled Jews to Britain and from there to America or sometimes Australia. She told me that Amos had loved me, and she was glad that I had given him what he desired so badly, even if it had ended his life. Richard had told her the details, and how I had tried to protect her from the knowledge of her fake husband's infidelity. He had also told her I had been planning to marry.

She had left behind a lover during the War, but many years later she learnt that he had died a few months after she had escaped. My lover had his whole life ahead of him. She suggested that both of us should make a new path in life. She didn't want anyone to trace me through him, or to harm him because he knew me. She advised me never to send anyone in Britain my address, as that way they could not pass it on to the police, who still wanted to question me over the underage girls I had hosted at Orchard House.

Paul's note was to tell me what had happened to Richard, and how sorry he and his father were to lose their business partner and lifelong friend. The police had contacted him again, to find me, as I was next of kin. Paul had told them that he had power of attorney in my affairs and that I now lived abroad under a new name. As they had nothing on me, and no longer needed witnesses against Richard, they had agreed to leave me alone and anonymous for the moment. There would be an inquest, and they may still need to talk to me, but they had accepted Paul's argument that I would be safer away from England if there had been any other men involved in the underage sex. They had told Paul that if they needed a statement from me, the police in Australia would arrange it, and they would give me witness protection if they considered it necessary for me to return to Britain. They had agreed not to release the news of Richard's death to the press until I had been contacted, so I didn't learn of it first through the newspapers.

He had written to my friend again, telling him that Richard had been framed and that I had no part in anything that he had been accused of, that everything I had done at Orchard House was legal, but that it would never be safe for me to return. They realised they had been at school together and had arranged to meet for lunch.

Paul would wind up Richard's affairs and sell the flat, and if I agreed, he would also sell Orchard House. Meanwhile he would find a caretaker for it. The money would be transferred to my bank account here. I could reply through Mrs Marek and Vera, who would pass my note on to Rebecca. He advised me to be careful what I wrote, as he was unsure who I could trust and didn't want any of my other friends involved.

I sat on the dark-red carpet on the bottom step of the stairway in the foyer of the exclusive Perth hotel and cried. Mrs Marek sat next to me, simply holding my hand.

I realised then that Lagan had set Richard up even before he had disposed of the girl, when he had asked him for cash and then used it to pay the hitman. When things had gone wrong and the hitman had been caught for something else, Lagan would have persuaded him to name Richard. He had framed my uncle for his own crime, then threatened to harm me if Richard exposed him as the mastermind behind the girl's murder. I had always known he was a rich and powerful man, although I had never known his real name. I would never be safe in England. If I told the police what had really happened, it could destroy him. Whatever influence he had, no one is entirely above the law. He would want to silence me before I could testify. He was totally evil, and I hated him with every beat of my heart.

Suppose I went to the police here and told them my story? Would they believe me? Or did he have influence even here, thousands of miles away? I couldn't even tell them his name because I didn't know it. Would I then live in fear of being shot or mugged when I walked down the street? Both my father and my uncle had died mysteriously, my father while in police custody. How could I have trusted anyone, even the police, after that?

What good would it do Richard? He was now dead. Rebecca lived her life only slightly within the boundaries of the law, and could also testify against Lagan, as she had seen the money change hands. I didn't want him to harm her. And Paul was now the son-in-law of a peer. I owed it to them both to say nothing. I had a new life here, and, so far, I had received no threats from Lagan.

Now, many years later, I ask myself why Richard had not simply fled on the plane with me and waited for things to die down. It was Lagan who had the most to lose. I wished I had tried to persuade him to, but it had all been arranged so suddenly and so swiftly that I had not even thought of it. Perhaps he believed in justice, knowing that nothing he had done was illegal, apart from hiding the accidental death of the girl in the icehouse and she might never be found. Perhaps he had simply underestimated the evil of that man.

Sometimes I thought about the girls that Lagan had brought with him to Orchard House, and what he had said on that last day. They had always seemed different from the normal escorts, not all over their men, seeming like docile convent schoolgirls, and Richard had thought they were pandering to some sort of fetish of the men for sex with reluctant fake virgins. But now I knew that at least some of them had been virgins, sold by the madam to those three men to ravish for their perverted pleasure, then train up as sex workers for her business. And I hadn't seen it because to me all the girls were the same, and a lot of them did not even speak English, so it was difficult for me to communicate with them. One of those girls—by then working on her own and much more sophisticated—had found out Lagan's real name and tried to get her revenge by blackmailing him. Had she really asked for the two thousand pounds, or had Lagan invented that to get money from Richard so he could frame him if worse came to worse? Lagan had clearly guessed who she was. She had been eliminated and my uncle blamed for getting rid of her.

It was late February when I received the note that I had been subconsciously dreading since the day I had received the last letters from Paul and Rebecca. It was addressed directly to Ethel Turner. All the previous letters had been sent to me through Mrs Marek. I did have a moment of hope that either Paul or Simon had found out my address and written to me directly, but I knew it would be from Lagan.

Both the envelope and the note were typed.

> *I know where you are*
> *you are being watched*
> *I know where your boyfriend lives*
> *do not contact him*
> *keep your mouth shut*
> *and never return*

It was only a few lines, only typed words on paper, but dark and menacing, the threat implied but unspoken. I dropped the note like a red-hot coal, and for a long time I stood by the desk shaking and feeling sick.

He had my address.

Should I flee from here, find somewhere else to live, hide out in some bolthole with not even the chance of a letter through

Mrs Marek from Paul? What had I done to harm him? Why was I exiled here, my hope of my happy ending with my lover made bitter by a threat to his safety if I so much as wrote to him? Did Lagan really know who and where Simon was? Who had told him? I knew it would not have been Paul, Richard was dead, and I had never told Rebecca the name of my lover. Was it nothing but an empty threat, a way to keep me here in fear of my life and his?

I carefully picked up the note I had dropped, my heart still racing, put it back in its envelope and took it to my room. I knew I should keep it, however much I hated to.

For a while I was frightened every time I walked in the street, wary of anyone coming up behind me, looking out for anyone who seemed to be watching me or following me. But there were only the usual faces of people in the street, hurrying on their own errands, wrapped in their own worlds, or hailing friends and stopping to chat. Ordinary people, who lived their lives unhindered by the dread that someone wanted to destroy them, wanted them dead.

By March, five months after I had left England so abruptly, I was studying at the university during the day and working at the hotel in the evenings. The course was easy enough. The lecturers were friendly and helpful to the students, and the students friendly to each other.

The anniversary of the day I had met Simon came round. One whole year had gone by since the funeral of Mrs Pearson, and so much had changed in that time. I had found the love of my life then lost him again. I had lost my uncle, my home by the sea. My whole life had been thrown into chaos, leaving me bereft of family and the friends I had once known, and leaving me fearful of walking alone in the street.

The pain of leaving Simon was so tied up in the pain of losing my uncle, that I could scarcely think of one without the other. But time does heal, and my life was so full with studying and helping Mrs Marek, that I had no time left to fall into the depression that had hounded me when James had died. I was one of the oldest in my classes, but the optimism of young people who were eager to make their way in the world was contagious. I had friends, and I sometimes went with them to dances and bars, but usually as part of a group. I never accepted a date unless I knew that the man understood it was only ever to be platonic. I said I had a lover back in England and would one day be returning to marry him. I was good to date when a man just wanted a partner at a function with no strings attached, so I was often asked out.

I had boyfriends, although none of them close. I remembered Richard once telling me how he had just drifted from one woman to another, always hoping that the next one would give him the joy he had felt making love to my mother, but it was never the same. That was not going to happen to me; I would never have another lover.

I occasionally went out with one of the postgraduate students, Alex, who was happy to have a platonic friendship. He told me from the beginning that women just didn't turn him on, and he understood from a friend that I might suit as a social companion for him. I would accompany him to weddings, dances, university dinners, anywhere he was expected to arrive with a female partner. He was fun to be with, and it suited both of us perfectly. I realised later that he was a closet gay, but then I just accepted that he was glad of a girlfriend who was happy to keep her distance.

The other anniversaries came and went: the day Simon had returned to the cottage for the summer holidays; his birthday when we had first slept together upstairs in the cottage; the week we had been lovers; and the last day I had seen him. I wished I could send him a card for his thirtieth birthday, to let him know I remembered him. But it was in the school holidays, so I could not send it to him at the school, as they might forward it to him at his mother's house, or worse, at a house where he now lived with a girlfriend or a wife. I could send it to the cottage, but he may no longer own it.

I finished my first year of studying accounting, accepted that my life was now here. I still worked for Mrs Marek, who treated me like a daughter, and when I had spare time from my studies, I worked in the salon of her hairdresser friend, Mrs Bukowski, doing manicures and facials for her clients while their hair was drying. I wanted to be always busy so I had no time for reflection and regret. She had managed to tame my curly hair when she had cut it short, and I always went back to her when it needed trimming.

In late November, when the university exams were over, I sat down and wrote a note to Simon. I wanted him to know that it was never as bad as the press had made out, that I knew my uncle would never have arranged the girl's murder, and that he had never employed anyone who was less than eighteen. I would enclose it in a Christmas card, with no return address, and I would send it to the school where he worked, in time for it to arrive before the term ended. That way if he had a new girlfriend, or even a wife, she would not accidentally find it. Neither Lagan nor the British police could intercept a letter sent to a school.

By now you will no doubt realise why I left England. Please believe me when I say I knew nothing about the underage girls, I simply hosted my uncle's clients with their wives or girlfriends. My uncle did nothing wrong, but he was framed by a man who was pure evil and wanted to save his own skin. Please don't think badly of me, but never try to find me, for your own safety as well as mine. I think about you every single day. The summer we were together was the only time in my life I have truly felt happy. Sadly, I don't even have a photo of you, but I can still see your face and hear your voice in my mind, and I remember every moment of the time we shared. I am studying at the university here for a degree in accounting and have now finished the first year. I am learning the names of the flowers and trees that grow in a vast park near where I live, and the birds that live there. We have seagulls here. They are like the ones at Deniton, but perhaps a little smaller. Every time I see a seagull, I remember how we stood on the beach together at dawn, watching them soar above the water. Please just forget me, go forward with your life and career, and find another girl who you can love and marry. I can never return. I will always love you. Ann.

I typed the envelope, addressing it to him at Harton School.

It was several days before I found the courage to post it, but I had to make the decision, as the days were running out for it to arrive at the school before the term ended. I slipped it into the post box at the corner of the street where I lived, thought about his hands touching it, thought about him turning it over, wondering who it was from, then slitting open the envelope and picking up the note that fell from the card.

Did he still think of me? Did he still own the cottage? Had he spent the summer there, rambling by himself, sleeping by himself? Had he wished I was there? Or did he despise me now, knowing how I had lived? Was he thankful that he had escaped from being married to me and involved in my disgrace?

Suppose I had married him and the police had raided Orchard House and found the girl we had buried in the icehouse. I would be an accessory after the fact, and Simon would have had a wife who was in prison. The school would have asked him to resign to save them embarrassment, and his mother would never have held up her head among her friends again. But Richard had said he would take full responsibility for that, and if I had denied any knowledge of it, they could have no proof, so I may have been safe. Admitting the truth would not have helped Richard, and there would have been no point in us both being jailed. But there would still have been a scandal; Simon would have been asked to resign from the school.

When the letter was gone beyond retrieval, I started worrying that the police may be trying to find me, and may have asked Simon to let them know if I wrote to him. They would know from the postmark where I was living, and I had been silly enough to say I was studying accounting. That would narrow it down.

Perhaps my fear of the influence of Lagan was exaggerated, but to me it was real. At first, I had thought he had sent me abroad because he had some regard for me, cared for my safety, valued the friendship we had shared in the years he had stayed with us. But by then I knew it was purely to get me out of the way if things did not go as he planned, as I was the only credible witness to his sins. Did he know my alias? Had he helped Rebecca arrange the passport? But no, Rebecca had said she was the only one, apart from Vera, who knew who and where I was. Yet Lagan had sent me a note, independently of Rebecca or Vera, addressed to me at the hotel; he had to know my address to do that. He wanted me to be too frightened to return, too frightened to go to the police and tell them what had really happened. And I was.

I liked the lecturer who had helped me to get into my accounting course. He now had a real name, Dr Philip Harvey, but at the hotel I never forgot to call him Mr Appleby. I would always talk to him when he came to spend the evening with one of the girls, and he generally left before midnight to return to his wife. I felt sorry for her, but it was just the way the world was. Richard had once told me that some men want sex enough to be prepared to pay for it, that back in the dawn of history, men who strayed had more children, but the children of faithful men had more chance of growing up, so nature had struck a balance. I also knew that a lot of men never made love to their wives, and some of them used that as an excuse to stray if they wanted to. Often the wives knew about it but didn't care, provided it was always kept private. Richard had said it was better if men went with escorts, as the girls were always discreet. If a man chased after a girl in the office, he was more likely to end up involved in an unsavoury and unwelcome divorce.

Alex invited me to a staff and postgraduate Christmas party for our department, held in early December at one of the yacht clubs on the Swan River. His friend Gary, a tutor in the department, was part of our group, although he had not brought a partner. I now knew both of them well, as we occasionally went out as a threesome. I guessed they were an item, but neither of them seemed to resent me being with them.

I suppose they understood I was not a threat to their relationship, and would not judge them. They both loved to gossip, so by then I knew a lot about the private lives of everyone in the department.

My lecturer, Dr Harvey, arrived at the dinner and came across to us, with a neat and pretty woman on his arm, and he introduced her as his wife, a little warily, of course, but he trusted I would not give him away. After all, he knew things about me that I wanted kept private, and I was more than willing to return the favour.

His wife was many years younger than he was—still in her twenties, I guessed—and I wondered how he could possibly want anyone else. I recalled I had once been told that she had previously worked in the department, and had been the object of admiration from several men who still worked there.

When he introduced us, he told her I was one of his best students, and she asked me, rather saucily, if he was one of my best teachers.

They joined our table for the dinner, and I was seated beside her. Her husband left her alone after the first course was finished, joining a group of the older lecturers at the bar, while the younger people danced.

I jived with Alex—he did not like dancing close up but he did enjoy the jive—and also with Gary.

One of the older lecturers was Greek. He was always full of energy and flirted openly with everyone female, but you could never take offense at it, and you knew he was harmless. He asked if I could tango, and we danced it together in a flamboyant and exaggerated way that we both enjoyed. His wife was a rather sour-looking woman, dressed in black, who spent her time sitting at their table in conversation with some of the other older wives, but she did not seem at all perturbed at her husband's exuberant flirting. I did wonder if she was actually his mother, but Gary assured me she was his wife.

After our tango, he rounded up some of the younger men to do a Zorba dance, first giving them instructions, then arranging them in a circle for the dance. Alex and Gary joined in, and I was left alone on our table with the lecturer's wife.

'You are very much younger than your husband,' I commented, as an opening. I had been surprised at this, and I wondered again why my lecturer availed himself of the services of our escorts when he had such an attractive wife at home.

'Twenty years younger,' she told me. 'I was a secretary in the department, and he was recently divorced. We've been married for eight years now. He has been very good to me, and we have two children. Phil tells me you have a fiancé in England, and that is why you go out with Alex. Is your fiancé older than you?'

'About six years.'

'That would be all right. Marrying a much older man has not really worked well for me. It seemed romantic and safe at the time, and I do care for him, but older men lose their vigour, and then they lose interest in their wives. He often works late and is tired and depressed when he gets home. But it's hard to leave when you have small children. What does your fiancé do for a living?'

'He's a school teacher.' But I didn't want to tell her too much about myself, so we watched the men doing the Zorba dance, some of them by now a little drunk, and I asked her about her children.

She seemed so nice, that I wondered if I could do something for her. The next time her husband came to the hotel, I asked him if he would meet me for lunch one day when he was free. I would buy him lunch in exchange for some advice on which units I should choose to study for my second year at university.

Perhaps it sounded a little artificial, but he agreed to meet me the next day. He knew I would not be making passes at him, as we had already discussed that. He had once asked me if I was available for the escort service, but had always respected my refusal and had never asked again.

We sat in a quiet restaurant in the park, looking down over the wide expanse of the river, the skyscrapers tall against the blue sky, the road bridges gleaming white above the sparkling water, sailing boats with their coloured spinnakers, a green area across the river that was the zoo, houses and trees, and beyond them all a range of hills in the distance. Perth is a beautiful city.

This was awkward, but I was used to making men feel at ease when talking about sex. I had been the hostess in a high-class gentlemen's retreat, and now I was receptionist in another. I started by telling him that a couple of the men in our department at the university had said he had a really attractive wife, that several of them had been in love with her when she had worked in the department, and now that I had met her, I understood why.

He seemed surprised, demanded to know who the men were, but of course I didn't tell him.

'She was beautiful when she was young,' he admitted.

'She still is beautiful, and she still is young. Do you still love her?'

'Yes, of course.'

'Do you sleep with her?'

He hesitated. He knew what I meant.

'Only occasionally. She has no interest in it.'

'Take her out to dinner somewhere where you can dance with her. Tell her she is beautiful and you still love her just as much as you ever did. Then ask her if she would stroke you occasionally when you both first wake up in the mornings. Tell her it would only take a bit of massage oil and a few minutes of her time, that you wouldn't expect anything else, and that it would be relaxing for you. Tell her you read an article that recommended it for older men; it is good for reducing stress.'

I handed him a bottle of scented massage oil.

'Give this to her, and ask if you could do something in exchange to please her so she enjoys it as well. No confessions, no recriminations, and no threats. Then stop spending your time with the girls at Mrs Marek's, and spend the evenings making love to your wife instead. She is worth ten of them. Sex feels much better when the man and the woman care about each other.'

He looked at me, dumbfounded, but he took the bottle of oil and put it in his jacket pocket. I changed the subject to accounting, and which units I would be studying for my second year at the university.

He never came to our hotel again, and I hoped he was not going to another establishment to avoid the embarrassment of seeing me. He was, however, perfectly friendly towards me when we crossed paths in the department at the university the following year. And so began and ended my one and only foray into marriage counselling.

Alex invited me to spend Christmas day with his family. He always asked a couple of friends, and his mother didn't mind, as she invited friends of her own. They lived in a high-class suburb near the university, in a house that backed onto the river—they even had their own little jetty—the garden shaded by trees and refreshingly cool on a hot summer day.

His mother seemed impressed with me and confided that her son had never brought a girl home before. She told me about her English relatives, who they knew and where they lived, and I realised she thought I was aristocracy and would know all the people she name-dropped. Just to make her happy, I told her about my friend Paul's wedding to the daughter of a peer, about the marquee on the lawn and dancing to the brass ensemble, trying to suppress my amusement as she gaped at me wide-eyed, taking in every detail of the story, asking me what they had served for lunch, relishing that her son now had a girlfriend who had moved in high circles. I couldn't recall the lunch, so I just told her asparagus canapés. I stopped myself just in time from telling her about Lady Ann Murphy and the photo in the social pages. But at least it diverted her attention from watching her son with his friend Gary, who had also been invited, and it was good to spend Christmas with a real family, even if it was not my own.

In February I received a large letter from Paul, sent inside an envelope addressed to Mrs Marek from Vera. It was a newsletter from Harton School. There was a note attached to the corner from Paul, saying he thought I might like this as a memento of James.

At first, I was puzzled about the reason he had sent it. It was years since James had been at Harton. I started reading the news snippets, old boys' achievements, teachers leaving and new teachers coming in, the rugby team's success. I turned a page, and my heart skipped a beat. There in the centre of the page was a photograph of Mr Davis, the science teacher, with two of his students, taken while they were on a camp in

Scotland. He looked so young and full of life, effortlessly in charge of the young men whose lives he helped to shape. He still looked exactly as he had when I first knew him, still the same smile, the cowlick, the brown beard.

He was still at Harton, so he would have received my Christmas card. He had read my note and had found a way to send me the photograph I had craved. But why did he not send me a letter through Paul, or a normal photo? Perhaps Paul did not entirely trust the privacy of the transport of letters through Rebecca, and did not want to reveal any connection between me and Simon. I went back over the few previous notes that Paul had sent me, and realised that he had only ever referred to Simon as my friend.

I sat with the photo in front of me and cried for an hour. I had no other photos of him, although I knew he would have some of me. When he had photographed the birds, he had taken some shots of me, and I had taken one of him, but cameras relied on film then, which needed to be developed. He had sent me half a dozen letters that autumn, while we were looking forward to half-term, but he had never sent me the photo.

Did he still have his photographs of me, or had he thrown them out in disgust? Did he still think of me? Did he blame me for breaking his heart? Did he think I had pursued him under false pretences and despise me for it? Did he think I was one of Richard's whores? Did he curse the day that we had met? Did he regret that he had ever loved me, and hate himself for allowing me to twine my poisoned vines around his heart?

No, for then he would not have asked Paul to send me the newsletter.

Karl 1991–1992

In June of 1991 I met Karl.

I was friends with one of the postgraduate accounting students, a neat studious girl called Anita, much closer to me in age and temperament than the undergraduate students in my year. She was Chinese, although her parents lived in Singapore. Perth is a very cosmopolitan city, and the university even more so; there were students from all over the world. Anita lived in one of the colleges across the main road, and I would walk with her through the underpass after lectures, as my bus stop was close to her college. She had a boyfriend, a postgraduate engineering student, who lived at another college; his name was Frederik and he was from Norway.

One afternoon he came over to our department just as we were leaving and walked back with us. He wanted to talk to me. Anita had mentioned to him that I had a lover in England and did not want a serious relationship with anyone here. He asked if I would go on a blind date to his college ball with a friend of his who was in a similar situation. His friend was always too shy to ask a girl out, and as their college was all male, there were few opportunities for him. They were both research students in the engineering department, and there were not many girls there either. Anita would pick me up from the hotel in her car, so I could arrive with her. His friend Karl would pay for me to go home in a taxi, as that way Anita could have a few drinks if she wanted to.

Since they both seemed keen, and had worked out the transport, I agreed to it. I could come to no harm at the college, and I could always leave if I felt out of my depth or didn't like the man I was dating.

'Does he have a girlfriend in Norway?' I asked, assuming that was what Frederik meant by a similar situation.

'Not exactly. Perhaps I should explain things, as it may make it easier for both Karl and you if you understand the situation. Can you spare half an hour? We can sit in the courtyard of Anita's college, and I'll tell you both the story.'

Karl and Frederik had first come to Australia six years before to stay on a farm in the wheatbelt owned by Frederik's aunt and uncle. They had both finished school and were on a gap year before they started university in Oslo. The uncle was a third-generation Australian farmer, the aunt a Norwegian woman who had met her future husband while she was here on a working holiday. They had six children, Frederik's cousins, all of them boys. The eldest boy Mike, then eighteen, was the same age as Frederik and Karl.

One evening Frederik, Karl, Mike and a boy named Jack from a neighbouring farm had gone out to shoot rabbits at dusk as they had on several occasions before. But this time things had gone horribly wrong. Jack was acting strangely, laughing one moment and becoming hot-tempered the next, trying to pick a fight with Mike over a girl from a nearby farm who had been Jack's girlfriend but was now Mike's.

They had bagged a couple of rabbits and were walking through an area of mallee on a ridge, Jack quite a way ahead of them. He had suddenly turned and started shooting. Mike was shot through the heart, Frederick in the shoulder and Karl in the groin. It had all happened so fast, and had been so unexpected, that they had not had time to react. It was hours before they were found by Frederik's uncle. Mike had been killed, but the other two survived, although both of them had lost a lot of blood. Frederik's uncle and Jack's father had spent all night searching for Jack, assuming someone had shot all four of them, while the police had set up road blocks to try to catch the killer. Jack's body was found the next day floating face down in a farm dam. It was only when Frederik had recovered enough in hospital to talk, that the police and the parents of the boys knew what had happened.

Frederik recovered almost completely, but still had the occasional pain in his shoulder if he overdid things. Karl was not so lucky. After a bit of reconstruction, he looked okay and functioned normally in the bathroom, but he had been left unable to make love to a girl or father a child. He had also damaged a hip joint and limped slightly. He could walk okay with support from a stick for balance, but he couldn't run.

They had gone through university together in Oslo, then returned to Perth, where they were both doing postgraduate research in chemical engineering, sponsored by both a European chemical company and a mining company with an office in Perth.

Karl would never ask a girl out, as he said it was not something you could tell a girl when you first met her, and it would be unfair to lead a girl on before you did tell her. He had intended to miss the ball, but Frederik had remembered that Anita had a friend who liked to go out but didn't want a serious relationship, as she had a boyfriend in England. Karl had agreed to give it a go.

I wore a long low-cut dress in a dark cherry red, and made my eyes up carefully; they were always my best feature. I wanted to look good for this man whose story had shocked me so dreadfully. I couldn't even begin to imagine the heartbreak of the two neighbouring families from the loss of their sons and the damage that had been done to the two boys staying in their care from Norway. And I could understand the reticence of the young man to ask a girl out on a date, the embarrassment of telling a girl what had happened to him. I was left with the feeling that both of our lives had been changed forever by someone else's crime. Even before I met him, I felt we shared a bond.

I had never been on a blind date before, but we would be in a room full of people, and it was only one evening of my life. I hoped I could give him some pleasure from my company, let him at least feel included in the excitement of a ball. I had enjoyed looking after the guests at the retreat; I would enjoy looking after my date. I would not throw myself all over him as the escorts had done to the clients, but I knew how to make men feel good about themselves.

Anita picked me up as arranged. We left her car at her college, where Frederik was waiting for us, and walked to the men's college. I was glad I had worn a jacket, as it was winter here, and the night air was cold, but I took it off before I entered the room. I wanted to look as glamourous as I could. Frederick led us over to the table we were to share for the evening.

I am not sure what I expected, but it was not what I found. Karl was tall, slender, blond and very Nordic looking, much more so than Frederik. He stood up as we walked over to the table—he looked steady enough—and his face lit up with a beautiful smile. I could scarcely imagine a man as attractive as he was ever lacking a date, but I understood his reluctance to ask a girl out. I greeted him with a few Norwegian words I had once learnt from Kristen and still remembered, and we both laughed when I didn't understand his reply.

There were two other couples at the table, but after the introductions they went away to dance, Frederik and Anita with them, leaving Karl and me alone together. He asked where I had learnt my little bit of Norwegian, and I told him about the au pair Kristen, who had looked after me when I was depressed after I lost my family. I asked about his family in Norway—he told me he had a younger brother and sister—and his research.

The research clearly inspired him, for he went into a lot of detail, leaving me struggling to follow, but I listened, fascinated by his perfect English and the gentle tone of his voice. He suddenly smiled.

'You didn't understand a word of that, did you?' he teased.

I had followed it a little. 'You are extracting rare elements from sand mined south of Perth so you can make better magnets,' was the best I could do, but he said that was right and apologised for having talked so much.

'Tell me about yourself. Anita said you have no family here at all, and a lover back in England. So why did you choose to study here and not stay with your boyfriend?'

'It's complicated.' I was deciding how much I should tell him, when we were interrupted by two young men who joined us at the table.

'Karl, who is the gorgeous chick? Fred says you are on a blind date, and you get the most beautiful woman in the room! Some men have all the luck!'

'Yes, Ethel is the most beautiful woman, so I am the luckiest man,' Karl agreed, and I laughed. But I couldn't help thinking that was not the kindest thing for them to say to a man who walked with a limp, even if they didn't know the full extent of his misfortune.

'I was lucky too,' I told them. 'I got a handsome Viking for my date.' I was rewarded with that lovely smile, and I felt he had relaxed a little, knowing that I was on his side.

One of the young men asked me to dance with him, since Karl couldn't, but I declined as politely as I could. Had these young men never learnt any tact? I wanted to be fair to Karl, as I was his date, but I didn't want to be rude to young men who may have been his friends.

'I'd rather sit here with Karl so no one can steal him, but you may join us for a while if you want. What are you studying?'

I can no longer recall what it was, but both of them were as totally wrapped up in talking about themselves as the young men at the parties in London had been. They even told me what make of car they drove, as if owning an expensive car made them more worthy of my attention, and they were quick to point out that Karl's car was an old wreck of a thing.

One of them asked if I would go on a blind date with him, or was I an escort you had to pay for. I sensed Karl go tense, clenching his hand where it lay on the table, so I put my hand on top of his, to warn him to say nothing, and looked the young man straight in the eyes.

'I'm sorry but I only go out with very special men, never with cheeky teenage boys.'

He dropped his gaze, but he retorted rather sulkily, 'I'm not a teenager.'

'And I'm not a paid escort. So maybe you should go and find someone your own age to dance with before one of us gets cross.'

A couple of girls came over to find the two young men, having returned from the ladies' cloakroom to find their boyfriends chatting up another girl, both of them giving me vitriolic looks for diverting their men, and they all returned to the dancing.

Karl poured me a glass of wine from a bottle on the table, his hand a little shaky.

'Think nothing of it,' I urged him. 'I was only eight years old the first time I was called a whore, so I am well used to it by now. I know I'm not, and I don't care about other people's opinions. Tell me what Norway is like; I have never been there.'

I wanted to avoid discussing the two boys, or needing to decide how much I would tell him of why I had left England.

He talked of long days with scarcely any darkness, long nights with scarcely any daylight, snow in winter, and endless forests with wolves and even a few brown bears, but they were very shy. When he had been at school and later at university, he and Fred had gone on long hikes with friends. He could still walk long distances okay. They always joked that he was good to have on a hike, as he couldn't run, so if they were attacked by a bear, it would easily catch him, giving the others time to run away. They had only ever seen a bear once, in the distance, and it had slunk away, more fearful of them than they were of the bear.

'Could you dance if we stayed at the edge and moved very slowly?' I asked him. 'You can lean on me a little if you need to.' I was conscious that most of the students were on the dance floor, and I wanted him to feel he fitted in.

'I haven't danced since I was a teenager, but I could manage it. I am quite steady on my feet most of the time, but sometimes if I move suddenly, I get a twinge of pain and I need the walking stick to balance. I'll give it a try, and if I fall, I promise I won't pull you over with me.'

It always felt good to dance with an attractive man, but I was careful not to get too close or lean against him. He seemed rather tense, nervous even, and we both understood the rules; it was always to be platonic. Yet I was close enough to feel the warmth and soft male scent of his jacket.

'You still haven't told me why you are here and not with your boyfriend in England,' he prompted.

What could I say? That I was fleeing for my life from a man who had framed my uncle for murder? It all seemed so cloak-and-dagger, yet I could think of nothing else that would sound plausible. I felt again that we had a bond between us; both of our lives had been changed forever by someone else's crime.

'It's complicated,' I said again, but I could go no further.

'You don't want to talk about it?'

I shook my head.

'That's okay. I won't ask again. How long are you staying here?'

'I'm not sure I will ever go back. Will you return to Norway?'

'We are here for two years. When we finish the research, we will return home, both of us hopefully with a PhD and a job at the company office in Oslo. But if all goes well, Fred and I want to eventually set up our own consulting company. Anita will do the accounting for us, and her father has offered to help us with the initial capital. She and Fred will be married next year. I'm to be best man at their wedding.'

Was there a touch of regret that his friend could marry and have someone to care for him? They had been friends since school, had travelled together, faced trauma together, studied together, but were soon to live more separate lives. I felt rather keenly the predicament of this man, the difficulty he faced finding a girlfriend and ultimately a wife.

There were other young men who tried to catch my attention that evening, attracted to our table like moths to a flame, interested in the mysterious blind date of their college mate, so I didn't get a lot of time to talk to him. Supper was served, and some of the students became a little drunk and rowdy. The music seemed to be louder than it had been at first. Frederik and Anita had disappeared; I assumed they had gone to his room.

Karl and I left the college. He helped me into my jacket, asked if I would be warm enough, offered to lend me a heavier jacket of his own from his room. I told him I was fine. We crossed the main road through the underpass and walked down to the river, where we sat side by side on a bench, listening to the quiet lapping of the waves, and watching the shimmering reflections of the moon and the city lights on the wide expanse of water, the seagulls on the retaining wall, quiet and sleeping, their clean grey feathers ruffled by a restless breath of air where the water met the shore.

I was reminded of standing by the sea with Simon, watching the sun rise and the gulls joyfully greeting a new day, but now it all seemed such a long time ago.

'Tell me about your boyfriend.' Perhaps he realised my thoughts were not with him.

'He is a teacher, maths and science. He is very quiet, as I am, but I loved just being with him, and he made me feel cared for and valued. We were planning to marry, but I had to leave England.'

'Didn't he want to come here with you?'

'I didn't give him the chance to. He doesn't know where I am. Perhaps one day I may tell you the whole story, but for now we can just enjoy the moon on the water.'

He suddenly took my hand and kissed the back of it.

'Thank you for tonight; you made me feel wonderful. Would you like to go out with me again?'

'Yes, of course. Did you ever have a girlfriend?'

'Yes, when I was a teenager and still at school. I even made love to a girl back then, but now I can't. I've taken a few girls out, thinking if we were friends for a while a girl might like me enough to stick around, but all of them eventually found someone else. Then one girl wanted me to come back to her flat and sleep with her the first time I took her out, and she was offended when I tried to tell her I didn't want to. I had only met her a couple of days before. She was groping me, and she got upset that I didn't respond, and said some rather nasty things about useless men who wasted her time. I can laugh about it now, but back then it distressed me badly. It was a long time before I found the courage to ask another girl out. In the end I just gave up. Fred said you were older than us, and you only went out with men who understood you had a boyfriend already and didn't want a sexual relationship. I was expecting you to be about forty, but you seem hardly any older than I am. You have been so nice to me, and you are so beautiful that I can hardly believe you're real. I would be happy to take you out whenever you want. Fred has Anita now, so I feel a bit left out. May I have your phone number?'

I went with him to the engineering department ball, a little more formal than the college one, and we danced again, this time a little closer. We got on well, and it was good to have company. He took me to dinners and film nights, usually with a group of people, sometimes with Frederik and Anita, but occasionally there were just the two of us. We started spending our Saturday afternoons together. Karl had a small car, and we would sometimes drive out to local landmarks, but usually we would simply walk in the park. He could manage long distances if he walked slowly, and I was happy to go at his pace. I would climb the helical tower while he waited below, ready to wave to me when I reached the top. He would stand on the lawn while I jumped between the stepping stones across a shallow lake the playground. We would buy ice creams at the kiosk, dodge the waterfalls and the fountains along the path in the water gardens, walk through the greenhouses, or just sit watching the swans on the lake.

There was a whispering seat at the War Memorial, set in a long curve. If two people sat one at each end, they could talk to each other in whispers although there was a good twenty yards distance between them. Karl explained to me how it worked with the sound reflecting around the curve, but I did not understand it; I only knew it was fun to sit there and say silly things to each other. He would pay me pretty compliments, or we would pretend to be spies exchanging information.

But the year was wearing on; the second anniversaries of my special days with Simon had all passed, along with my twenty-sixth birthday. I was so busy I scarcely felt the time slipping away from me. In my spare time I still did facials for the clients of the hairdresser Mrs Bukowski, and many of them asked for appointments at times when I would be there.

I still thought of Simon every day, but time had erased the worst of the pain, and I never expected to see him again. He became part of a life that might have been, the last lingering hope that we might meet again fading with every day that passed.

I eventually told Karl about James and Richard and Orchard House and Lagan, but not, of course, about the girl in the icehouse. But I told him as little as I could about Simon. It seemed unfair to talk about a love affair to a man who could never enjoy one.

One afternoon, as we sat in the shade watching the children, carefree and wild, in the playground by the lake, he told me his version of what had happened on the evening that they were all shot. It didn't differ much from Fred's account, except that Karl had not recalled what had occurred at the time but had gradually recovered the memory of it.

'Sometimes I lie awake at night and go through it all in my mind, trying to see a way we could have prevented it. When Jack fired the shot, we just thought he had taken aim at a rabbit, and even when Mike collapsed between us, neither of us realised what had happened. I recall there was a lot of blood, and Fred and I tried to stem it, not actually understanding why Mike was bleeding. But then we were both shot. Fred believes Jack was trying to get another shot or two at Mike, but as we were trying to help him, we were both in the way. I don't think there was anything we could have done differently once Jack had fired the first shot, but we might have called off the shooting expedition if we had been thinking more rationally. The first two times we went out shooting, Fred's uncle came with us, and we learnt all the rules. You always stayed together as a group, you always checked the others were beside you when you raised a gun to shoot a rabbit, and you always kept the gun pointing downwards when you were walking. But that time we were on our own. As soon as Jack and Mike were bickering, and Jack was going off ahead of us and on his own, we were breaking the rules, and we should have called it off and gone back to the house. Sometimes I blame myself for not realising that something was wrong about the way Jack was behaving, but we were scarcely out of school, in a foreign land, and guests of Mike's family. And sometimes I just relive that night, and imagine that Fred and I protested at Jack not following rules, and we all returned with Mike to the house. He would still be alive. Both of them would be. Do you ever think like that, imagining if things were different?'

Did I? Yes, but it was not something I could ever discuss with anyone. I had not followed the rules either. When the au pair had died, we should have called the ambulance, let the police do their worst. It had been an accident. Richard had told me they had both fallen asleep with the tie still around her neck, and she had turned and strangled herself. He might have got away with it being the accident that it was, and we should never have tried to hide it. Then when I met Simon, I would not have worried that I could ruin his life, and I might have gone back to

Harton with him when he left that summer. And when the black-mailer struck, Richard would have had nothing to lose but his reputation; he could have quietly disappeared and left Lagan to his fate.

But I still had to answer Karl.

'Yes, sometimes I do. And sometimes I think that the things that might have been can feel just as real as the things that are. But in the end, we just have to pick up the pieces and go forward with our lives. Nothing was your fault and nothing was mine, but we can't change what happened.'

As part of our accounting course, we studied stock exchanges and how listed companies did their accounting. We were given some company reports from Australia, Britain and the United States so we could study differences in their accounting meth-ods. I opened one of the reports for a long-established British company, and there were my three bunny hunters, directors of the company, their photographs smiling at me from the page. So now I knew their real names. Did they still do the bunny hunt-ing at another retreat? Did they thank their stars that they had not been involved in the scandal when Richard was arrested? I remembered that long-ago evening when I had sat on the ter-race with Richard and his then current au pair, whose name I no longer recall, and we had laughed at the sounds from the woods.

But I never saw a photo of Lagan, and in a way I'm glad. If I had seen him pictured on a yacht, successful and wealthy, with a film star beside him, I would have screamed with rage. To this day I don't know his real name, or where he had made his money. There are a lot of rich men in the world.

Sometimes I dreamed of getting my revenge on him. I dreamed of a shipwreck where I was in a lifeboat and he was drowning in the sea, and I would push him away with an oar and leave him to be devoured by sharks. I dreamed of leading the police to him so he was caught red-handed murdering a girl—but just in time to save her, of course—preferably in a country where murderers, even attempted ones, were still hanged. I dreamed of walking along a line of men in a police identity line, looking into his eyes, seeing the fear, knowing that I could destroy him and that the police would keep me safe if I did. But most of all I dreamed of visiting the hitman in prison and persuading him to tell the police the truth.

I took photographs of birds and flowers, planning which of them I would send to Simon with his card in November. I gradually learnt the names of them all, the trees, the flowers, the birds. I still lived in the hotel with Mrs Marek, manning the desk in the evenings, and looking after the hotel accounts for her. No one from England ever contacted me directly, but Rebecca still occasionally enclosed a note for me when Vera wrote to Mrs Marek, and Paul sometimes sent a school newsletter through Vera when it included a photo of Simon. He never sent any more letters, but there was an occasional indirect message passed on from him in the letters from Rebecca.

November came around; exams were finished. Frederik and Karl went back to spend the northern winter in Norway, and Anita went home to Singapore. It would be early March before we all met again. Anita and Frederik would be married in July, in the break between the two semesters.

I still sometimes went out with Alex, sometimes with Gary as well, sometimes with a group of students from my year, but I found I missed Karl after he left.

I had now been in Perth for two years, so I applied for my citizenship, at first a little apprehensive that they would discover that Ethel Turner had a death certificate somewhere in the British records, as well as a birth certificate and a passport. If they did, and they wanted to deport me, I would throw myself on the mercy of the British Embassy, tell them the reason I had left England, and ask for asylum here, or at the very least police protection if they sent me home. But it appeared the immigration people trusted the British Passport Office to have checked my bona fides, and my citizenship certificate was issued. I could now do so much more in my new country, even buy a house or land. I then applied for an Australian passport, and there was no problem with that either.

I decided it was time I got a car of my own, so I applied for a driver's licence—I could already drive, of course, but my British licence was in Ann's name—and bought a Volkswagen Golf. It gave me far more freedom. I no longer had to rely on buses and trains.

Orchard House had been sold, as well as Richard's flat. Some papers had been sent to Mrs Marek for me to sign as Ann Berrington and return through Vera, and the money had arrived in my bank account in Australia. A lot of money, as the house had increased in value considerably since we had first bought it, and I had all of Richard's estate as well. Rebecca had enclosed a note for me with the forms, instructing me where to sign, and telling me that Paul had taken over Richard's clients, had changed the name of the business, and he now had a son.

I thought back to his wedding day, the marquee on the lawn, the lovely old man who was now his father-in-law, dancing to the brass ensemble with the earl's youngest son Percival, my photo in the social column under the wrong name. Paul had his happy ending, even if I could never have mine. His cute blonde wife now had a child—he had clearly managed to do his conjugal duty—and all was right with his world.

There was nothing in Rebecca's note about Simon. Had Paul met him for lunch as he had once told me they planned to? Had they talked about me? Had Paul told him about my mother being a cocaine addict and my father a thief? Had Simon realised that Paul was the boyfriend I had chosen not to marry? Had they agreed that they had both been lucky to escape from being tied to me? Why hadn't Paul sent his own note to me to tell me about the child? We had been friends as well as lovers. Surely, he still cared about me at least a little. He had sent me the newsletters, after all.

Sometimes I wished Simon would find me, arrive one evening at the hotel, walk in, tall and confident, with his beautiful smile, tell me he would stay and live here with me, since I couldn't return to him. I had asked him not to try to trace me, but he would only need to ask Paul, who would direct him to Rebecca, and she would know where I was. Even just a word from him, to say he didn't think badly of me, would have been solace to my soul. Yet I still would not send him my address. I was still frightened that Lagan could harm him, or the police would force him to tell them where I was.

I sent him another Christmas card, this time just to say I had finished my second year at the university, thanking him for sending the school newsletters, and I enclosed a photograph I had taken of the seagulls on the river and one of black swans on a lake with water lilies in a park at the other end of the city. One part of me wanted him to get on with his life and find someone new, but another part of me wanted him to think of me when he stood on the beach or slept in the cottage and wish I was still with him. Did he still own the cottage?

I invested some of the money I had received for the house and Richard's share of the accounting business in the share market, and I made enough in dividends that I could have lived independently if I had wanted to.

I still followed the British newspapers, reading them each morning in the library at the university. There was never any news of a body in an icehouse, but I could never be certain that I had not missed it.

When I walked in the street, I would look at everyone I passed, with some strange hope that one day I would see Simon, yet with a fear that he would no longer recognise me. I knew he could never be here, as he was still at Harton, but hope is never constrained by logic. I still lived in a shadow of fear, watching for men lurking in the street near the hotel, turning suddenly if I felt a step close behind me as I walked through the city, but there were only the office workers, the shoppers, the tourists, teenagers meeting in groups.

The university year had finished. I was again invited to the department Christmas party with Alex and Gary. Dr Harvey was seated at our table with his wife, but this year he danced with her instead of spending the evening at the bar with the older men. Had my interference actually worked?

I danced the tango once again with the Greek lecturer, the other dancers stopping to watch our somewhat risqué dance moves. We were by now good friends, and we flirted outrageously whenever we met, both of us knowing we were safe from any misunderstanding.

I spent the Christmas of 1991 with Alex's family again. His mother was all over me, saying I had been friends with her son for over a year now, and making hints about weddings and grandchildren. She had made asparagus canapés, as she recalled I had said I liked them. I did tell her Alex and I were platonic, that I had a boyfriend in England, as I didn't want her building her hopes up, but it did not deter her. Alex and Gary went for a walk by themselves after lunch, but I found a couple of dear old chaps to talk to among his mother's friends—so she didn't realise her son had left me by myself—and let them make a fuss of me, bringing me glasses of iced punch and plates with little pies and quiches and the asparagus canapés. They were both a little drunk, but they were still polite to me, paying me pretty compliments and saying Alex was a lucky man. However, I was grateful for the chance to spend Christmas with a family, and I helped his mother wash up afterwards.

Paul sent another newsletter, again with a photo of Simon, but there was no letter with it, not even a stick-on note. I found that a little strange. But part way through the newsletter I found a note, written in tiny writing between the lines below a photograph of Simon.

> *I hope this reaches you. I believe some of the letters I send never get through. Why do you never send back? Paul.*

My first reaction was complete shock. Letters? I had received no letters from him for months. Were they being intercepted somewhere between Rebecca and Vera? And I had sent back short letters to him, through Vera. I was left with an uneasy feeling that something was wrong. I wrote a note to Paul for Mrs Marek to include when she next wrote to Vera.

> *Thank you for the newsletters. It is good to have the news from James's old school. I have not received a letter from you for months.*

But then I realised that if someone was reading the correspondence, then my note was unlikely to reach him, as it would expose their meddling. Were any of my notes reaching him? So I screwed it up and started again, with just the first two lines, and I underlined *newsletters*, hoping he would understand from it that the newsletters were all I had received. Surely Vera and Rebecca would send that note on to him.

Karl and Frederik returned in late February, ready for the new university year which started in early March. They came with Anita to see me at the hotel, and Mrs Marek served tea for us all. I still helped her by manning the desk in the evenings, and with the running of the hotel. But the guest numbers were dropping off, as a couple of new five-star hotels had been opened, and most businessmen preferred to go there. She couldn't pay me much, as there was now precious little profit, but it didn't bother me; I had means of my own and was grateful for a home with her.

Karl and I resumed our friendship, going out occasionally and walking together in the park on most Saturday afternoons.

I was never in love with him. I considered him as a friend in the same way that Anita was, and I knew he liked my company as I liked his. Perhaps I flirted with him just a little, but he seemed to enjoy it, and he never took it seriously. I was giving him the illusion of having a girlfriend, the pleasure of pretending that he could be my lover. He was sometimes romantic, buying me presents, touching my waist to guide me across a room, paying me compliments on how I looked or dressed. But Alex treated me like that as well, and he was gay, so I thought nothing of it.

Frederik and Anita were married in July. Her parents came over from Singapore for the wedding, and Frederik's aunt, uncle and cousins came to Perth from their farm in the wheatbelt. It was a small affair, held in the chapel of Frederik's college. Karl was best man, and I was the only bridesmaid. Afterwards we had a reception in a private room in one of the top hotels.

When they returned from their honeymoon, they moved into a flat together, and Karl and I saw them less often.

I knew it depressed him a little to lose the close companionship he and Frederik had shared for so many years, especially as Karl himself was never likely to have a wife of his own, and I tried to keep him company when I could.

At the end October they would return to Norway. Their research was coming to an end; they were writing it up to submit for their degrees, tidying up their commitments at the university. I knew I would miss Karl.

We had only a few short weeks left. We walked in the park, and I could feel he was heavyhearted at the prospect of leaving. We did all the things we usually did, me climbing the tower, Karl waiting while I stepped between the stones across the lake, both of us dodging the spray from the waterfall, sitting at either end of the whispering seat at the War Memorial.

'I love you, Ann. Will you come back with me to Norway? We could get married and make a life together.'

Whispered words, from his heart to mine, echoing along the stone in the warm sunshine, past the names of the long-dead men whose hopes and dreams and loves had died with them. Sometimes he had whispered silly compliments to me, but he had never said that. And he had called me *Ann*; it had taken me a few moments to realise the significance of that.

What had I done? Had I been totally unfair to this beautiful man, allowing him to dream of a life where he had a permanent companion in spite of his injury? Perhaps it was inevitable that he would fall in love with me, but I had never even considered it. I had assumed that falling in love was impossible without the sexual attraction. But perhaps he did feel that, in spite of not being able to act on it. I had wanted to make him happy, but I had never intentionally led him to believe I could love him. From the start I had told him I was in love with Simon and nothing could change that.

And what should I do? Here was a chance for me to make a new life with a man who cared about me, to leave behind my fear of being found, for Lagan would never trace me to Norway. I could leave here and not tell anyone where I was going. I liked his company, and I didn't care about the sex, or the children. I felt that this was the right thing for me to do. But I would also be leaving behind forever my dream of being reunited with Simon, and I knew I couldn't do it.

'I'm sorry,' I whispered back.

He stood up and walked back towards me, tall and beautiful, with his thick blond hair, his slight limp, and his patient resignation to the blow that fate had dealt him. He sat beside me, took my hand in his and kissed my palm. I pulled out my handkerchief to wipe the tears I could no longer hold back.

'Don't cry, Ann. You still love him, don't you?'

'Yes, I can't help it. How did you know my real name?'

'Fred calls Anita *Ann*, and every time he does, you turn your head. You told me your story, and I knew approximately when you came here, so I looked up the British newspapers, and there was your photograph with your real name. Now when I dream about you at night, I call you Ann in my mind. You haven't heard from your lover for three years. If you were mine and you were lost, I would go to the ends of the earth to find you, and I would never rest until I had. Yet he hasn't. Can't you let it go? Make a new life in Norway with me.'

I could only shake my head.

'Are we still friends?' he asked.

'Yes, of course.'

'Will you think about it?'

I nodded.

'I can't offer you sex or children, but I can offer you life-long love and protection and financial security, although you seem to have that already. And we always get on well. It isn't just sex that binds men and women together, but wanting to be with the person who can make your life feel complete. Being together is better than both of us living our whole lives alone.'

'I wanted to make you happy,' I told him. 'I didn't realise you could fall in love with me. I thought you couldn't feel that way about a girl, like my friend Alex who is gay. I thought we were friends, like I am with Anita. And I did tell you I loved someone else.'

'I was in love with you from the first moment I saw you walk across the room with Fred and Anita. I thought this beautiful sexy girl can't possibly be my blind date. When the young guys came and asked you to dance, I expected you to go with them, but you didn't. You said you wanted to stay with me. Then you actually managed to follow what I said when I told you what Fred and I were researching, and I held you up close to dance. I knew by then that I was totally under your spell. I can still feel desire for a woman; I just can't make love to one.'

'I'm sorry,' I said again. 'I do like you, but I can't let go of my dream.'

'Is there anything I can do to make you change your mind? I could stay here in Perth, find a job and a house, and we could live together until you can go back to your other lover.'

'That would not be fair on you. Do you really dream about me at night?'

'Every night. I think how good it would be just to hold you, to kiss your face, to wake up in the morning with you beside me, to make breakfast for you and watch you dress for the day.'

Was that something I could give him, a small way to make amends for totally misreading the way he felt for me? I recalled Richard once telling me that my body was my gift to give to a man if I felt he deserved it, and this man did.

'Can I make a bargain with you? Next weekend we will go away together, stay in a hotel room on the Saturday night, and I will sleep with you. I can give you a massage, you can hold me as close as you like, and we can spend the whole night together so you wake up beside me. You can make the breakfast, and I'll even let you watch me dress. In exchange, I want you to try to find someone else when you get back to Norway. There are girls who would be happy to love you for who you are. If all a girl cares about is how good a man is in bed, then she's not worth having. There are ways a man can give a woman pleasure without going the whole way, and even ways to have children if that is what you both want. You will meet girls where you work, and your sister will have friends. You know now what it feels like to fall in love with someone, but it isn't something that can only happen once in a person's lifetime. It will happen to you again. Do we have a bargain?'

'Yes, absolutely.'

I booked a holiday apartment with a double bedroom, a bathroom with a spa bath, and a small living area with a kitchenette, at an upmarket resort in a seaside town called Broadsea, three hours' drive south of Perth. I had never been there before, but Mrs Marek had, and she recommended it. I packed a little black dress and told him to bring a jacket and tie so we could dress up for dinner, as well as his bathers and his pyjamas.

We drove down on Saturday morning, blessed with a warm and sunny spring day, had lunch in a café near a long jetty, checked in at the resort, and spent the afternoon swimming and lying on the sand on a beautiful pristine beach. We had dinner at the restaurant at the resort, smartly dressed, sat for a while in their bar, then decided to walk on the beach in the moonlight.

I let him unzip the black dress, watch while I changed into jeans and a tee-shirt, and we walked barefoot on the cold sand, the water softly lapping, the glint of moonlight on the dark velvet of the sea, the gulls asleep on the sand, undisturbed by our presence. I was still unsure how far this would go, but I let him kiss me, enjoyed the feel of his body against mine, and we wandered back hand in hand to the resort.

Over the fifteen months I had known him, we had spent some good times together, and now I was going to give him a night he would never forget. I hoped he would enjoy this, and I would not leave him frustrated and bitter at what he had lost.

I ran the water to fill the huge spa bath, adding the bubble bath that the resort had supplied. The jets of water foamed it into a bath full of froth. I left the door open, so he could watch me from where he was lying relaxed on the bed. I pulled off my tee-shirt and bra, my back towards him, pulled off the jeans, so I was left wearing only skimpy black knickers. I recalled once thinking it was hard to put knickers on elegantly; I now realised it was equally hard to get them off elegantly. I wished I had stayed to watch how the strippers at Orchard House had managed. But I didn't think he would care whether I undressed elegantly or not.

I stepped naked into the bath, ducked below the rim before I turned around, asking if he wanted to join me, assuring him I would close my eyes until he got in and there was plenty of foam.

For a moment he stood, amused but hesitant, at the bathroom door, but then he pulled off his clothes and stepped into the bath with me. We twined our legs together, hidden below the foam, and splashed and touched and laughed like any lovers might.

I had brought massage oil with me, and after the bath I gave him a massage, every inch of him, but I asked him first whether I could get personal. He did respond slightly to my touch, although I hadn't expected that, and he said it felt good, he was not completely dead.

We lay together, his body covering mine, as close as he could get to making love to me, and he kissed me with as much passion as any man would, touched me with shy fingers, setting me on fire. I was not expecting to enjoy it as much as I did. I was not sure how much pleasure he got from it, but when I asked him, he told me it was as good as it could get for him.

'Life could have been better for me, but I don't get depressed or curse God, since the guy standing next to me, Fred's cousin Mike, was shot dead, while I'm still here. It would be good to have you sharing my life forever, but I love you and you're beautiful, and you are here with me now. Tonight I want nothing more.'

We lay side by side, lost in a world of gentle touch and his whispered words of love, until we both finally slept.

I awoke to the smell of burnt toast—his attempt to make my breakfast was clearly not a success. I slipped into my pyjamas and went into the living area to help.

He was dressed in his jeans and tee-shirt, standing in the kitchenette, looking in dismay at a plate of charred toast.

I made the obvious joke about chemical engineers who couldn't even make toast, turned down the setting on the toaster, and we tried again. He pulled me against him, and the toast was forgotten while we smooched. Once again, the toaster failed us, and he joked about hotel owners who couldn't even make toast. We realised it was faulty and was not turning off when it was supposed to.

We left it to cool down, opened the window to clear the smoke, and returned to the bedroom. He had wanted to watch me get dressed; that was part of our bargain.

We were eventually ready to try again on the toast, but the coffee provided in the rooms by the resort was only instant, the milk in small capsules, so we decided to have breakfast at their café, with real espresso coffee and warm croissants, before walking hand-in-hand along the beach in the cool of the morning.

'You did enjoy last night, didn't you,' I asked him, still concerned I had left him frustrated.

'Yes, absolutely. I wish I could have you with me every night of my life. If you ever get back with your lover, thank him for allowing me one night in bed with you, and tell him he's the luckiest man alive.'

I laughed, and assured him there was no way I was ever telling my lover what we had done.

'I wanted to make you happy,' I said, still not confident that I had done the right thing by him.

'We make our own happiness, Ann. We can only be happy if we accept the things we can't have and enjoy the things we can have. Why don't you write to your lover, tell him where you are, and ask him to come and join you. And if he doesn't want to, then let him go, and make a life for yourself that is not just regret at what might have been.'

'I don't want to put him in a position where he has to let the British police know where I am. They may be looking for me.'

We stood on the edge of the sea, the gentle little waves washing over our toes, and I was reminded of a long-ago dawn when I had stood on the edge of a colder, rougher shore, so long ago and so far away.

'Would you like me to write to him from Norway, tell him you still care for him, and ask him to come to stay with me in Oslo for a week or two. You could fly to Norway and meet him there, and sort out whether you wanted to be together. He wouldn't know your address here, only mine in Norway.'

I looked at him, scarcely believing what he was saying.

'You would do that for me?'

'Yes. Even if I can't have you for myself, I don't want to think of you spending your life here alone, wasting years wanting a man when you won't even give him a chance to find you. Either contact him so you both have the chance to get back together, or let him go and make a life with me. I would like to make you happy, but I can only do that if you allow yourself to be happy.'

I knew he was right, but I said nothing, and we stood for a while, his arm around me, looking out over the sea.

We were together as often as we could be for those last few weeks. Fred and Anita went on ahead, and we took them to the airport. They would be staying with Anita's family in Singapore for a couple of weeks before flying on to Norway.

I knew Karl was hoping I would change my mind, but I didn't. He promised to keep his side of the bargain, but he said he would wait for six months, in case I decided to join him in Norway. Perhaps I did waver, but I didn't let him know, as I didn't want to disappoint him any more than I had already.

I drove him to the airport, let him kiss me one last time, watched him walk away, turn to wave as he went through the gate, both of us knowing I should have gone with him, perhaps neither of us really understanding why I hadn't.

Being reunited with Simon would only ever be a dream, and I could have made a life with Karl that would have been fulfilling and happy for both of us. But I couldn't do it. I still clung to my faith in a fairy-tale ending where I would be reunited with my lost love. But even as I watched Karl go, I knew that was but an excuse; I knew that I was afraid to love someone new and risk losing them as I had lost everyone I had ever loved.

By the end of November I had finished my degree, and I intended to look for a job in the new year. I sent a card to Simon, and I spent that Christmas, 1992, with Alex's family again—we were still friends—although his mother was less exuberant and no longer hinted at us being an item. But she was still friendly, I was now one of her usual Christmas guests, she liked to show me off as her son's friend, even if I was not his girlfriend, and she was grateful for my help to clean up afterwards.

Alex and Gary had set up house together in a flat. They had a room each, and two men sharing a flat was perfectly normal and legitimate, but I think his mother was starting to realise that her son was not really interested in me, and I was the only girl he had ever brought home.

Broadsea 1993–1995

Even in the three years that I had lived in Perth, the city landscape had changed, with new buildings, new roads, new shops and new hotels.

In January of 1993, a developer made Mrs Marek an offer for her hotel, and she decided she would retire to Broadsea. She was by then over sixty, and could get a government pension if she wanted to. Mrs Bukowski, the hairdresser, would retire with her. They would look for a small house close to the sea and live there together. Mrs Marek knew I would be fine on my own—I would buy a flat or a townhouse and find a job—and I didn't want her to alter her plans for me.

I drove them down the coast road to Broadsea, where Karl and I had spent the weekend together, and we met with an estate agent and looked at some houses. The beaches were beautiful, sheltered from the west by a curve of the coastline, calm and sandy, and the gulls soared lazily across the water.

Oh, how I had missed the whisper of the sea. I knew as soon as I saw the beaches at Broadsea again that I would move there with them. It was a tourist town, with cafés, shops, caravan parks and resorts, some more upmarket than others. The town had a jetty, no longer used for commercial shipping, which extended over a mile from the shore into water deep enough for small ships to berth.

The two ladies bought a retirement villa, in a gated community with a shared pool and tennis court, close to the sea and close to some shops. I bought a much larger house near to them, with a garden that more or less backed onto the beach; there was only a small wooded reserve and a footpath between the back fence and the seashore.

The developer would convert the hotel in Perth into luxury apartments, as the council would not allow it to be demolished. Perhaps that had helped Mrs Marek in her decision to sell, as it was a beautiful building from the Edwardian era with verandahs and a narrow corner tower; it would have been a shame to knock it down. We had, in truth, been making less money over the last couple of years, as Perth now had some new international hotels with better facilities than we could offer our businessmen.

So the hotel was sold, our staff found new jobs, the escorts were transferred to the jurisdiction of another madam, and we moved to Broadsea. By the end of February I was living by myself in a nearly-new house, with the two ladies in their villa less than half a mile away. And I had a job, working three days a week, doing the accounting and the payrolls for one of the resorts, an easy walking distance from where I lived.

There were no escorts, no gentlemen, just families with their children, excited young voices in our playground and on the beach. There were honeymooners, retirees, school leavers celebrating, poised between the safety of childhood and the complexity of their lives beyond.

But most of the teenagers and young adults preferred the beaches further south, which had no shelter from the west and therefore better surf, so my resort was mainly families with small children, who could play on the safe sheltered beaches of Broadsea, and retirees recapturing the romance of their youth.

We hired out small cottages, scattered over an area of lawn and peppermint trees with a swimming pool and a tennis court. A family with children could stay in a cottage, cooking for themselves or eating in our restaurant, dreaming for a few glorious days each year that they too lived their lives within the sound of the sea.

Every paradise has some evils, but ours had few. There were sharks, but attacks were rare, and mainly confined to the surf beaches, south and west of us, not our sheltered bay where the children were safe near the shore in water too shallow for predators. There were jellyfish, almost invisible, with a sting that was painful but not lethal. There were deadly snakes in the swamplands, but bites were uncommon and fatalities rare.

Karl had written to me before we left the hotel. He and Fred were working in Oslo, Anita was learning the language, and they now lived in apartments in the same building. I was welcome to join him, but even if I didn't want to, he would love me to keep in touch. I sent him my new address, and told him I now had a house and a job here in Broadsea.

I joined a birdwatching group. There were inland lakes and swamps around the town with birdlife as rich and diverse as anywhere in the world. I extended beyond seagulls and black swans to spoonbills and ducks and coots and dusky moorhens with their babies, like tiny black ducklings, following their mothers among the reeds. We had greenshanks and marsh sandpipers—which breed in Northern Europe and migrate here for our spring—and graceful pure-white egrets, poised like statues, mirrored in the dark water of the lakes. Along the shore there were cormorants and shags, pelicans and terns and Pacific gulls, larger than the normal seagulls and usually solitary.

Our resort had magpies and wagtails and cute kookaburras, which sat on the picnic tables, coyly begging for scraps of meat from the barbecues. They would take food from your hand. Ducks would wander from cottage to cottage, hoping for scraps of bread, although we did have signs up asking residents not to feed them.

I photographed them all. There were photos of black swans with their cygnets on the small island nests that they built in the shallow water of the swamps, grey herons nesting, rather surprisingly, in trees, white ibises leisurely feeding on the insects on my lawn or in graceful effortless flight, and one of a moorhen with her tiny black chick.

I found a local wildflower group, and one afternoon each month we went on an excursion along the local beaches or through the wetlands, learning the names of the flowers and the trees, and every new name I learnt made me think of Simon.

One magical afternoon I found a sea bindweed, with its soft pink flowers and strange rounded leaves, just like the one outside the gate to the beach at Orchard House, and once more I felt that shift across time, taking me back to the day Simon had pointed it out to me and taught me the name. I photographed it, of course, and I proudly wrote the Latin name I had learnt for it on the back of the photo, *Calystegia soldanella*. I would send it to Simon at Christmas.

I joined a local investors' club, where my knowledge of accounting was welcomed, although most of the members were men, much older than me, and more inclined than I was to take risks by researching and trading small mining stocks.

I had friends, although none of them close. I could have found a kindred soul who was single and wanted a wife, but I always kept my distance from any man who showed any interest in me.

At the end of that year, 1993, I sent the photos of the moorhen with her chick and the sea bindweed to Simon with his Christmas card. I told him I no longer lived in Perth, I now owned a house by the sea, in a birdwatcher's paradise, and I still often thought of him.

Another year has now passed, as years do, each one seeming to slip by more rapidly than the one before. It is now May of 1995, and I have reached the end of my story. Perhaps one day things will change, and I will take it up once again.

I have now lived in Broadsea for more than two years, and they were happy years for me. Families come back each year to our resort, and each year their children are a little older, but I always remember them, and they always remember me. I like to watch them play on the beach and forge their childhood memories of holidays by the sea.

I have a good deal of money invested in safe blue-chip shares, and working three days a week suits me. I transferred the resort accounts onto a computer system, and the manager asked me to computerise the booking system as well. I have freedom to pursue my hobbies, photographing the birds and the flowers, and searching the British newspapers for any remaining vestiges of the past life of Ann Berrington.

Sometimes I just sit and read my journals from my life in Surrey and the time I lived at Orchard House. But I remember every moment of every day of the weeks I spent with Simon; for those days I need no reminders. And I always have jazz playing softly in the background when I am at home.

I still hear from Karl. He married a Norwegian girl, a friend of his sister, and they are expecting a child, legally his, but conceived with a donation from his younger brother. I cried with joy when I read the letter, for I had felt very guilty that I had inadvertently led this man to fall in love with me then declined his offer for me to share his future life. He has moved on with his life, and I am glad of it, but I am still trapped here in my solitude, dreaming of my lover, still clinging to the hope that something will change and we will be back together.

Alex still lives with Gary in their flat. He sometimes phones me, and I have coffee with him on the rare occasions I drive up to Perth. Did his mother miss me the first Christmas I was not at her party? Perhaps she did. I had liked her, and she had only wanted what she thought was best for her son.

After the house and the flat were sold and the money transferred, Paul never wrote to me again. He still sent the occasional school newsletter, usually containing a photograph of Simon, but never accompanied by a letter or a note. That still made me uneasy. Was he sending letters that never came through? Or did he simply want me to fade out of his life?

He had performed his last duty to me when he sold my house. He had managed to distance himself from the scandal that surrounded his partner in the accounting business. Why would he want to risk his reputation by any further contact with me? Does he still thank his stars that I refused him when he proposed to me? Did he grow to love his beautiful younger wife? I hope so. He had traded choice for upper-class status, but at the time he had seemed happy with his bargain.

Perhaps class doesn't mean as much now as it once did, but we still all have the right to choose our friends, how we spend our leisure, who we invite into our homes and who we marry. If we choose friends that share the same values and ethics as we do, then I see no problem with that. It is not classism when it is choices we make in our private lives. We need to embrace differences and diversity, not deny them an existence by consigning everyone to some dreary mediocrity. We should celebrate the whole range of humanity, the different points of view, the different talents and contributions that we can bring, as unique and wonderful people, to the lives of those who share the world with us. And we should celebrate the differences between men and women instead of trying to eliminate them, the differences that have made our civilisation develop into the world we have now, giving us the framework to bring up children who will, in their turn, leave the world a better place than they found it. Men and women should complement each other, not compete.

I have thought a lot about the love between men and women. When you get older, you see it more objectively than when you are young and a part of it. I have seen both sides of it, the lust and the devotion. There is love we feel for our family, and sexual attraction that begins with lust. But there is a love in between that encompasses both, a strong and heady chemistry between two people, an obsession with the other person that can distort rational thought, a romantic love that can start with a need just to be together, then mellow into an affection that can bind two people together and last for a lifetime. A love that can make both partners feel that their lover makes their own life complete. Even the ancient Greeks understood it, recognising lovesickness as a depressive disease, cured only by the union of the lovers. Eros of the Greeks and Cupid of the Romans show that they understood its power. Their gods commanded forces of nature that were beyond human control, and that was how they regarded love.

Perhaps for men there is more of the lust and for women more of the devotion, but it has existed since the dawn of man, and it keeps families together, so the children can survive to have children of their own. It is more than just a social contract giving men access to sex and women to financial security.

Romantic love can work its chemistry across social and geographic barriers and those of age, but for the most part, it works between young people who move in the same circles, who are tired of playing the field, and are, consciously or sub-consciously, looking to settle down with a partner. Nature takes over from there, providing the fireworks to make attraction happen. Sometimes it can last a lifetime—some of my retiree couples, both at Orchard House and here at Broadsea, were still romantically devoted to each other—but sometimes an underlying incompatibility wins out, as it had for Simon's parents, and sometimes it is one-sided and bruising as Karl's love for me had been.

I tell myself that what had happened between Simon and me was merely chemistry, but it had meant so much more to both of us. I was twenty-three, living a lonely and isolated life, starved for the company of any man who was remotely eligible, and at twenty-nine he would have been thinking that he was facing a lifetime of solitude and celibacy without a wife, but was wary of making the same mistake as his father had. From the day we first met the fireworks engulfed us. But then we were parted, and for me the lovesickness has never healed with the five years that have passed since we were lovers.

I once found a reference to Julian in the business section of one of the British newspapers, which I still read in the local library. He is now in his early thirties and is the managing director of a retail chain that his father founded and is still chairman of. Does he, or his horrible mother, ever worry that somewhere in the world is a woman who could come forward and claim that he raped her when she was fifteen? Of course I never would, but if they worried about it even fleetingly, it would be revenge enough for me.

I would imagine that I was a celebrity, being interviewed on an afternoon chat show, watched by thousands of women across Britain. His mother would be older now, but still painted up like a cheap plastic garden statue of a peacock. She would sit on her plush Louis sofa, in her vast drawing room in her vast house on her vast estate, a gin and tonic in her hand, crossing her fat thighs in her tight skirt, settling in to watch her favourite chat show. She would not recognise me at first, as I was then just a schoolgirl friend of her daughter, who stayed at her house for less than a fortnight.

The chat-show hostess would ask about my first sexual experience, and I would tell her I was raped at fifteen, in a little temple summerhouse, by the heir to a country estate, who was now the managing director of a large retail company. I was staying there for the holidays with a schoolfriend. It was definitely rape, as he didn't ask me first, I was so young that I scarcely even knew what he was doing, and he was so much stronger than me that my resistance was futile. I would tell the hostess that his mother had come in and found us, with his jeans down around his knees and my knickers, which he had ripped off me, lying on the floor. His mother had blamed me for her son's indiscretion and had thrown me out of the house.

The hostess would ask me who this dreadful man was. He could still be charged. Men should never be allowed to get away with these things.

I could see the horror on his mother's face as she recognised the incident, the increasing panic that was making her feel sick. But she couldn't run to the cloakroom to throw up; she had to wait to see if I was going to name the man, right there on television with thousands of viewers. Oh, my god!

No, no, I would say, gently and politely. No point ruining him now. No good would come of it. He would lose his job, his friends would shun him, the customers would boycott his shops. Think of the employees, the shareholders, the suppliers who would never be paid. If I had wanted to complain, I should have done so at the time. Then he would have got off with a warning, he had done me no real harm, and by now it would all be forgotten.

But the relief came too late for his mother; she had already thrown up her gin and tonic all over the plush Louis sofa.

Oh, the sheer joy of imagined revenge.

Sometimes I think about Simon's mother, but I want no revenge on her. I feel for her, and I know that if I had been her daughter-in-law, I would have come to love her. She had wanted her beautiful intelligent son to have the love and companionship of a wife, and she had almost succeeded. She would have been bitterly disappointed that it didn't work out, and forever wracked with guilt that she had mistakenly encouraged him to love a woman who had ultimately broken his heart. I could imagine her horror at seeing the newspaper with my photograph and the headline about my uncle. I would not blame her if she spends the remainder of her days dreaming of revenge on me.

When Paul sent me the Harton School newsletter for the summer term of 1994, he included a brochure for Orchard House Hotel, now owned by the Kershaws, who run it as a private hotel, just as Mrs Pearson once had. There are photos of the rooms, and I recognised my own room in the tower, with the same brass bed where I had once lain with my lover.

But I cannot think of Orchard House without thinking of the young woman. Do the current guests walk down to the beach, oblivious to the existence of an old icehouse only a few yards away from the path to the sea? An icehouse that hides a sad secret, buried now for more than six years. Does the forlorn ghost of a long-forgotten girl scream silently to them as they walk down the path? Does she plead for someone to take a dozen steps into the woods and find her remains, so she can be laid to rest with her own people, in her own country?

I know that what we did that night was terribly wrong, but at the time it seemed to be the only thing to do. Richard was the last family I had left alive, and I loved him. He had not deliberately killed her, and although it would not have been consciously in my thoughts at the time, I could never have faced losing him. He had shut me up in an isolated life where he was all that I had left. He had wanted to protect me as he had never been able to protect my mother, but in doing so, he had made me so emotionally dependent on him that I was little more than his slave.

I cannot make amends. I do not even know her name, and her passport is now tiny fragments of ash in the soil near the garden shed. She had a mother, a father, a family, friends, schoolmates, teachers, all of them people whose lives she had touched. Her family may still wonder what has happened to her, but to everyone else who knew her, she would be just a vaguely remembered acquaintance who has faded into the vast jumble of people we once knew but no longer care about or even think of.

Every day, even now, I think of Richard, long dead but still living in my memory, still treasured and loved every day of my life, just as James is. He had tried to give James and me some semblance of a normal childhood, with outings and toys and books, while my father shut himself up to count his ill-gotten gains, and my mother lived in her own fuzzy fantasy world.

There are so many questions that will never be answered. Was Richard really my father, or was that a delusion of his? Was it something he believed because he wanted it to be true? Had he really loved my mother? Had he been trying to keep me safe by setting me up in an isolated house, alone for most of the week, so I was almost totally under his control? Had he wanted to protect me to salve his conscience that he had allowed his brother to destroy my mother? Why had he been so obsessed with money that he had stashed so much away for me, money that I have never touched, millions of pounds in a Swiss bank account that neither he nor I had ever needed?

But most of all I wanted to know how and why he had died. I know he would never have arranged a hitman for the girl because he had very little to lose if she had gone to the press. He could have simply retired and lived the rest of his life on the Swiss money. Lagan was the one who had brought the girls to our retreat. If they had been underage, then Richard would have no more criminal responsibility than if he had been the owner of any hotel where Lagan met his girls. Lagan had traded my safety for Richard's silence, but I will never believe my uncle took his own life. It was all too convenient for Lagan. If there was an inquest, I was never contacted about it, and neither Paul nor Rebecca had ever mentioned it in the letters they sent to me.

Still so many questions but never any answers. All of us live in a tangle of our own thoughts, memories and motives; we can never get inside another person's mind.

I scarcely now remember my father, as he was barely a part of our lives, always at work or shut in his study. Yet I loved him, as all children love their parents, almost no matter how badly they are treated. He did not treat us badly at all, but was just never there. Why had he not been bailed? Did he think he was safer in police custody than he would have been out of it? Had he been unable to live with what he had done to my beautiful mother, fuelling her drug addiction and blackmailing her to stay with him by threatening to separate her from James and me? Or had the drug dealer—or one of the clients—had so much power that they could have a man murdered in police custody and cover it up with a suicide verdict? Yet more questions with no answers.

In my garden I have a small slab of limestone, surrounded by gazanias and pansies, with a brass plaque inscribed with their Christian names: *Eloise, Giles, James* and *Richard.* I am still too fearful to have my real surname on anything I own. They are all buried in a cemetery in Surrey, my parents side by side, James quite close to them, and Richard a little further away. Paul had arranged the headstone for my uncle, and had once sent a photo to me through Vera. Does he still tend the graves as his last gift to me, or are they now neglected, overgrown and forgotten?

Mrs Marek and Mrs Bukowski still live in their retirement villa, close to the sea. They can walk to the nearby grocery store, or take a bus or a taxi the three miles into the town of Broadsea. Sometimes if I am going into town, they come with me. I have tea with them on Thursday afternoons, and Mrs Bukowski still occasionally trims my hair.

I have no other close friends, although I know a lot of local people who share my interest in birds, in wildflowers and in trading shares.

I have no children, and as far as I know neither has Simon. But he has the boys he teaches, whose lives and futures he shapes, and I have the children who stay at my resort, treasuring for all of their lives the happiness of the seaside holidays of their childhood.

I see their sandcastles on the beach and it transports me back to the sandcastles that I built with Richard and James, with Paul and with Simon, and the ones I never built with Richard and the children that Simon and I could have had, but for a blow of fate that was not of our making. The eternal tide washes away the sandcastles and the footprints, the gifts we leave for the sea in exchange for the memories and the dreams.

Every morning and every evening I walk on the beach, stand staring at the horizon, knowing the same sea touches the beach at Deniton, wondering if my lover sometimes stands on a beach halfway around the world, thinking of me.

Does he still own the cottage? Does he spend the school holidays there? Does he still walk on the beach at daybreak? The British newspapers give the time of the sunrise in England, and I sometimes stand on my beach at the same time, usually early afternoon here, on days when I know he will be on holiday. I think about him looking out over the sea, sharing the same moment, connected by the same sea, the same air and sky and sunlight.

Sometimes I ask myself if things could have been different if I had stayed in England, but I know I was right to accept the choice that fate made for me, the chance of a new life beyond the one that could only have led to me being jailed with Richard for helping him to hide the girl in the icehouse, or disposed of, as the blackmailer had been, by a man who was pure evil. Simon and I could never have been together. I would never have allowed him to wreck his life and his career by tying himself to me.

Should I have married Karl and returned with him to Norway? Perhaps. I was never in love with him, partly because I had initially thought him incapable of feeling love for a woman and it had seemed useless, as loving Paul had seemed useless because he was destined for another. But Karl is happy now, and so am I. I like my solitude, even if I do spend a lot of it in reminiscence.

I have tried not to waste my own life by drowning in regrets. Perhaps I have succeeded, perhaps not. For none of us can know what might have been; we only know what was; we cannot change the past.

Each Christmas I send Simon a card to let him know I am still alive and thinking of him. I usually word it carefully, as I still do not know if he has a wife. Every year I send one of my bird photos. Perhaps he knows that I live in Broadsea, as letters have postmarks, but I have never told him my address.

But last Christmas, 1994, when I sent him a card—this time with the photo of the black swans with their cygnets on their island nest in a shallow lake—I was a little bolder. Perhaps I had one glass of sherry too many on the evening I wrote it.

I read and re-read the Harton newsletters that Paul sends to me, although I never receive any letters from him. Sometimes I just sit for hours, looking at the photos of you. I wonder if you are married, and whether you still own the cottage by the sea. I have no way of knowing. I have never forgotten that summer. The red fox, the sandcastle washed away by the tide, the nights in the cottage, and the whisper of the sea. There was never anyone else for me, but fate and circumstances kept us apart. It was never safe for me to return. I hope you sometimes still think of me, and if you do, please think of me kindly and bear me no ill-will. Do not reproach me or despise me. I think of you every day of my life, and every night I dream of those few precious weeks that we shared. I remember every moment of every day we were together. I will never stop loving you. Ann.

After I had posted it, I realised I must have gone raving mad. Suppose he had a wife and she found it. Suppose the school secretary opened all the mail. What had I done? Perhaps I should never send a card again and just let him forget me.

Had I fallen in love with Simon only because he had been the one man in my lonely isolated world who cared about me? Had he fallen for me because he had finally found a young woman who shared his love for quiet companionship? I had been very unfair to lead him on as I had, when I had known that there could be no way forward for us. And since then, I had used the excuse of my undying love for him to prevent myself falling in love again. I had lost every man I had ever loved—my father, my brother, my uncle, my lover—and I had never wanted to feel that hurt again.

He could have contacted me if he had wanted to, by asking Paul to send me a note through Rebecca and Vera, but he hadn't. I could have sent him an address, but I had feared he would say he no longer loved me and would ask me to stop sending him the cards. It was not because of the police finding me through Simon, for I had long ago realised the police could easily find me here if they wanted to—Paul knew my new name, I had a driver's licence, and I owned a house. It was because I would rather not hear from Simon at all than know he no longer cared. He could have traced me if he had really wanted to, but he had chosen his career and his safe way of life over finding me. I recalled Karl telling me that if I had belonged to him, and I had been lost, he would search for me to the ends of the earth. Simon had never tried to find me.

I suddenly saw it all for what it was. A foolish, romantic delusion.

I was a woman who had once had a brief affair with a man and was trying to keep herself in his memory, trying to preserve his love, trying to make him regret what he had lost, trying to prevent him from moving on with his life. It was not even his fault that we had parted. I needed no revenge.

Why should he still care that I was still alive? Was I just upsetting him with every letter that he could never reply to? And I realised with a shock of guilt that he could not even ask me to leave him alone. For five years I have been stalking him.

That card will be the last I ever send.

Once more I stand on the beach, watching the sun set across the water, the darkness seeping across the world, ending yet another day in the journey of humanity through time. From the known to the unknown, from the memories of yesterday to the hopes for tomorrow, we are all but a fragment of something vast and eternal.

It is finished. My story is written and printed and lying on the desk in my study, with instructions on where to find my will, although I hope I still have many years ahead of me. I have left everything to charity: the house, the share portfolio, the money, the funds in the bank account in Switzerland. There is no way now to return the money to the men and women who my father cheated all those years ago, and I have no sympathy for the cocaine users or the clients of my uncle who paid him to supply them with a venue for their depravity.

But today something happened which has left me restless, unable to collect my thoughts, and I know it will change my life. Perhaps there will be more story to come.

This afternoon when I visited Mrs Marek, there was a large envelope for me, sent by Paul through Vera. It was another school newsletter from Harton. I leafed through it expectantly until I found the photograph of Simon.

He still looks the same to me, the same neat beard and beautiful smile, the same face I have always loved, his hair still with the cowlick that had reminded me of James. In front of him, on the desk, is a framed photograph of black swans on a nest, surrounded by their soft brown cygnets. It is turned towards the camera. Beside it is one of a girl with a mop of wild black curls, swept back by the wind. And there is another, of a red fox. I didn't recall him photographing the fox when we saw it, but perhaps he had seen it again.

There is a news article below his photograph. He is taking long service leave at the end of the school year and will be away for six months. He will stay for a while at his cottage in Deniton on the south coast, where he will enjoy his time swimming, taking solitary walks, and putting together his photos of birds into a book. And he is hoping to travel. He has always wanted to visit the Broadsea wetlands, in Western Australia, famous for the diversity of its birdlife. He has a friend who lives there.

He is wearing the tie I gave him all those years ago, maroon with a thin gold stripe, the tie I had bought for the birthday that my brother didn't live to celebrate. He still owns the cottage, and there is no mention of a wife to share his solitary walks. After all these years he is still sometimes there where I remember him, where we lay together in the darkness, lost in a love that joined our souls, listening to the whisper of the sea.

And I know this is a message for me from half a world away. The photo of the swans is the one I had sent to him at Christmas, and the girl is me, although the photo is too small and indistinct for anyone else to identify the subject and realise the significance. Was he hoping I would see the photographs, recognise the tie, read the words, understand that he is telling me he still thinks of me, and he would like us once more to be together—if not in his part of the world, then why not in mine?

Does he lie in his room in the cottage wishing I was beside him? Does he wander along the cliff paths, remembering the precious days we shared, when he taught me the names of the birds and the trees and the flowers? Does he stand on the sand at the edge of the sea, looking out to the horizon, wondering if I am standing on a faraway beach, thinking of him?

I recalled the message I had once received, written in tiny print beneath a photograph in a newsletter, so I fetched a magnifier and went over this newsletter until I found a new note, written in light pencil close to the spine between two pages, which were then stuck very slightly together.

> *My letters are clearly not reaching you, but I believe the newsletters are. Write to me or your boyfriend directly and SEND US YOUR ADDRESS. Paul.*

I found my pile of school newsletters and went back through them. The messages were there, but I had missed them. Sometimes notes in tiny writing. Sometimes seemingly random words on random pages, underlined or highlighted, even individual letters underlined that together made a complete word where Paul could not find the word he needed. Always similar messages.

> *You are not getting my letters. Write directly to my office or to your friend. Send us your address. Do not trust the messengers.*

For over five years they had been trying to get me to contact them directly, and they had never given up.

Tonight I will write to Paul at his office and let him know how to contact me. I will type the envelope and post it from a town halfway between here and Perth, with a fake name and address on the back. No one will intercept the letter. How could they?

How could I have been so blind as to think they could? How could I have been so utterly stupid as to think anyone could have enough influence to check everyone's mail? And the British police could easily find me if they wanted to, whether Paul or Simon had my address or not. I had thought Paul no longer wanted anything to do with me, I had been worried that Lagan would harm Simon, and yes, I had trusted the messengers; Rebecca and Vera were my friends. Were they discarding the letters Paul sent and only sending on the newsletters?

And I will send a letter to Simon, addressed to him at the school. It is May now, and he will not be on leave until July. And this time I will give him my address, tell him if he wants to visit Broadsea, he can stay with me. I will tell him why I had to leave England, and why I was too frightened to ever return. I will tell him about my father and my uncle, although he will know some of it already. I will tell him how his love for the birds and the flowers enriched my life, and how I never loved anyone but him.

But I won't tell him everything; I will leave out the dead girl. That secret will die with me if she is never found. And if she is found, if they can tell that she died during the years that I owned the house and Richard lived there, there would now be no way they could prove I had any hand in helping to bury her. I have had my five years in the wilderness, my atonement for what I had done.

No one will now care about tracing the men who were clients of my uncle nearly six years ago. Whatever Lagan had done, it would now be forgotten, except, of course, by the girls he had violated. I had never known his real name and I would rather not know. I don't want to see his name in a coveted spot on a list of the world's richest men, or pictures of him on some billionaire's yacht surrounded by beautiful women. I am unlikely to see a picture of him rotting in a coffin, or hanging from a gibbet, or his head in a basket below a guillotine, and nothing less would satisfy me.

Perhaps Simon will write back. Perhaps he will forgive me. Perhaps, after everything, he may still care for me.

Perhaps he will come here, stay with me in my house by the sea. I will tell him the names of the birds, proud to be teaching him as once he had taught me. We will stand together on my beach, looking at the sunset, watching the dolphins and listening to the cry of the gulls.

Perhaps one day I will return to England, travelling as Ethel, then living there as Ann. I will live in the cottage by the sea, next to a house I once owned, with the man who is the other half of my soul. The vicar may by then be retired, and no one but his wife would ever remember me. No one will associate me with the shy secretive girl who once lived at Orchard House, a girl who was wanted for questioning over charges laid against a man who has been dead for over five years.

I will find the grave of the child whose name I borrowed and leave white roses for her, and I will scatter meadow flowers on the earth above the icehouse, the last resting place of a girl whose name I never knew.

And Simon and I will once more tread the paths we once shared and stand side by side, looking out over the sea, our souls united, one with each other and one with the sky and the wind and the eternal whisper of the sea.

Unearthing Secrets 1995

But I must resume my story, as it did not end where I intended it to, with my letter to Simon and my hope that he might join me in exile.

Only a few days after I had sent the letter, too soon for Simon to have even received it, the doorbell rang. From my upstairs window I could see a sleek black Holden Commodore parked in the driveway, and there were two men in dark suits at the door. Was this the police, or were they assassins sent by Lagan? Had he finally caught up with me? Was this retribution for sending my address to Paul and Simon?

But no, it was almost certainly the police, as assassins were more likely to lurk in lonely places and strike in secret. Had Paul given my address to the police now that he finally knew it? Had they caught up with my fake identity? Or had they found the girl in the icehouse? I had to keep my head. The identity was not strictly a crime—the worst they could do was to deport me—and I could deny all knowledge of the girl.

I had no choice but to answer the door; they had looked up and caught a glimpse of me at the window. I could see my neighbour mowing his front lawn. If they murdered me at the front door, there was at least a witness. I went downstairs.

The door had a glass panel, so I could see them, but I also had a black mesh security flyscreen door. Most houses here have flyscreen doors, but not all of them are made from the strong steel mesh that I had chosen for mine. I had installed it when I first bought the house, not just from my fear of Lagan or the police finding me, but as a sensible precaution for a woman who lived alone. Would the steel protect me from a bullet? I doubted it, but it would protect me from a knife or a hatchet, and the lock was strong. I was glad of the sound of the neighbour's mower, and I hoped his curiosity about my visitors would keep him lingering in his garden.

The men were from the Australian federal police, who dealt with national and international matters, rather than the local state constabulary. They showed their badges, introduced themselves, both of them quietly spoken and patient with my reservations. Could I trust them? I had to stay calm. I would not allow them into the house.

'How do I know you are not here to murder me?' I asked them, trying to sound far more light-hearted than I felt, still behind the flyscreen door, talking to them from the safe shadow of the black mesh. I could see the men clearly, but I would be scarcely visible to them.

They countered by asking why I thought anyone would want to kill me. They had simply been asked by Scotland Yard to contact Ethel Turner. I had done nothing wrong, but they would be grateful for any help I could give them on a case the British police were working on. Could they come in and talk to me for half an hour or so?

I hesitated. My heart was thumping, but I did my best to keep calm. How could I trust them? I had no idea whether their identification was real. I suggested we talk outside, where we were in full view of my neighbour and anyone in the road. They accepted that.

I had no chairs on my front verandah, so we agreed to stroll down to a café, only a street block from where I lived, that fronted onto a park by the beach. I asked them to wait out near my gate while I fetched my handbag and locked the house. I refused their offer to drive there, as there was no way I was getting into a car with them, so they walked with me, commenting on the beauty of the beach and the soft warmth of the late autumn sunshine, all the time assuring me that they were not here for anything I had done wrong.

I would have been on more confident ground if I had known why they actually were here. It took every ounce of strength I had to keep calm. I knew that keeping my head was the only way I would survive this, yet I could not calm the rapid thumping of my heart, and my legs felt weak. Had they found the body in the icehouse? I had always kept up with the newspapers in the local library, but I may have missed it. All I could do was to deny any knowledge of how she came to be there. Had they discovered I was using a fake identity? Were they here to deport me? But no, they had said I had done nothing wrong.

I ordered takeaway coffee and muffins for us all, forcing myself to chat normally to the man who ran the café, and we sat at a picnic table in the park, shaded by a peppermint tree, a little away from the café and the path along the shore, but still in sight of the café staff and the other patrons.

They asked if they could record the conversation so they could send it back to the detectives at Scotland Yard. I agreed to this, knowing I would need to take care with what I told them and that I had no choice but to accept that they really were the federal police. I would stick to the truth as much as I could.

They asked me first why I would think someone wanted to kill me. They had been concerned about it. I decided to be straight with them.

'Some years ago, in Britain, my uncle was charged with hiring a hitman to murder a girl who was blackmailing him, a crime he didn't commit. The man who paid for the girl to be murdered threatened that he would kill me if my uncle told the truth, so I believe my uncle intended to take the blame, to protect me. A friend arranged for me to live here, with a new identity, for my own safety. My uncle was released on bail and was then murdered, although it was made to look like a suicide. I don't know how much influence this man has, or if he knows I'm here. I don't want to testify against him; I would be too frightened to. I don't trust the police either. My father was also murdered, while in police custody, and it was also passed off as a suicide. I assume you know I live here under a false name, but that is for my own protection. I left England in fear of my life, as I was the only credible witness who could have vindicated my uncle and exposed the real killer. He had already had one girl murdered, and I didn't want to be the next one. It isn't illegal to live under an assumed name, provided it isn't done for fraud.'

I knew I sounded defensive, perhaps they even thought I was paranoid or crazy, but I still did not know why they were talking to me. This may have nothing to do with Richard, or even Lagan. Had I said too much?

One of the men gave a low indrawn whistle, and for a long time neither of them said anything. I suppose they were surprised at it all.

'We are not here about the identity, Miss Turner. This does involve the disappearance and possible murder of a girl, but not, as far as we know, the one your uncle was accused of murdering. We were not given that information. With your permission we will pass on everything you say to us today, but your safety will be a priority.'

Had they found the au pair? I knew my whole future would depend on my keeping calm and denying any knowledge of it. Even if he had still been alive, Richard would never have given away that I had helped bury her, and I knew he would not want me to admit to it. I was so close to being back in touch with Simon. I was so hoping he would come here and I would see him again. Fate could not be so cruel as to have me arrested now.

They then gave me the background on why they wanted my help.

The British police had arrested a Russian woman, living in London, for trafficking underage girls for sex work. The girls came from Eastern European countries as illegal immigrants with the promise of living and working in Britain as au pairs or being trained as ballet dancers. In some cases, it was actually illegal for them to leave their home country, so they were smuggled out, and were then completely in the power of the Russian woman. They were hired out as prostitutes, many of them under the legal age. They were unable to leave the Russian madam's employ, as they had nowhere else to go. She hardly paid them enough to buy clothes. A few of them had managed to leave and set up independently as escorts, usually with the help of one of their clients, but not many. Sadly, the Russian woman had stayed under the radar for over ten years, and there were a lot of girls involved over that time.

They had also arrested several men who had paid for sex with the girls. The girls had been interviewed, they had confirmed the identity of the men, and most of them were being returned to their home countries. However, two of the girls were adamant that the sister of one of them had disappeared about eight years ago when they were taken to a house near the sea. They had then been around fifteen or sixteen. They were told they were being taken to a hotel to do housework there, but they were tied up and raped, and in the morning one of the girls had been missing. She had been with them on the Saturday but was not there on Sunday morning. The men had told them that she had been taken to the train station and given her fare back to London, but the girls all lived together in the Russian woman's boarding house, and they had never seen her again. The Russian woman had later told them the missing girl had gone to live with a client, but her sister knew that she would have contacted her if that was the case.

All of the older girls had been treated the same way when they first arrived at the Russian woman's boarding house. They were taken to a house near the sea by three of the men and were raped. They then had sex with the same men at the boarding house later, so they learnt what to do to please men and could be hired out as prostitutes. The younger girls had been taken to a different location, but their stories were similar.

The police believed the house near the sea had belonged to me, and that I was living there at the time. They wanted to know if I had been aware of what happened to the girls there, and if I could recall a girl going missing, so they had some confirmation of the girls' story before they treated the disappearance as a murder investigation. They had contacted the missing girl's family in Russia, who confirmed they had lost touch with her at about that time. If I had known that the girls were underage, or knew anything about the fate of the missing girl, the British police were prepared to give me immunity from prosecution over it in exchange for information, unless I had murdered the girl myself, which they considered highly unlikely.

My first feeling was utter relief that this was not about Richard's au pair, although I knew I still had to be careful. But

I was beginning to realise that this involved Lagan, not Richard, and I might finally get my revenge. A girl had gone missing; I knew where a girl was buried. Not the same girl, but did that matter? At least she might be found and laid to rest with a family, even if it was not the right one.

'I had nothing to do with hiring the Russian girls, and neither did my uncle. I worked for my uncle, managing a private retreat where he brought clients of his accountancy business on weekends. We did sometimes have clients who brought their girlfriends or mistresses down with them, and we always kept those clients anonymous, but it was mostly married couples. They had a weekend at our retreat for a small cost, and it kept the clients loyal to my uncle's firm. I was in charge of the gym equipment and the pool, and I assigned the rooms and took the guests for yoga classes and beach walks. There were three Italian men who regularly brought Russian girls. I don't know their real names, as we usually only used Christian names or nicknames. I don't know if the girls were actually from Russia, but I thought of them as the Russian girls. My uncle thought the language they spoke was Russian. Some of them did look young, but my uncle assured me that the agency they came from looked after that. I just thought they were escorts like the other girls. He said they were paid to act like reluctant virgins, and I had no reason to doubt that. We had other men there who sometimes played rather unusual sex games, and my uncle always assured me that nothing we did was against the law. I do recall a girl not being there the following day. One of the men said he had driven her to the train station. The girls spoke no English. I can also speak French and German, but not Russian, so I could never communicate with them. I don't know the name of the girl. There were so many different ones, and I was never very good at remembering names. I only knew the men by their nicknames, so I can't help with that either.'

'Do you recall when this occurred?'

'Not immediately, but I always keep a journal, and I would have written about the girl going home early as it was unusual, so I could give you a precise date. It would have been some time in 1986.'

'A date would be very helpful indeed, Miss Turner. Can you give us the nicknames?'

'Lagan, Antonio and Marco. I thought of them as the *tre amici*, the three friends. Lagan seemed to be the ringleader. He often came down, sometimes with his friends, occasionally by himself. He was my uncle's friend, and he paid a lot to stay at the retreat, but I don't know exactly how much as my uncle looked after the money. I just wrote cheques for the bills that came in for laundry and gardening and so forth. Sometimes the Italians brought three older escorts, who were strippers, but more usually they brought young girls. In the end a girl blackmailed both Lagan and my uncle. She sent a note to each of them, saying she would go to the press with the story that Lagan had raped her in my house when she was fifteen, and would tell the police that a girl had disappeared. She demanded two million pounds, to be put into a Swiss bank account. Lagan suggested I leave England until they had sorted it out, as he and my uncle didn't want me involved. He said the girl had asked for an extra two thousand pounds in cash so she could get to Switzerland, and he asked my uncle for it. We always had cash in the house. Lagan then gave the money to a hitman who murdered the girl. The police traced the cash to my uncle, and he was blamed for arranging the hitman. I believe he intended to plead guilty because Lagan told him he knew where I was and would kill me if he didn't. Then my uncle died, and I believe Lagan murdered him so the case was never brought to court. By then I had left England, so I know very little of what happened afterwards.'

'Are you okay with us sending this information to the British police?'

'Do I have a choice? But I won't testify against him because I value my life. Can you keep my address secret? I don't know if Lagan knows where I am now, but he once sent me a threatening note when I lived in Perth, telling me he knew where I was and where my boyfriend was, and I was to keep my mouth shut and not contact anyone. I don't know how you found me, but I would rather stay as hidden as possible.'

'We were given your current name and your bank account number, and asked if we could trace you. The British police simply wanted any information you could give them regarding the missing girl. We will tell them that you believe yourself to be in danger. From what you have told us today, it is likely that they will want to talk with you further. We will have your statement typed up and fax it to them, but we won't include your address at this stage. Do you still have the note the man sent you?'

'Yes, I do.'

They asked me to find the note, photocopy it, and look up the date of the girl's disappearance in my journal. They would be back in touch with me in few days' time.

It was a huge relief to tell someone my story. I did trust these men were genuine; even Lagan would not have enough influence to control the police here. They had been sent to ask if I could recall a girl going missing, and they had been rewarded with a much more complicated story.

It was a week before I heard from them again. This time they had a man from Scotland Yard with them, Inspector Fullerton, who had flown to Perth then driven down to Broadsea specially to interview me.

It was a beautiful day in late May, almost winter here but still warm enough to sit outside on my rear verandah. Two ibises wandered over the lawn as they often did, a flock of small honeyeaters chattered and splashed in my bird bath, and gulls circled beyond the peppermint trees that separated the house from the beach. I made coffee for them all and provided them with cheese and crackers. I now felt a little more confident that they really were the police and not assassins.

The British detective started by telling me that the police were okay with my changed identity and were confident that I had done nothing wrong. They were not trying to incriminate me in any way. They wanted information about the missing girl, were grateful for any help I could give them, and they were interested in what I had said about my uncle.

We went through my background, everything from where I went to school, the parties, my mother's addiction and my father's alleged suicide, my uncle looking after me when I had lost my whole family, the years we had hosted clients at Orchard House, the Russian girls who were different from the usual escorts who came with the men, the blackmail attempt and why I had left England, my life at the hotel in Perth, the note that Lagan had sent saying he knew where I was, my three years at the university, and my decision to move here when Mrs Marek retired.

This man was so calm, and guided me in such a structured way, stopping me occasionally with questions, helping me to keep my story in order, asking me if I still had the note from Lagan. I went indoors and found it, showed it to the inspector and gave him the photocopy I had made. He asked who the boyfriend was, but I was not prepared to give them his name, and he seemed to accept that I did not completely trust them.

When I reached the end of my story, I was shown a range of photographs of men who were alleged to be clients of the Russian madam, and asked if I recognised any of them.

'We understand that you are reluctant to testify against these men, but we have them in police custody, and we would be grateful for your help. A girl may have been murdered, we are hoping to find her body, and we want justice for her. If what you have told us is true, then we may also be able to get justice for your uncle, or at least clear his name.'

I pointed out the three Italians; I did not recognise any of the remaining men.

'We picked those three up at the airport, on their way back to Italy. The girls who we interviewed recognised the same three from the photographs. Can you recall their names?'

I knew Lagan; I was not sure which of the others was Antonio and which was Marco. But I did my best, and they said I had got them correct. They told me that Lagan's nickname was from his surname, which was Lagano, but the other two had used their Christian names.

I told him everything I could recall about the weekend the girl had gone missing. I had found the dates from my diary, the week-end of the 18th and 19th of October in 1986. The three Italians had been there with three girls, as well as myself, Richard, and his au pair. I always slept in the tower—the only room that was on the second floor apart from unused attics—and it was a con-siderable distance from the guest bedrooms. The au pair was always assigned a room on the ground floor near the kitchen, although some of them actually slept with Richard in his room on the first floor. I had heard nothing untoward that night. I had not even heard the car drive out early the following morning to take the girl to the station, but I had heard it return. I had been organising breakfast by then. It was one of the other men who had been driving, not Lagan. It was the green sports car. Lagan's car was red, the third one black, but I could not recall if the green car belonged to Marco or Antonio.

Inspector Fullerton then asked if there was any place I could think of in the house or grounds that could be used to hide a body. A cellar below the house or stables? A well? An icehouse? Many Victorian houses had them. It was possible that the body of the girl had been taken away in the car and buried somewhere, but they were hoping the car being driven out and returning was just a decoy and she was still somewhere in the house or grounds.

I put down my mug to hide that I was shaking, but this man was trained to notice reactions, and he would have seen it.

'I'm sorry, but I find it upsetting that a girl could have been raped and murdered in my house. I never thought to question their story that the girl had wanted to go home.'

But I still had to answer their question.

'There was no well that I know of. A small stream starts from a spring at the base of the cliffs across the lane from the house and runs through the garden, so there would never have been any need for one, even before piped water. The water once flowed into in a cistern near the kitchen door, but that had been filled in and converted to a flowerbed by the time we bought the house. We did have a cellar below the kitchen, which we used to store the wine. It was used right up until I left, so I don't think you could hide a body there. It is just a single room and is quite well lit. There are attics that we never used; you could search there. The house is Victorian, so well past the time of priest holes. But we did have an old icehouse. I used to point it out to my guests when we walked down to the beach, and explain what it was used for, so the men would have known it was there. It was built into the slope of the ground as you went from the house down to the shore. We never opened it, as obviously it was no longer used for ice, so I don't know if it was still intact inside. I'm not sure you can even see it any more. I recall the bank collapsed around it, and the door was covered.'

I could hardly deny the icehouse since I had pointed it out to my guests. If they spoke to any of my retiree couples, they would remember it.

Was this my opportunity for revenge? If they found the au pair we had buried there, they would think she was the missing Russian girl, and Lagan would get the blame. He had framed my uncle for the murder of one girl. Perhaps I could frame him for the murder of another.

'I understand you sold the house to a couple who run it as a private hotel.'

'Yes, that's right. Paul Brady, my late uncle's business partner, looked after the sale and sent the money to me. You haven't told me how you found me. Did you talk to Paul?'

'Yes, we did. The girls recalled that the house was in a village between high cliffs and the sea, there was a small Norman church, and the house had locked gates, a tower and a path down to the sea, so we eventually found it. We took several of the girls there, and they confirmed it was the right place. The current owners gave Paul Brady's name as the contact. Mr Brady knew your new name, but not your address. He was reluctant to give us the name of the woman who did know how to contact you, as he didn't trust her and didn't want her to know the police were trying to find you. He stressed that he was concerned for your safety. He had your Australian bank account number and asked if we could find you from that. The police here easily traced you. Mr Brady has been very helpful. I spoke to him again after we received your statement, and he confirmed your story about your uncle taking the blame. He also told us some of what you have just said to us, that most of the men who came to the retreat were clients of his and your uncle's accounting firm, although he knew nothing of the escorts or the girls that Lagan took down.'

The inspector told me they were now reopening the investigations into the murder of the prostitute by the hitman and the death of my uncle.

He showed me the photo of the girl who had been murdered, but I did not recall her as one of our guests. I explained that there were a lot of girls and I was not good at remembering names or faces. However, I was able to tell him, word for word, what the blackmail note to my uncle had contained, as I had written it into my journal, and I told him how Lagan had cheated Richard into giving him cash to give to the girl.

'Your uncle died from an overdose of a prescription sedative, and although we know he himself had no prescription for the medication, it was assumed to be a suicide. The girl he allegedly murdered was also from Russia, although she apparently spoke very good English and shared a flat with a British girl, who identified her and also identified the hitman as the man who had collected the victim for a date. The British girl was very helpful at the time. She knew her friend was trying to blackmail a man who had hired her as an au pair and raped her when she was fifteen. At the time she was murdered, the girl no longer worked for the Russian madam, so the woman was not investigated at that time, but we now believe there was a connection. We talked again to the girls who were at the boarding house when we raided it, and several of them recognised the victim as a girl who had previously worked there, but had moved out to work by herself. They immediately knew her name when we showed them her photograph. I also checked the report into your father's death, and the conclusion was that he took his own life. That can sometimes be difficult for relatives to accept, but he was on suicide watch and was left alone due to a mistake. We did have an internal enquiry, and protocols were changed.'

I knew I would have to finally accept that. Had his guilt over my mother's death been too much for him? Whatever had happened, the police were unlikely now to look into it further. But I was glad that they were looking into the murder of the blackmailer, so my uncle's name could be cleared, and hopefully Lagan could be charged.

'Miss Turner, would you come back to England and show us where the icehouse is? The Kershaws had no knowledge of its existence. It may save us digging up the whole of their twenty-acre garden. We will pay the return fare, of course, and we will do everything possible to ensure your safety. We will find you somewhere safe to stay and give you a security guard. The three men you fear are in custody. While you may think of them as being part of an international criminal gang, we believe they are only small operators with limited resources. We will bring you back here afterwards.'

'How long would it take? I do have a job here, I work three days each week at one of the resorts, doing their accounting, and they would need to find a temporary replacement.'

'A couple of weeks should be sufficient. We can arrange a flight for you in a few days' time.'

'Would I be able to see Paul Brady and another friend?'

'We can arrange that, but we would like to keep this as quiet as possible. Mr Brady told us that he doesn't trust the woman who knows your address, and from the details he gave us, we believe he has good reason. So for the moment we would ask you not to contact her. Do you still have the letters she sent and the envelopes? If so, bring them with you, with the note you received from the man you called Lagan, and the journal.'

I told the manager of the resort that I needed to return to Britain for a few weeks. He was good about it. He had previously done the accounts himself and would go back to that for a short while, as it was much easier now that I had computerised it. I had never taken a holiday although I was entitled to, I had often helped in reception or the café at times when we were understaffed, and I often helped him on weekends when the resort was booked for a wedding or a business conference and he needed a hostess. He told me to stay for as long as I needed to. He would cope, and it was coming into winter when there were fewer bookings.

Reunited 1995

I was accompanied on the flight by an Australian diplomat, who was returning to the embassy in London, so I was not on my own. This time I travelled first class, and I was able to get some sleep on the plane. When I had first come to Australia, I had been tourist class, as Paul had thought that would attract less attention.

Inspector Fullerton had returned to England on the day after he had spoken to me, but the federal police had arranged the travel companion and the tickets and had driven me up to Perth to catch the flight.

At Heathrow the diplomat and I were waved through customs, with only a glance at our passports, before we were driven to the Australian Embassy. Inspector Fullerton was waiting there for me, and there were some formalities and paperwork. I was being given immunity from prosecution for any minor offences that may come to light from my evidence. That included the identity, and whether I had been aware that the girls who were brought to my retreat were underage. They had no reason to believe I had done anything wrong, but they wanted me to be confident that I would not be incriminating myself when they interviewed me.

It was strange being back in England after more than five years; it seemed as if I had never been away, as if the years in between were but a dream.

I stayed in a flat with two young policewomen, and they could not have been more kind to me. It had been arranged that they worked different shifts, so one or other of them was always at home. If I went out of the flat, even if it was only for grocery shopping with one of the policewomen, I would be accompanied by a young plain-clothes detective for my protection. His name was Alan Claymore. I was to call him Alan, so it appeared we were simply friends. I was given a number to call, and he would meet me at the door.

I offered to help the policewomen with the extra costs, but they were not allowed to take anything from me; the police were paying them to put me up. So I helped with the housework, and when we shopped, I bought flowers to brighten up the flat.

Three days after I arrived, a young detective drove me and Inspector Fullerton down to Deniton, Alan accompanying us.

Everything was the same, the village, the lane, the cottage, the gates, Orchard House. I strained to look at the cottage, hoping I might see Simon in the garden, but I was sitting on the far side of the car. It was, in any case, a Monday during term time, so he would be at the school. The gates to Orchard House were open; you no longer needed to ring the bell.

The Kershaws, who ran the house as a small private hotel, were expecting us. They were very courteous to me, as they knew I was the previous owner of the hotel, although they had dealt only with Paul. The police had explained that they were investigating a historic murder and would like to look over the house and grounds. Two other police officers and a photographer were already there waiting for us.

Nothing had changed inside the house. We looked in the cellar and the attics, and the old stables, which had been converted to garages.

The Kershaws knew nothing about the icehouse—Richard and I had covered it well—but I recalled exactly where it was.

I found a spade—the same one we had used when we buried the girl, still in its old place in the garden shed—and I led the six men down the path towards the shore, breathing the familiar salt smell of the sea, with the soft touch of the wind on my face, the whisper of the waves on the beach, the gulls circling above the sand, the fresh green of the trees, some in soft-coloured blossom. It was all so beautiful and so familiar that it was hard to believe we were there on such a gruesome errand.

So many times I had walked down that path and looked across to where the icehouse could once be seen, thinking about the sad lost soul of the girl we had buried, and I went straight to it, dug away at the earth where I knew the door to be, and uncovered a corner of it.

They took photographs of the door and the surrounding bank, before one of the men took the spade from me and cleared away the years of leaves that had rotted down to beautiful black soil. The meadow flowers, in the bloom of early summer, were scattered discarded and bruised as the soil fell away from the door. The lock was still broken, and the door succumbed to the force of two of the men pulling it open.

I already knew what they would find.

There was a ghastly stench—of rotting earth and a thousand dead rats—released from its confines then clearing a little. And I felt nothing but immense relief that now the young woman would be laid to rest, even if it was not with her own people.

'Take her away,' the inspector said tersely, and Alan took my arm and led me away down the path, asking me to show him the beach. If they found a body, they did not want me to see it. They had no wish to upset me.

The path was the same, the gate no longer locked, no longer needing the code that I still remembered from all those years ago. The sea thrift was still there and the sea bindweed, the gulls soaring in the wind, the clean sand. A pile of glistening seaweed, torn by the sea from its hold on the rocks and washed up on the beach, waited for the waves to reclaim it, or the sun to dry it out and leave it half-buried in sand, beyond the reach of the tide. I breathed in the cool air from the sea, trying to erase the smell of death that still filled my head, the nausea that was churning at my stomach.

A man was standing on the beach, looking out over the water, his back to me. I recognised him at once, and I stopped, frozen in shock. How could he be here? Had my mind conjured him up from some fantasy world? It was a weekday; he would be at the school.

Alan had instantly moved in front of me.

'It's okay,' I said. 'He is a neighbour and would wish me no harm.'

'Are you all right, Ethel?' Alan asked me, seeing I was shaking, and taking my elbow to steady me. 'I'm sorry, I should have taken you away before they opened the door. Would you like me to take you back to the house?'

'I'll be fine.' My voice seemed to come to me from far away, and I scarcely even knew what I was saying.

For a moment I thought I would faint. Simon was here, not twenty yards from me, his hair ruffled by the wind, in the same checked shirt he had worn when we had sat together on the sand on his birthday.

Hearing our voices, he turned to look in our direction, and for an eternal moment we gazed at each other. He hadn't changed. Still the same beard, the same hair, the same smile that made my heart melt and my knees weak. He took a few steps towards me then stopped, seeming unsure, but by now we were close enough to speak over the rush of the waves and the call of the gulls.

'Ann?' he said at last. 'Are you a ghost? You've had your hair cut.'

I could say nothing. I threw myself against him, his shirt warm and soft beneath my face, his arms around me. I was crying; I couldn't help it.

'Alan Claymore, Scotland Yard.' My bodyguard flashed out his identity card. I suppose he saw that Simon and I were much more than friends and didn't want any misunderstanding.

'Miss Turner is helping with a police investigation. She is not in any trouble. I am protecting her while she remains in England.'

'Simon Davis. I teach science at Harton School, and I own the cottage next door to here. Ann and I were once very good friends. What are you investigating? I know Ann did nothing wrong.' He was still holding me, my face against his shoulder, his hand stroking my hair and my cheek.

'We are digging up an old icehouse, in connection a possible murder. We brought Miss Turner back to England because she knew where the icehouse was located. We know her real name, but we are sticking with Ethel Turner while she remains here. We don't yet know if there are any credible threats to her life, but we are not taking any chances. I wanted to keep her out of the way while we investigate the icehouse, so we came down to the beach. We may find nothing, but finding a body is never a pleasant experience, and we wanted to spare her that.'

'Why are you here?' I asked Simon, finding my voice at last. 'Why aren't you at the school?'

'It's half-term. I still come here every holiday and some week-ends. I received your letter, and I wrote back, but it may not have reached you yet. I was hoping you might let me join you for the summer, and we might carry on where we left off. I was standing there looking out towards Australia, wondering what you were doing, and you turned up behind me.'

I longed for us to be alone, to feel his mouth against mine, his naked body against mine, but Alan was with us, and we had to behave.

'May I take Miss Turner back to the cottage with me for a while and allow you to get back to your investigation?'

'I'm sorry, Mr Davis, but my job is to look after her. I can wait a little further along the beach if you two would like to talk in private.'

We sat side by side on the sand as we once had many years before, both of us savouring for a moment the realisation that we were back together.

'Do you have someone else now?' I asked him. It was all I could think about. We were finally together, but I didn't know if he was now married. I so desperately wanted him to still be single and unattached so we could go back to being lovers. So much had happened since the last time I had seen him, yet it seemed like yesterday.

'No. I could never find another girl who shared my love of seagulls.'

I laughed, slipped my arm through his and rested my head against his shoulder.

'Are you still mine?' he whispered into my hair.

'Yes, if you still want me. Did you sometimes think of me?'

'Every single day. I still can't believe I'm not dreaming. Ann, why didn't you let me know where you were so I could join you? I kept thinking that if you still wanted to be with me, you would have let me know where you were.'

I looked at him, his eyes holding mine, and I realised he had been just as afraid that I no longer wanted him and would find someone else as I had been afraid that he no longer wanted me.

'When I first arrived in Australia, I received a threatening note from the man who framed my uncle for the murder of the girl. He said he knew where I was and where my boyfriend was, and I was not to contact anyone. I didn't want him to harm you or Paul. I thought you would no longer want anything to do with me and would find someone else. That was why I sent the cards to the school. I didn't want your wife or girlfriend to read the letters. And I was afraid that if I gave you my address you would write back and ask me to stop sending you the Christmas cards.'

'Paul didn't have your address, and I didn't want to send letters through someone else. He told me that the woman who knew it would never give it to him. Her excuse was that the police were looking for you and could charge you over hosting the underage girls, and if they asked Paul for your address, he would be obliged to tell them. He always thought that was just a concocted reason so he could not send to you directly and she got to read all the letters he sent. He had spoken to the police, and they had nothing on you. He didn't know who we could trust and was concerned that his letters had been intercepted. He was not sure you had received some of them. He several times asked you to send letters directly to him at his office or his flat, but you continued to send through Vera, so he thought you may have never received his letters. If you had sent one of us your address, we could have sent letters back to you and no one else could possibly have intercepted them. Neither Paul nor I could understand why you didn't realise that. The man you are frightened of can't sort through everyone's mail.'

I realised that now, but I really had been convinced that the police were looking for me. I let him continue.

'We didn't know how to get through to you. I knew from the first card you sent that you were studying accounting at the university, so I tried telephoning the department there and asking if they could ask you to contact Paul or me. But the secretary said they were not allowed to confirm whether you were a student there, they could not give contact details for their students, and they were unable to pass on messages. I had never felt so frustrated in my life.'

The secretary had never told me that someone was trying to contact me, but there were a lot of students, and she would only have been following protocol.

'In the end I asked Paul to send you the school newsletters, and he arranged it. Your brother had gone to Harton, so it would seem quite natural for Paul to send them to you, and we hoped they would get through. We sent the first one because you said you didn't have a photo of me, and that way we could send you a photo without the woman realising the significance of it. Paul didn't want to send a photo directly, as he didn't want her to find out who I was. We knew you received that one because you mentioned it in a Christmas card, so we tried sending you messages in the newsletters, asking you to contact us directly and send your address. In the last one I was trying to tell you that I still cared about you, after you sent me the note last Christmas. I set the photo up very carefully, and the wording. The sixth-form boys put the newsletters together, and the student who did the photos was quite happy to do it the way I wanted, although he didn't know why. I was so happy when I got the letter with your address.'

'I'm so sorry,' I responded. 'Rebecca wrote that the police were looking for me, and she didn't want me to send Paul my address as he may have been obliged to give it to them. I now realise that was futile, as the police found me anyway, and unnecessary, as they haven't charged me with anything. They just needed information.'

'And now you are here. I always knew that one day my elf princess would come back, or I would find her again. I have never given up hope. How long have you been back in England?'

'Only since Friday. The police wanted me to show them where the icehouse was, as it was buried when a bank collapsed, and the Kershaws didn't even know it existed. The police think a girl was murdered here. She disappeared one weekend, but the men told me they had taken her to the train station, and I had no cause to doubt that. My uncle did supply escorts for some of the clients, but most of our guests were dear old couples who trusted him with their personal accounting, and I enjoyed pampering them for a weekend. The underage girls were brought down by three Italian men, friends of my uncle. I did ask Richard if they were too young, but he said the agency supplying them would look after that. None of the escorts my uncle arranged were less than eighteen, and I was never an escort. I was worried you would think I was, and I hated to think what your mother and the vicar's wife would have thought of me.'

'I never blamed you for anything, and I could never think badly of you. My mother was disappointed, but mostly because she had wanted me to find a wife and things had gone wrong. She had been so thrilled that I had finally got a girlfriend. But she didn't believe you could be involved with anything illegal. Mrs Mason was shocked and quite upset. She had always thought there was something strange about the locked gates, but she thought you were all naturists, and the gates were locked so your guests could run around in the nude. When she read the story in the newspaper, she was convinced you were a victim of your uncle. She could never believe you would do anything wrong, and even now she sometimes asks me if I have heard from you.'

Mrs Mason? Yes, of course, he meant the vicar's wife. I had never been good at remembering names. I recalled he had once told me he knew the name of every boy he taught.

'May I tell her that I've spoken to you?' he asked.

'No, better not. You can tell her you are coming out to Australia to see me. That's if you still want to. Just ask her not to tell anyone else. She was always so kind to me.'

'Of course, I want to. I did think about going to Australia, but I was not sure how I would find you when I arrived, and you may have been married to someone else. I thought if you wanted me to find you, you would have given me some way to trace you, even if it was only a phone number. I had a recurring dream of knocking on your front door and it being opened by some handsome bronzed Australian man who was now your husband. And you are not in the phone book. When you mentioned in a card that you had moved to a house of your own, I thought I might trace you that way. I phoned the Australian directory helpline, but they had no record for you, and said you may have a silent number.'

'I do have a silent number. I'm sorry, I feel bad now that I didn't send you the phone number. I was just so worried that the letters would be intercepted. I realise now that was silly of me, but I was very frightened that Lagan might target you.'

We could hear Alan talking on a two-way radio behind us, but he was too far away for us to hear the conversation. He joined us, asked me to go back to the house with him, and whether there was a way we could return without going back along the path past the icehouse.

'There is a public footpath that runs from the lane to the beach, beside the wall on this side of the garden. If we take that we can return through the front gate.'

'They have found human remains. In fact, they believe there may be two bodies, but they will need to take out the first one before they can be sure about the second, and they will need the forensic experts here for that. You may come back with us if you wish, Mr Davis. The inspector said that was all right. He was happy for Ethel to have a friend with her.'

We sat in the lounge at Orchard House with the two detectives and Alan. Simon knew the Kershaws, of course, as they were neighbours, and he told the inspector his name and where he worked.

'Before Ann left, I was hoping to persuade her to marry me, and more recently I was hoping to travel to Broadsea and stay with her. She had finally given me her address.'

I sat beside him on a sofa, his arm around me and my hand in his. The Kershaws made sandwiches and tea for us. A forensic team would arrive shortly, and the bodies would eventually be taken to the morgue. The Kershaws were asked to keep their guests away from the path to the beach—the police would tape the area—and instead send them around to the public footpath. But beyond that they could carry on as usual.

With all that arranged, they asked me if I had any idea of the identity of the second body.

'I don't recall any of the other Russian girls going missing, but I may not have noticed it. There were a lot of girls who came here, escorts and my uncle's au pairs.'

I didn't want to incriminate Richard, but I wanted the dead au pair to be returned to her family. I wanted closure on the part I had played, but I would never admit that I had helped hide her.

'Do you know where the other girls came from? We have the Russian woman in custody. Were all the girls from her agency?'

'No, they weren't. Only the girls that the Italians brought with them. The others came from Rebecca Feldman, who runs a modelling agency and supplies au pairs and escorts. Her girls are all over eighteen, and my uncle said it was perfectly legal. You could ask her if she recalls any of her girls going missing. Richard had a succession of au pairs; they looked after him at our flat in London in the week and came here with him to help with the clients on the weekends, and I believe they all came from Rebecca. I always tried to help them with their English. The last one he had was called Lottie, but I don't think that was her real name. I don't remember her disappearing, but he did suddenly stop bringing her, and he did without an au pair after that, which I did think rather odd. She did sleep with him. They did kinky stuff, bondage and whips. I thought he had fallen in love with her; she was around for much longer than any of the others. He never told me why she had left, and I never asked, as the au pairs rarely stayed with us for long. Rebecca came here sometimes on the weekends, and she may recall who the last girl was, as Richard would have hired her through Rebecca. Her husband Amos was in partnership with my uncle, running the retreat here, but one night when he was here, he had a heart attack and died during the night.'

I thought I had given them enough information to find Rebecca, and for her to identify the girl, assuming she kept records. I wanted Lottie to be identified.

'You mentioned a journal, Miss Turner. Would you be prepared to lend it to us to copy, so we can go through it and get the dates?'

I was not prepared to. I explained that there were personal things in it, and notes about men who came here without the knowledge of their wives. If it ever fell into the hands of the press, they would have a field day. I offered to extract details of dates and the Christian names of the guests for all of the weekends.

'That would be very helpful,' the inspector agreed. 'If you could photocopy the pages for the weekend the girl went missing, then black out anything you don't want us to read, we would be grateful for that.'

Perhaps they could have demanded the diary, but they needed my cooperation in their investigation. I suggested the Kershaws may still have the hotel registers. We were required to keep track of the guests here, so we could account for everyone in the event of a fire, but we accepted Christian names. They did have the books, still below the desk in the hallway. The au pairs and the escorts would have signed in with their names; most of my journal entries would only contain the names of the men and just the expected number of the girls, as I was never given the escorts' names in advance. I generally labelled their rooms as *au pair* or as *escort*. I kept no records of which rooms I assigned to the guests, but I remembered which Lagan and his friends had slept in, as I always gave them the same ones at the end of the house, with the best views of the sea. I showed the detectives the rooms they would have used, as well as my old room, Richard's room, and the bedroom downstairs which I always assigned to the au pair. Neither the au pair nor I had slept near the Italians' rooms.

The inspector looked briefly into all the rooms, but said there would now be little or no useful forensic evidence there. I recalled there were plans for the house that had been created when the renovations were done, and the Kershaw's still had them, so Mrs Kershaw made a photocopy of the room layout, and I pencilled names in the rooms that would have been used that weekend.

When we left to return to London, leaving the forensic team to work on the icehouse, I was reluctant to part from Simon, but he gave me the phone numbers for the cottage and the house where his mother lived near Harton School. He was living there during the week, as his mother was away on a Mediterranean cruise. She had taken up travelling with a friend— they went to all sorts of exotic places—and she was now often away.

I remained at the flat with the policewomen for several more days, working on extracting notes from my diary, so they knew which weekends the Italians had been there and which day the Russian girl had gone missing. They compared my notes with the information they had from the hotel registers. It was helping them to determine when each of the Russian girls had been taken to the house, and to help establish if any of them were less than sixteen at the time, as that was a more serious crime.

Each afternoon Alan came to collect me, and we would walk in a park for an hour or two, so I could get some fresh air, while he gave me a progress report on the investigation. He offered to accompany me if I wanted to shop, but I had no need for new clothes.

They had identified the second body, which had been found on the floor of the icehouse, as the Russian girl who had gone missing. The girls they had interviewed knew her name, as she was the sister of one of them. They had contacted her family, and had been sent her dental records. They were still working on identifying the first girl they had found, whose body had been lying on the steps leading down into the icehouse. They knew she had been left there at a later date and were not assuming the same man had killed her. Rebecca Feldman was assisting with the identification, and the dates I had given to them were very helpful in establishing who she was. Rebecca kept very good records of the girls she employed, unlike the Russian madam, who had kept no records at all. At this stage they had a possible name for Richard's last au pair, and were liaising with the police in Finland to contact her family and establish if she was actually missing, or had returned home. Rebecca had not been told I was in England or that they were reopening the investigation into the murdered blackmailer. They still did not want me to contact her.

Of course, there were headlines. The police discovering the remains of two girls lying for years in an old icehouse was too good a story for anything but the front pages. But my name was not mentioned and neither was Orchard House. The press release from the police had been scanty, with no mention of the village or the house where the girls were found, but speculation and imagination filled any gaps. It was believed to relate to the recent arrest of a Russian woman who was alleged to have supplied underage girls for sex and kept them prisoner in her boarding house. By some miracle they had not yet related it to the six-year-old story of Richard Berrington and the murdered blackmailer. But sooner or later they would.

Paul visited me at the flat one evening after work, showed me photos of his two children—they were so sweet and beautiful—and talked about Richard and the long-ago days when we had been lovers. He had become good friends with Simon, and they often met for lunch. Paul still had his flat, where he stayed in the week to be close to work, going home to the estate and his wife at the weekends. It suited them both, and he was happy with his marriage. It had worked out well so far, although he was a little concerned that his wife was getting rather too fond of an equerry who looked after her horses on her father's estate. I was not actually sure if he was being serious, but I advised him to pay her more attention if he was worried that she would stray, and not to tell her he had been here to see me.

He told me that Percy's sister, Lady Ann Murphy, had been livid when the story of Richard's arrest had first surfaced and the newspaper had used the picture that had once been incorrectly labelled as being of her. She had talked about suing the paper, but her father had talked her out of it. Percy had dined out for weeks on telling his friends everything he knew about me, although it was precious little.

Percy was now married to a friend of Paul's wife. Paul's mother-in-law was Percy's mother's cousin, so the families often met and exchanged news. There was a house party every Christmas either at his father-in-law's estate or at Percy's father's estate, and the men had a few glorious days to themselves, playing billiards, enjoying exquisite cigars and drinking craft whisky, while the ladies gossiped to their hearts' content in the drawing room.

Lady Ann had also been married for a short time, but after she slapped her husband's face in public at the races when she caught him flirting with her best friend, the marriage had ended in divorce. Lady Ann had done very well financially out of it, however, and was now engaged to an even wealthier man than her first husband. Paul and Percy had joked that Lady Ann had put her friend up to it, so she could get rid of a painfully boring but very wealthy husband and get herself a decent settlement. They were wondering if a similar thing might happen with the second husband, although he was old—positively geriatric—and he would likely have a heart attack on his wedding night and save her the bother.

I asked about some of the friends I recalled from the parties with our old set, but Paul knew very few of them now. It seemed he moved in much more aristocratic circles.

I phoned Simon every evening, but only for a short while, as I was using the policewomen's phone. He offered to put me up at his mother's house while I was in England. It was on the edge of a quiet town, and I was unlikely to be found there by whoever it was I was frightened of. I suggested this to the inspector, and he agreed to it, but wanted someone to be with me during the day while Simon worked.

They would need me here for only a few more days while they identified the second girl and put together their evidence against the Italians. The were quite open with me as to what they had found so far. They wanted me to know what the men had said, in case I noticed any discrepancies with what I recalled. The Russian girl had died from a blow to the back of her head, damaging her skull and breaking her neck, but the cause of death had not yet been established for the other girl.

I agreed to sign a formal statement of what I recalled of the weekend the Russian girl had disappeared. She had been raped and murdered in my house, and I owed her that. If they needed my evidence at a trial, I would not be identified by my new name.

At first the Italians had denied everything, blamed the Russian madam for supplying underage girls, claimed it was not a crime if a man believed the girl to be old enough, and they had refused to answer questions about the missing girl. Antonio had taken her to the station. That was all they knew. How were they supposed to know where she had gone after that? She could have taken the train to anywhere.

But now her body had been found, they had turned on each other like starving rats, contradicting each other, swearing they were not involved, each blaming the others, and all of them blaming the girl for resisting when she had been paid for sex.

Antonio and Marco both said the girl's death was nothing to do with them. It was Lagan who had killed her, in self-defence. She had fought back like a wildcat and had hit her head on the bedpost when he had tried to fend her off. He clearly hadn't tied her down properly. The madam should never have sent them a girl like that. Richard had suggested they put her in the icehouse; he didn't want anyone prying into what they did at Orchard House. Antonio had been asked to take the car and drive to the station in town, then come back, so the other girls would believe she had returned to London by train. That was the only part he had played in it. They couldn't charge him with anything.

Lagan denied all knowledge of the girl's death. He had lent her to Richard, and she had slept that night with Richard, not with him. He had slept with Richard's au pair. Richard must have killed her. He was well known for playing games of strangling girls. Lagan only knew she had disappeared the next morning, when Antonio said he had driven her to the station. It was years ago. They went through heaps of girls; how was he supposed to recall one of them going missing?

I was haunted by the horror that I had hosted these men in my house. All three of them had been good looking, suave and totally charming. I had joked that Lagan was my Latin lover; I had allowed him to kiss my neck, breathe into my ear, walk with me on the beach and swim with me in the pool; I had given him massages, laughed off his attempts to persuade me to sleep with him. My own gullibility was the worst thing; I had not seen him for what he really was. To me they were just men who were prepared to pay for sex with girls who were happy to sell it to them. I had always been a little troubled with married men bringing their escorts and mistresses, as it seemed deceitful, but I had come to accept it all as harmless fun between consenting adults, perhaps even blamed some of the wives for not giving their husbands the attention they craved.

The date I had given them for the girl's disappearance had been very helpful. They had compared it to the hotel register and had traced the au pair who was with Richard on the night that the Russian girl had disappeared, as she had signed in with her full name.

She was now married and living in Manchester. She recalled going to Orchard House on several occasions. She remembered three rather sleazy Italian men, but not the girls who were with them, although she had thought that some of the girls at Orchard House looked very young to be escorts. She did not recall a girl going missing, but said she may not have noticed, as she would not have known who was supposed to be there. She denied ever sleeping with Lagan, and said she had never slept with Richard either. She had been given her own room downstairs at Orchard House, and she had slept in a small bedroom in Richard's flat. It was awkward, as it was so small, and the wardrobe had sliding doors because there would not be room to open normal hinged doors. She said she had liked working for Richard, as he was always a perfect gentleman, but when her sister got a job in Manchester, she had moved there with her, and they had worked there together, looking after an elderly lady, who was the great-aunt of the man she had eventually married. She remembered me, as I had taught her some English words, and she said I was sometimes at the flat in London with Richard. I had given her a few clothes I no longer wanted.

The inspector believed they now had enough evidence against Lagan to charge him over the death of the Russian girl. His alibi for that night was in tatters.

The police had established the identity of the girl on the steps. She was the girl I called Lottie. Her full name was Lotta Hakulinen, and she was Finnish. Her family had confirmed she had not contacted them since the time I last recalled seeing her.

They had not been able to determine conclusively how she had died. There were no bones broken, no bullets, no evidence of a knife being buried with the body. She may have been strangled, as there was a small amount of damage to the hyoid bone, but if so, it was not with any great force and may have occurred accidentally.

They asked me whether I would have missed her if she had died in the night and Richard had hidden the body. I answered very carefully. The last entry I had for her in my diary was a weekend when we had no other guests. She would have stayed for three nights, as Richard normally came down on Friday evening and returned to London early on Monday. I was not always in the house when he left in the morning, as I usually walked along the beach. As there were only three of us, I would not have made a formal breakfast. The au pair would have made breakfast for Richard, and I would have fixed my own when I came in from walking. Richard may have already left before I returned. I did not recall missing her, but I would have been busy that Monday morning, as I intended to spend the week in London. I had to leave the house tidy, ready for when we returned the following weekend. I always drove up to London separately, and Richard would normally have left before I did. I couldn't recall if she was with us in the flat in London that week, as Richard did not always have an au pair. I had a record in my journal of where I shopped during the week I was there, but nothing else. If I had wondered why she was not at the flat, or where she was the following weekend—when I had noted in my journal that Richard had come down to Orchard House alone—I would just have assumed she had left us. The au pairs rarely stayed long.

I had, in fact, made no mention of the girl in my diary that weekend beyond the note that she and Richard had come on the Friday. There are some things no one includes in a personal journal.

They asked about the strangling games that Lagan had mentioned. I did know that Richard and Lottie were lovers, and that they did play some sort of sex games. His room was not close to mine at Orchard House, and his love affairs were his own business, but at the flat, where the bedrooms were adjacent, I sometimes heard them laughing and squealing in his room. He had kept Lottie for longer than the other au pairs, and he had never hired another one after she left. I had taken over cleaning the flat when I stayed there.

Inspector Fullerton was not sure if they could obtain enough evidence to pin Richard's death on Lagan, but he said he would try. They had interviewed the hitman once more—he was still in prison—and he had identified the photo of Lagan as the man who had hired him to get rid of the blackmailer, claiming the man had said his name was Richard Berrington. Perhaps he resented that he was in jail while Lagan walked free, but he said he was prepared to testify against him. They were charging Lagan with arranging her murder.

On the Friday of that week, the inspector and the younger detective came to the flat where I was staying, wanting to talk to me again. They wanted to know more about Rebecca and how she fitted in.

'She was my uncle's friend. She took me in hand when my brother died. I was sixteen and seriously depressed. She organised for me to do lessons in deportment and massage, and she encouraged me to train in physiotherapy, so I could run the gym at the retreat for Richard. She was very kind to me, and I don't want to get her into trouble. I realise that what she does to get people new identities isn't really legal, but it may have saved my life.'

'We are not charging her with anything at this stage. We know what she does, and she normally keeps within the law, so we leave her alone. There are many perfectly valid reasons why people want to change their identity. Many of the people she helps are victims of domestic violence, or girls who simply want to evade ex-lovers who are stalking them. She has even helped us with information on occasion, as she does have a few contacts in the criminal world. But we are concerned that she may have duped you. You trust her explicitly, don't you?'

'Yes, I do.'

They asked me again what had happened on the day she came to the house with Lagan, and I went through the details with them. Lagan had brought her with him because he wanted me out of the way while things were sorted out, and Rebecca could give me a new identity and a new home in another country. He thought I would not leave with him without Rebecca with us. Lagan had always claimed he was in love with me, and I had assumed he really did care about me when he organised for me to leave, but I later realised it was to prevent me from being a witness to what had happened. The blackmailer had asked Lagan for two thousand pounds, so she could get to Switzerland, and he had asked my uncle for it. Rebecca would be able to confirm my story that Richard gave the cash to Lagan. She had even referred to it in one of the earliest letters she had sent me. I had the letter with me, and I offered to give them a copy of it.

'Did you ever see them together apart from that one time? We have gone through the hotel records, and they were never both there on the same weekend.'

'No, I don't think so. Rebecca only ever came on weekends when we had no clients as guests. Her husband Amos came with her until he died, and usually Paul Brady as well. He was my uncle's business partner, and he and I were close friends before he was married.'

'Did you know that the man you call Lagan is her nephew?'

I was left reeling in shock. I had trusted her and believed everything she had said about keeping me safe from him. 'No, I had no idea.'

'Initially, we only told her we were investigating the au pair, and she was very helpful with the identification. She told us none of the girls she supplied were underage, and to her credit she did tell us that you had no part in providing the escorts. Your uncle ran the business, and you just hosted the weekends and helped in the gym. She knew about the missing Russian girl from the recent press stories but said she was not one of her girls. She claimed she had very little association with the Italian men. They occasionally hired three of her escorts, who special-ised in sex games, but that was all. We then told her we had flown out to Australia to talk to you, and asked her to confirm that your uncle had given the cash for the blackmailer to Lagan. She immediately denied it. She said you had made that up to try to vindicate your uncle.'

The pieces were gradually slipping together in my mind. It was not just Lagan who wanted me to be out of the way and too frightened to return, but also Rebecca, trying to protect her nephew.

'We had already established that the envelopes you showed us for the letters you received from her and the note that you believed was from Lagan were both typed on the same type-writer, so we delved a bit deeper into her connection with Lagan.'

They had discovered that Rebecca's sister Rachel had been married to Lagan's late father, who was an Italian count. That was in 1943, when Rachel and Lagan's father were both working for the French Resistance. Lagan had been born in 1944 and had been brought up by his grandmother in Italy when he was orphaned as a small child. His real name was Conte Edouard di Lagano. Antonio and Marco were brothers, and cousins to Lagan on his father's side.

'We believe Mrs Feldman exaggerated the danger to your life, in order to persuade you to stay out of England so you could not testify against him. She made sure that your friends didn't know where you were, and that all letters came through her. Paul Brady told us that he never entirely trusted her, and he was right. He believed that some of the letters he sent to you through Mrs Feldman didn't get through. You confirmed this in a note you sent to a mutual friend in a Christmas card. Mrs Feldman knows that we have spoken to you but not that you are here in England. We have also spoken to Mrs Vera Gilmore, who sends the letters on to Mrs Marek. She has the address for Mrs Marek, who she has known since they both lived in Poland before the last War, but says she doesn't actually have a current address for you, as you no longer live with her friend. Mrs Marek passes the letters on to you. We told her we were simply trying to trace you and that you were not in any kind of trouble, so she gave us the address for Mrs Marek, suggesting we contact her. We don't believe Mrs Gilmore is involved in any of this, and we don't believe either Mrs Feldman or Lagan has any Australian connections.'

I sat very still for a while, taking it in.

'So, Rebecca wrote the note?'

'We are not saying that, but certainly it was written on her typewriter, and she knew your address, so if it was from Lagan, she knew about it. They were trying to frighten you, so you never returned to Britain and never told the police that Lagan was involved in the murder of the blackmailer. At the same time, she was assuring you she had your interests at heart.'

On Saturday afternoon Alan drove me to Simon's mother's house, on the outskirts of Harton town, in his own old and rather battered car so I didn't arrive there in one of the black police cars. He handed me over to Simon, who made coffee for us all, found some biscuits, and talked with Alan for a while on the precautions we should take. He was intending to take me out to dinner, and wanted to know if that was allowed. It was, provided we kept it all low key.

The police considered that I was unlikely to be in any immediate danger. There had been no direct threats, no indication that the three Italians knew I was in England, and the police already had my statement, so eliminating me would only get them into more trouble than they were in already. I was free to return to Australia whenever I wanted, and they would arrange it. If they needed any more information from me, they had my contact details there. They would take me to the airport and would organise someone to meet me off the plane and drive me back to Broadsea. If they needed me here for Lagan's trial, they could bring me back or organise a video conferencing link.

Simon had arranged for me to do volunteer work at the school on the days that he worked so I was never alone at the house. There was a group of mothers who were helping convert the labels on the books in the library to a new computer system. Most of them worked one or two days a week, but I could work every day. If the inspector wanted to talk to me, he could telephone the house here in the evening.

Alan eventually left, shaking hands with Simon and wishing us both the best. We waited until the car was out of sight, then Simon gently closed the front door, and we stood looking at each other for a while, scarcely believing we were alone together for the first time in nearly six years.

We finally kissed, the passion as strong as it had ever been.

Simon took my suitcase up to the spare bedroom, but he asked me, rather shyly, whether I would sleep in his room with him. He would like us to return to being lovers if that was what I wanted, but a lot of things had changed since we had parted, and I could have some time to think about it.

I told him I didn't need time. We spent the rest of the afternoon cuddling on the sofa, the soft jazz music in the background, while I told him about my life and my home in Australia, and the years we had been apart simply melted away.

We went out to dinner, danced as we had once before, while I breathed in the familiar scent of his jacket, felt the warmth of his beard against my cheek. It was like starting out as lovers from the beginning again, the touch, the whispers, the longing for each other that had to wait until we returned to the house, where we went up to his room to spend the night reliving the joy of that long ago summer.

We spent five perfect weeks living together in his mother's house—the first three of them by ourselves—planning when we would marry and how we would get over the problem with the names. Was I to be married as Ann Berrington, or as Ethel Turner? If we were to live in Australia, it would need to be as Ethel; if we lived in Britain, I would prefer to return to being Ann. I suggested we marry twice, once here and once in Australia, but Simon was worried he would be charged with bigamy. He was happy to have one wife, but was not sure he could cope with two.

I spent my days at the school. I was introduced as Miss Turner, the fiancée of Mr Davis. We said my Christian name was Ethel, but I preferred to be called by my middle name, Ann. That worked for us, as Simon always called me Ann.

The mothers were wonderful, and although I was a lot younger than most of them, I was welcomed into their group. I worked at a desk in the library, checking the books off against a computer-printed list after they had been given their new labels. Some of the older boys would come over to talk to me as I worked. This was very flattering, of course, as they were years younger than me. Was I really engaged to Mr Davis? Wasn't he too old to be engaged? One of them even asked if I could marry him instead. Surely, I would prefer a younger man. I smiled at their self-confident chatter, happy to listen to them. They were so like Percival and the young men I had once known from the parties with Paul. They talked about their homes, their girlfriends, what they hoped to study at university, the cars they would drive, all the great things they would do in their lives, until the head librarian came over to shoo them off.

The volunteers had a small sitting room, where we congregated for mid-morning coffee and where lunch was served to us at noon. The work was tedious—there were thousands of books—but the chat among the ladies made the time fly faster. I did watch the clock a little, as I looked forward to the end of the school day at around four, when Simon and I would return to the house, make dinner for the evening, watch a film on the video player, and then retire to his bedroom.

One afternoon, on my way back to the library from the ladies' cloakroom in the school foyer, I stopped to look at a framed photograph of the boys who had left in 1981, looking for James. I found him; he was standing beside the friend who had also died in the accident.

The headmaster walked past and stopped to talk to me. I had met him, of course, and to tell the truth I was a little afraid of him. 'If you are looking for Mr Davis, he left in 1978.' He pointed out another photograph, further along.

'I was looking for James Berrington. I knew him.'

'Berrington? Ah, yes. That was very sad. He was killed in a motor accident, along with Carmichael. He was in his first year at Cambridge and had recently lost both his parents in rather distressing circumstances. Did you know him well?'

I looked at him, unable to answer, and he gave me a shrewd glance of recognition. Apart from James's hair being straight and mine curly, and the difference in our ages, we could have been twins.

'I believe he had a younger sister. Do you know what became of her?'

He knew who I was.

I still did not answer, so he gently took my arm and guided me further along the corridor, where he pointed out the photo from Simon's year, asking me if I could pick him out. I did, of course, and I also found Paul.

At least the headmaster hadn't thrown me out of the school grounds.

Simon's mother returned from her cruise, and I met her travelling companion. I had expected an elderly lady, but the companion was man, a retired army officer, long-ago widowed. He was an absolute gentleman, very polite and highly educated. His name was Martin Ellery, and I was to call him Martin as Simon did.

He had first met Simon's mother last summer at a fete at Harton School—he was an old boy, and she was helping to serve tea and scones. After a few day trips to local historic houses, they had spent a week together exploring Wales. They then visited Paris in the autumn. This spring they had gone on a long Mediterranean cruise. They enjoyed travelling together and were hoping to visit other parts of the world.

Mrs Davis had not changed much, but she did look suntanned and more natural, her makeup a lot less garish than when I first met her. Perhaps the admiration of her gentleman friend had made her realise that men could like her for what she was, not for how young she pretended to look. I had been a little apprehensive about what she would think of me after the way I had treated her son, but she seemed so glad to have him engaged at last that she was prepared to overlook my past. She even asked me to call her Alice.

Simon joked to me in private that Martin must be deaf to put up with her unending chatter, but when I watched them together, I realised he just turned off, occasionally agreeing with her, but not actually listening to what she was saying. Sometimes she would pull him up on it, ask his opinion, and he would pretend he hadn't quite heard her properly the first time.

Simon and I were planning to marry as soon as school broke up for the summer. We would honeymoon for a week in the cottage at Deniton then would go on to Broadsea. If Simon liked living there, we could stay indefinitely. The headmaster at Harton had asked his secretary to make a list of contacts for independent schools near Broadsea and would give Simon a reference if he wanted to apply for a job at any of them. There was always a shortage of teachers, particularly in maths and science, and independent schools usually welcomed teachers with excellent references from prestigious British schools. There should be no problem with getting the necessary work visa, since Simon was marrying an Australian. It would tie in nicely with his long-service leave, as the Australian school year started in early February. The headmaster would like a decision by November whether

Simon was returning to Harton so he could find a permanent replacement for the following term.

Nothing was expressly said, but I believe the headmaster was rather relieved that Simon would most likely be leaving. He knew who I was, although he had never actually said so, and he did need to consider the reputation of the school. A science teacher who was married to a girl whose mother had been a drug addict and whose uncle had been charged with supplying underage girls for sex and murdering a prostitute was not an ideal employee at a top British school. But he was always very civil to me when I was working in the library, and he told me he would miss Simon very much, as he had been part of the school community from when he was a boy.

We had a quiet wedding in a local church. Alice and Martin were married at the same time, and Martin's two adult children, who attended with their partners and five small children between them, were witnesses to both ceremonies. As I was still trying to lay low, we invited only Paul and his wife as our guests.

We all had lunch together at a local hotel, and Alice and her new husband left for their honeymoon in Sweden.

Simon and I spent our wedding night in the cottage where we had first been lovers, and we stood together on the beach at dawn as we had that first morning, our feet in the swirling foam at the edge of the vastness of the sea, feeling part of the eternity of the sunrise and the endless ebb and flow of the waves on the shore.

Epilogue 2015

It is now over twenty years since Simon and I were married.

Tonight, as we stood on the beach at Broadsea watching the sun set, I recalled the story I had written so many years ago, and now I will finish it. This is my life of sex, crime, loss, love, revenge, atonement and happy endings.

The three Italians and the Russian woman were all jailed—Lagan for life—so the girls had some revenge and some justice.

Lagan was convicted of arranging the murder of the blackmailer, as well as the manslaughter of the Russian girl and a whole string of offences against underage girls. He died in prison of natural causes two years ago. He was then close to seventy. I hope that there is an afterlife, so his soul can rot forever in the worst torment that hell can offer.

He was never charged with murdering my uncle. The coroner had initially found Richard's death to be a suicide, and the inspector told me that they could not get enough evidence together to convict Lagan of killing him.

The inquest into Lottie's death was left with an open verdict. It was likely that she had accidentally died from strangulation during sex games with Richard, but there was no way now to confirm it. They were not investigating her death any further unless new evidence came to light.

Simon and I live in Broadsea, with our two sons, James and Richard, but we still own the cottage at Deniton, renting it out as a holiday let managed by the Kershaws, who still own Orchard House. The icehouse door was refurbished, and a plaque was attached with the names of the two dead girls. There is now a neat path to it from the main path to the beach, and Mrs Kershaw tells her guests stories about its past that are much more ghoulish than those I was able to tell.

Alice went to live with Martin in his home in Surrey, quite close to the house where I was brought up. The house near Harton was sold, since she no longer needed it. Simon was the legal owner; it was part of his inheritance from his father.

We stay at the cottage for a few weeks each year in the British winter, when we have the longest school holidays here, and we spend most Christmases at Martin's house, which is large enough for his own two children and their families to stay overnight as well as our family, although some of the children sleep on mattresses on the floor.

Alice and Martin, now both in their late seventies, still travel a lot, and most years they visit us at Broadsea. We all build a sand-castle together on our beach, and although I always wish my uncle was still with us, Martin is a wonderful step-grandfather.

Paul is now a member of parliament, respected and success-ful. We rarely hear from him and never see him, but I follow his career on the internet news sites, and I am glad he achieved the lifestyle that he wanted. He is still with his wife, so she did not run off with the equerry. Does he ever think of the long-ago days when we were lovers, or the cold January morning when we stood on the beach at Deniton, when I could have accepted him and changed the course of both our lives? Or does he try to forget he was ever involved with me and thank his stars that

I never agreed to marry him. I thank my stars, as I would then never have met Simon.

Lady Ann Murphy is on her fourth husband, having divorced one and outlived two others. I occasionally find news items regarding her marital exploits. She now has plenty of photographs in the social pages and women's magazines, so I hope she has forgotten the one where she was mixed up with me.

Karl still sends me emails at Christmas with a photo of his family, usually playing in snow. He now has four children, presumably all artificially sired by his brother. I like to think I helped him, and I'm glad he didn't pine away for love of me as I almost did for love of Simon.

Alex and Gary now live openly together as a couple. I never saw his mother again, so I have no idea how well she accepted it.

Julian is now the chairman of his family's retail company, having replaced his father when he retired. I no longer want revenge on his mother, however much I had once enjoyed planning it. Does he still remember me and the morning his mother caught us in the act? I can laugh over it now, and I am sure he does. But his mother was a painted-up tart, and I still sometimes wish I had told her so at the time. It was a lost opportunity.

I have lost contact with all the other people I knew in England, but we have friends here, the staff at the school where Simon still teaches, and at the resort where I still work, as well as the groups we both now belong to, the birdwatchers, the wildflower enthusiasts and the investors. I still often visit Mrs Marek and Mrs Bukowski in their villa, but I have never had any further contact with Rebecca. I will always be grateful for the help she gave me after James died, but I can never forgive her for how she later betrayed me by making me believe I was in danger, making me so frightened to contact anyone that I almost lost all chance of ever being reunited with Simon.

A year ago two businesswomen came to talk to our investors' group about a charity they were setting up. One of the women would manage it while the other was partly bankrolling it, but they would appreciate some extra help with the costs. Many of our members were well-heeled retirees and a good audience for their venture.

They had obtained a government grant to buy an old block of flats, which they were converting to accommodation for girls who were homeless or at risk of becoming so. They wanted money for the renovation and the initial set up costs for the charity, and ongoing funds to run it. Girls would live four to a flat, and would be given help to find a job. The charity would train them, buy work clothes for them and subsidise their wages working in boutiques and coffee shops, until they were confident enough to get a mainstream job and rent a flat or a room for themselves. Their aim was to keep the girls safe from living homeless on the streets, falling into prostitution, or being vulnerable to drug addiction.

I drove up to Perth to talk to them again, listened to their business plan, suggested that I could fund deportment classes for the girls as well as the retail training, so they had more confidence in themselves. Their project seemed to be a good use of the money still sitting in the bank in Switzerland, so I gave them a significant amount of what they still needed, transferring it directly to them from the Swiss account, and I pledged an ongoing amount as well. I could easily afford to, and it eased my conscience a little. Simon didn't mind. He knew about the Swiss money, but we had never used any of it. We had everything we wanted.

I looked over the flats and met some of the girls they were already helping. One of them was a girl with soft brown hair and soft brown eyes, a sweet round face that reminded me of the Russian girls, and that same way of stealing a glance at you—hoping for understanding or help, but not knowing whether you were a friend or a foe—that I had seen in Lagan's girls but had not then understood. I told her that my mother had been a drug addict, and I had seen what men could do to girls who were vulnerable, using their bodies with no thought for their souls. I wanted her to know that she deserved better than that, and there were people who cared about her.

Reading the first part of my story, written when I despaired of ever seeing my lover again, makes me feel so grateful that Simon and I were reunited and have had so many years together. I could so easily have spent the rest of my days alone.

Perhaps now I do believe in happy endings, but the sadness for the people I have lost still haunts me even now, as Simon and I stand together every evening on the beach, looking out to the horizon, with no need of words between us, content with our lives in this beautiful corner of the world, and spend each night together in the house near the shore, lulled to sleep by the soft whisper of the sea.